Dangerous to Love

CHAPTER ONE

CAINE ALEXANDER was no knight in shining armor. His aversion to damsels in distress was as legendary as his ability to avoid them. A man could get killed playing hero.

So what, he asked himself, was he doing in Little Falls, Arkansas, an Ozark Mountains community so small it wasn't even a dot in *Rand McNally,* trying to protect a feisty redhead who insisted she didn't want protection?

And how the hell was he supposed to protect her when he couldn't even find her?

Swallowing a sigh of frustration, Caine reached across the red-and-white-checked tablecloth for his second buttermilk biscuit—one of the soft, made-with-lard-in-cholesterol-heaven, melt-in-your-mouth variety. The silence in the Down Home Café was as thick as the homemade butter he slathered on the biscuit—smothering and unnatural.

Normal chatter, the give-and-take of conversation between friends, the kind he'd expect to find in a small café that so obviously depended on local patronage, had disappeared the moment the small bell hung above the entry door announced his arrival.

He was as conspicuous as a nun in a red-light district.

And apparently about as welcome.

Why, he asked himself for the hundredth time, had he volunteered for this job? In the eight years he'd spent as a member of the army's special forces, he'd learned that "Never volunteer" was the first rule of survival. He'd endured torture, knife wounds and bullet holes, but never on a voluntary assignment. Trouble didn't need an invitation. A man was a fool to offer one. Brother-in-law or not, Danny Carelli owed him big time.

Caine reached for the honey dish, a heavy pressed-glass compote with matching lid that held an oozing wax comb—obviously another local product. Dribbled on the hot buttered biscuit, it redefined the word "sweet."

It failed, however, to sweeten Caine's mood.

Damn Vicki Winslow. Why hadn't she agreed to do the sensible thing and enter the witness protection program? They'd told her it wouldn't be forever. If, by the time they were convinced she was safe, she wasn't happy in her new life, she could resurrect herself.

But Vicki Winslow said no. She'd done nothing wrong. She wasn't going to disappear.

Stubborn woman, Caine remembered thinking when Danny had related the tale. The justice department had made its offer, a take-it-or-leave-it deal, and the lady had turned it down. As a federal marshal, Caine's brother-in-law had done everything, professionally and legally, he could do. That should have been the end of the story.

Even as Danny cursed and complained about Vicki Winslow's decision, Caine had heard the admiration in Danny's voice and known his Sir Galahad of a brother-in-law wasn't going to let it go.

Maggie, Caine's sweet little sister, had stood beside her husband, her hands folded serenely over the bulging belly that housed Caine's future niece or nephew, her eyes snapping sparks of outrage. "It isn't fair," she'd said. "Someone has to protect her."

How stupid could he be? The two of them had played him like a Nintendo, set him up like a plump, park pigeon. And he, Caine Alexander, tough-skinned survivor in this dog-eat-dog world, had rolled over and played dead.

"I'm free at the moment and have nothing special planned," he heard himself telling Danny. "You stay with Maggie. I'll guard the Winslow woman."

Oh, yeah. He'd been set up all right. Volunteering was breaking rule number one.

Doing the job gratis was breaking rule number two. He hadn't acquired blue-chip stocks and six-figure bank accounts by giving away his services. Still, he owed Danny, if for no other reason than the man made Maggie happy, so maybe rule number two was no biggie.

It was breaking rule number three that really rankled. He didn't do bodyguard jobs. Ever. His security company specialized in electronic protection—remote sensors, hidden cameras, security alarms. Playing bodyguard meant he was going to have to get up close and personal. Human Super Glue.

To do the job right, he'd have to have Vicki Winslow living in his pocket. They'd be occupying the same space, breathing the same air. There was no privacy on a guard job—no time-outs, no way to escape the togetherness—not for the guard and not for the guarded.

From what he knew of her, Vicki Winslow wouldn't like it. He already knew he would hate it. Which was why he'd made rule number three in the first place.

He'd planned his strategy carefully, talked the manager of Vicki Winslow's apartment house into a three-month lease, hoping he could stay close but remote, at least long enough for her to get used to the idea. He'd bought the apartment-house doorman a fifth of imported brandy and donated his personal season tickets for the Washington Redskins as thanks for present and future favors. He'd checked burglar alarms and installed security cameras outside the entrances to the Winslow apartment. Then he'd moved in next door.

Twenty-four hours later Vicki Winslow had split.

The woman wasn't dumb, he admitted with a grudging admiration. He'd lost her trail completely. If Danny hadn't dug up the Little Falls connection, he'd still be running in circles.

Still, Caine had found no concrete evidence that Vicki Winslow was in Little Falls. Not yet. But instinct told him Danny was right. Somewhere in this dead-as-the-day-before-yesterday countryside she was hiding. And if he could find her, so could other hunters.

So here he was—at the back of beyond with his pants fly flapping in the wind. He had no excuse for being here, no cover story, no backup, and there wasn't a health club in sight.

He preferred jogging concrete sidewalks shadowed by grime-coated city buildings to hiking fresh-air trails shaded by towering vegetation. He was used to subways and schizophrenic taxi drivers, not rusting pickups and mud-splattered four-by-fours. He could translate curses in six different languages, but the speech of the slow-moving, slow-talking natives of Little Falls, Arkansas, seemed to defy understanding.

He preferred his air pollution in the form of exhaust fumes, not woodsmoke and barnyard. He preferred his trees civilized: groomed, pruned and planted in concrete boxes, not growing willy-nilly across the landscape. He preferred his women sleek, sophisticated and sane, not obstinate, opinionated and outrageous.

Caine reached for his third buttermilk biscuit. The sign above the Down Home Café's chalkboard menu boasted "The Best Biscuits in Little Falls." He wasn't about to dispute that claim, even if the Down Home was the only café in the two-block-long, slightly widened area of Highway 62 that served as the town's main street. They were certainly the best biscuits he'd ever eaten. Even purgatory, he supposed, had its compensations.

THERE WAS A STRANGER in town, a tall, dark, dangerous-looking stranger. Vicki heard the news twenty minutes after the man advertised his presence by parking his Mercedes in front of the Down Home. Talk about obvious. His imported, big-city wheels were as out of place in Little Falls as a pig in Aunt Abby's parlor. Under other circumstances, Vicki might have found it funny, but right now, a stranger's presence was anything but humorous. She tried to ignore the tingles of fear racing up and down her spine.

"If he's one of them, he's pretty dumb, driving straight into town," Harve tried to reassure her. "It's probably a false alarm. You stay put. I'll check him out."

"I made a mistake coming here. I'm sorry, Harve," Vicki told her cousin, unable to keep the weariness or the dismay from her voice. "If it's not this one, it'll be the next one, or the next. This time, I should have told Aunt Abby no. I didn't intend to put you or anyone else at risk. I'll start packing."

Harve grabbed his Stetson from the peg by the door and set it firmly on the back of his head. "Dammit, Vicki, hold up a minute. There's no need to panic. You're staying right here." He slapped his hand against the doorframe as if for emphasis.

The sound brought a chitter of indignation from under the couch, swiftly followed by a small furry head. Glittering black eyes glared at Vicki, then her cousin.

"You woke up Sweetpea," Vicki protested as the small pet skunk exited her hiding place, holding her bushy flag of a tail in its at-alert position. Sweetpea stood still for a moment, as if assessing the scene, then slowly lowered her tail and wrapped herself around Vicki's ankles.

"Yeah. Well, she'll live. She's sure adopted you. Maybe we shouldn't have disarmed her. She'd be a formidable deterrent if anyone came poking around."

Vicki let out a reluctant chuckle. "That might be a case of the cure being worse than the disease. I was visiting the summer that mother skunk decided to den under the cabin."

"We all remember that summer," Harve said. "I had to bury my letterman's sweater, and the cabin wasn't habitable for a year."

Vicki felt herself relaxing as Sweetpea's antics and the memories of that long-ago summer worked their magic.

Harve seemed to sense her mood shift. "Look, Vicki," he said, "I know it's hard, but try to relax and don't worry until we decide there *is* a problem. Right now, we don't know if this is one of the bad guys or an innocent stranger. Even if it turns out he's looking for you, it doesn't mean he's going to find you. I'm driving into town to check him out. You stay inside until I get back. The shotgun's loaded. I don't reckon you've forgotten how to use it, even if it has been over ten years. The dogs will alert you if any stranger comes poking around."

"That's just it. I can't stay in this cabin the rest of my life," she started to complain, but Harve was already out the door, pulling it shut behind him. She swore—a four-syllable, extremely unladylike expression.

Sweetpea chittered, disturbed by Vicki's agitation, until she was picked up and stroked. "It's all right, girl," Vicki said, curling the small animal into the crook of her elbow. Sweetpea gave one last squeak of protest, then draped her head over Vicki's arm and closed her eyes.

Vicki looked at the already slumbering skunk for a moment, wishing she could make her own problems go away as easily. Was she really in danger? Maybe she was being paranoid. Her friends and co-workers seemed to think so.

But then, they'd thought she was crazy when she first accused her boss, Roy Henderson, director of the For Children's Sake foundation, of embezzling foundation funds. Even Senator Marvin Van Brock, chairman of the board of directors—the man who'd suggested she apply for the job of assistant director, then given her his personal recommendation—had demanded she stop her "unfounded" accusations when she took her suspicions to him. He'd been supported by foundation attorney, Ben Sinclair, the prominent Washington, D.C. lawyer who volunteered his time to advise the foundation. She'd been hurt by their lack of faith in her judgment.

When officials considered her evidence seriously enough to bring charges, both Senator Van Brock and Ben had apologized. Senator Van Brock asked if she was interested in the director's position. Ben presented roses and explained away his lack of support as a lawyer's characteristic sense of caution.

With Henderson behind bars, both said that the "unfortunate incident" was over. In a meeting the day after the trial, the six men on the foundation board of directors had given her a unanimous vote of confidence and urged her to return to work, telling her the foundation needed her.

She wished she could believe they were right, wished she could believe that it was all over. But she couldn't help remembering they had been wrong before.

Henderson's embezzlement of funds from a charity for children's relief had outraged both Washington society and law enforcement. It was her discovery and, in large part, her testimony, that had convicted him, but little of the stolen money had been recovered. Officials now believed Henderson was involved with someone else, someone who was possibly the mastermind behind the scheme. They'd find him, justice department officials assured her, but it would take a little time.

Until then, Federal Marshal Daniel Carelli believed she was still in danger.

Should she have listened to him? Vicki wondered. Should she have accepted his assistance and simply disappeared? But that would have meant cutting herself off from family and friends, letting them all think she was dead.

It wasn't as if she had much of an immediate family left, she admitted. There was only her great-aunt Abigail, the family matriarch, and Harve, who was a second cousin, plus a half-dozen or so scattered once- and twice-removed cousins. The family ties stretched thin, but she'd been taught that kinship was something you didn't ignore, no matter how diluted the bloodline. Besides, Aunt Abby was eighty-seven. There were no guarantees she'd still be around for Vicki's resurrection two or three years from now.

It was Aunt Abby who'd sent word, who'd told her to come to Little Falls. "The family managed to hide Cousin Alphonse for three months when the Yankee bluecoats were thick as fleas on a hound dog's back," she'd written. "Not many strangers around these days. Spotting one will be as easy as finding a crow in a cornfield. This family takes care of its own. You get yourself home where you belong."

Then William, the twice-removed cousin who'd delivered Aunt Abby's note in person, shoved an envelope stuffed with one-hundred-dollar bills, a plane ticket to Little Rock and her cousin Camille's Arkansas driver's license into her hand. "In case you need it for identification," William explained. "You and Camille both have red hair and look enough alike to pass. Aunt Abby said to leave your car in the garage, don't cash any checks or use your credit cards. And don't pack a suitcase, in case someone's watching your place. Cousin Harve will pick you up in Little Rock."

She hadn't tried to protest. When Aunt Abby ordered, the family marched. The Tremaynes claimed that if Aunt Abby had been a general, the South would have won the war.

That had been two weeks ago. Only fourteen short days, and someone had already tracked her down, Vicki realized, her despair tainted with exasperation. Harve had made a halfhearted effort to convince her this stranger was an innocent, but Vicki suspected the worst. The family also had inbred survival instincts. They knew when they were in danger.

Vicki wasn't good at waiting—never had been. Dammit all, anyway, she swore, her temper rising to match the fire-glow color of her hair. She'd done the right thing in testifying. It wasn't fair that she was the one being forced to skulk around like a criminal while, even from jail, her scum-ball of a former boss continued to threaten her.

What was she supposed to do? Hibernate until the legal eagles did their jobs? Sometimes, she thought, vigilante justice had its good points.

But sitting here bemoaning her fate wasn't going to accomplish anything, either. And Harve was right. With the dogs on guard, she was safe—for the moment, anyway.

The cabin was hidden deep in the woods of Tremayne Mountain. Except for occasional use as a hunting or vacation hideaway, it hadn't been lived in for more than twenty years, but in spite of that, Harve kept it in good repair. Even the gasoline generator that supplied electric power had fired up at the first crank of the engine.

And Aunt Abby was determined to keep Vicki occupied. Idle hands make devil's work was her aunt's motto. "The family papers need cataloging," she'd told Vicki. "It'll give you something to do, and it's a job that needs doing. Once the excitement dies down, there are other things. Mae's youngest wants to learn to use a computer, and your cousin Jackson, over in Benton County, needs his farm accounts computerized. Don't worry about not pulling your load. We'll keep you busy.''

Remembering the conversation now, Vicki couldn't help smiling. Her great-aunt had been as good as her word. Harve showed up at the cabin the morning after Vicki arrived hauling a top-of-the-line laptop and a steamer trunk of papers dating back over a century.

''Told Grandmother that generator power fluctuated too much to run a regular computer,'' Harve said, ''but this should work.''

With a snort of exasperation, Vicki laid Sweetpea in the corner of the couch and turned her attention back to the papers she'd been working on when Harve arrived. If truth be known, she hadn't gotten very far in her cataloging. She kept stopping to read. Some of the earliest papers, letters from family members left behind in the east, farm account ledgers and personal diaries penned in spidery script so precise and ornate it looked like calligraphy, were fascinating.

Vicki's attempts at diversion worked, and morning slipped into early afternoon before she realized it. The sound of a truck in front of the cabin roused her, but didn't excite her. She was sure it was Harve. The dogs hadn't made a sound.

''Well?'' she demanded as soon her cousin opened the cabin door.

"The man's here for a reason, all right, and it's probably you," Harve said without preamble. "I don't think he's one of the villains, though. His name is Caine Alexander. Says he's on vacation, just traveling. Likes the look of this area. Thinks he might stay around for a while."

Vicki felt her stomach roll. "And what in that story makes you think he's not a bad guy?" she asked, not bothering to hide her exasperation. "Is he wearing a white hat?"

"No, Miss Smarty, he's not wearing a white hat. Not wearing a hat at all," Harve answered. "Get the red down, Vicki, and think a minute. From what you've said, the men involved are cautious, careful and very well organized. They wouldn't rush in here unprepared. This one smells like a fed. You slipped out of town pretty slick. Probably didn't give the poor guy time to grab a hat. It's not hard to see he feels like a fish out of water, although I'll have to admit he's pretty good at covering it up."

"You're wrong, Harve. He's not a fed. They offered me protection—on their terms. I turned it down. I'm on my own."

"Bullcorn. That's what they wanted you to think, an extra inducement to get you into their program. Even if you did refuse their offer, they aren't going to hang you out to dry. You're an important witness."

Vicki shook her head. "Was. I was an important witness. My testimony's all on record. They don't need me anymore."

"Even if that's so, how's it going to look if they go around letting ex-witnesses get killed? Not much of an incentive for the next guy they need on the witness stand. They've got a good reason for keeping you alive and healthy."

Vicki wanted to believe Harve was right, but she wasn't convinced the justice department would send anyone chasing her all the way to Little Falls. "They explained all that to me," she told him, "but they also explained there's no budget to cover private guards. If this . . . this Caine Alexander is here looking for me, it's not to make sure I stay healthy."

"Double Bullcorn. Come on, Vicki, snap out of it. You've been around government long enough to know there are always discretionary funds, hidden budget items. I say this one's not a black hat. And, I might remind you, we Tremaynes are famous for our judgment. Besides, Cousin Myrtle says he has a good aura."

Vicki hesitated. Murphy's Law and common sense both said the man was bad news. On the other hand, Harve was an excellent judge of character and Cousin Myrtle's aura reading was famous in six counties. "Suppose, just suppose you're right," Vicki said after a moment, "what do we do now?"

"Well, I guess that's up to you. If I'm right, he might be a good man to have on our side. But you're out of sight up here. He'll never find you without help. Every one in town knows to call me if strangers are hanging about. If Alexander sticks around we'll know it. The Down Home's the only place in town for him to eat."

"What happens if you're wrong? If he really is the enemy?" Vicki asked. "If he suspects I'm here, Henderson's associates won't leave a tree standing on the mountain until they find me."

"We'll deal with that if it happens, when it happens," Harve said. "You're home now, Vicki. Time to stop running and take a stand. *'Si vis pacem, para bellum.* If you want peace, prepare for war.' Vegetius said that back in the fifth century. Near as I can tell, nothing's changed."

How could she have forgotten Harve's penchant for using obscure ancients to make a point, as if, by virtue of being dead, they'd possessed great wisdom? But this time, she realized, Harve might be right. If she'd been willing to run, she would have followed Carelli's advice and gone into the witness protection program. She still didn't believe the man at the Down Home was here to help her, but her cousin might have a point when he told her not to panic.

"All right, Harve," she said finally, "we'll play it your way for now, even if the idea of a last stand makes me nervous. I just wonder if Custer ever read Vegetius."

CAINE ARRIVED at the U.S. marshal's office in Fayetteville shortly before noon. Time enough, he figured, to identify himself and see if Danny had forwarded any new information.

"Might as well go back to Little Falls," Rodney Baxter told him after he checked out Caine's unofficial credentials with Danny. "You've already blown your cover. Have supper at the Down Home. If the family decides to let you stick around, that's your best place of contact."

"I wasn't that bad," Caine protested. "I know that local was vetting me, but he could be the nosy sort. I think I handled it pretty well for the spur of the moment."

"And did you happen to catch the name of the local?"

"His name was Harve—Harve Tremayne. Dressed like a cowboy or a farmer—worn jeans, plaid shirt, cowboy boots run-down at the heel and a tan cowboy hat. About thirty-five, six foot two, maybe a hundred and ninety pounds."

Caine might as well have saved his breath. The marshal was wiping tears of laughter from his eyes long before Caine finished describing the boots.

"Good ole local boy, Harve Tremayne," Baxter said, once he managed to get his guffaws under control. "His full name is Harvey Gibson Tremayne III. He's your pigeon's second cousin and her closest kin, unless you count his grandmother, Abigail Tremayne, who's Vicki Winslow's great-aunt. Good ole Harve is a Harvard grad, who also happens to be chairman of the board and a major stockholder in Tremayne Diversified, a Fortune 500 company. In his spare time he runs a quarter-horse farm that grosses six figures annually, pilots his own plane and plays benevolent benefactor to his hometown. Offhand, I'd say you were right. Vicki

Winslow is probably in Little Falls. They pulled out the big guns for you."

"Do you happen to know her shoe size?" Caine asked in disgust.

"Nope. Never saw the lady. No reason to worry, though. The information on Harvey Tremayne is common knowledge, but the Winslow connection isn't. I wouldn't have discovered the relationship if Danny hadn't contacted me last week to check out relatives Miss Winslow had left in the area. Her mother was born here in Fayetteville. Maiden name, Ashley."

Caine wasn't in the mood to be humored. "So how'd we get from Ashley to Winslow to Tremayne?" he asked, simply because he knew it was expected of him. The how didn't really matter. That the connection was so easy to find was the problem. If both Danny and Baxter could unearth it in a couple of days, so could anyone else.

"Now, that was a bit tricky," Baxter bragged. "Took me half a day at the library to find it. Doesn't involve the Tremaynes directly. Started with two sisters named Smith."

Half a day? If that remark was meant to reassure him, Caine thought, it wasn't working.

"Anyway," Baxter continued, "a Smith girl married a Tremayne two, no three, generations back. That's the present Abigail Tremayne. And Miz Abigail had a sister, who married an Ashley, who had a daughter who married a Winslow. The result is your Ms. Winslow. The connection's there, but not obvious. Your Ms.

Winslow is related to Abigail Tremayne through her family, not directly through the Tremayne line.

"Direct enough that it took you only a few hours to find it—at the public library, for God's sake," Caine said in a growl.

"In the genealogy room of the public library," Baxter clarified. "I doubt if an outsider would stumble onto the connection—not unless he knew what to look for. Like I told Carelli, the Winslows never lived around here. Offhand, I'd say your girl made a good move, unless she left a easy trail?"

"No. She didn't leave an easy trail," Caine admitted, beginning to feel a little better. "Look, is there any way we could pull those records off the shelf for a while?"

"I thought about that," Baxter said, "but I decided the gap in the records might look too suspicious, so I flagged them, instead. They're part of a special collection, you see. Not on the regular shelves. Anyone wanting to see them has to make a special request. The librarian takes names, addresses, checks ID. Until further notice, she'll alert me if any nonlocal makes a request to see those particular volumes. Not usual operating procedure, of course, but like most Southerners, Ms. Gillicutty has a profound respect for law and order—especially when it's directed toward outsiders. I thought, unlikely as it seemed, that if any of Henderson's accomplices were bright enough to think of it, it would give us a bit of warning."

It was a good idea, Caine admitted, and told Baxter so. Maybe, just maybe, they weren't blown out of the water. Yes, he was definitely feeling better. He hadn't actually tracked Vicki Winslow to Arkansas. It was Danny who suggested Little Falls as a possibility, and Danny's records weren't exactly public.

Of course, Caine hadn't found her, either—not yet. The family could be on alert simply because they knew someone might be looking for her. Or they could be laying a false trail.

But Baxter thought she was here, Caine reminded himself. And so did he. That feeling in his gut had told him so the minute he stepped into the Down Home.

"So," he said, "assuming we're right and she's in Little Falls, I've still got to find her before I can protect her. Got any ideas?"

"Nothing besides my first one," Baxter said. "Go back to the Down Home. Tremayne will find you. And ditch the Mercedes. Get a pickup, or a Jeep," he added. "Even if the locals have made you, no need advertising the fact that you're an outsider to the wrong people."

Caine grunted, silently gnashing his teeth, but somehow, he managed to keep his expression placid. He'd accept Baxter's advice about the vehicle, he decided, but he'd be damned if he'd show up again at the Down Home like a park-bench bum waiting for a handout. He was here to find Vicki Winslow, and find her he would. After all, a man had his pride.

LATE AFTERNOON found a satisfied Caine Alexander crouched under a tree at the edge of a clearing watching a thin spiral of smoke rise lazily from the chimney of small log cabin.

Bingo! If he was a betting man and hadn't already given them away, he'd bet his fifty-yard-line seats at RFK Stadium that he'd found Vicki Winslow's hideout.

The cabin and its accompanying forty acres of woodland were listed on county tax-assessment roles as unimproved acreage with unoccupied vacation structure owned by one H. G. Tremayne III. February certainly wasn't prime vacation time, and the rutted, ungraveled logging road into the cabin showed signs of recent use.

On the north and east, the property abutted two other parcels owned by Mr. Tremayne: one with improvements valued in the high six figures; the second, a large unimproved parcel that encompassed most of a ridge known locally as Tremayne Mountain. On the west was a ten-acre improved property with a pre-1860 two-story house and auxiliary structures owned by an A. Tremayne—probably Aunt Abigail herself. The south boundary line was a seldom-used county road.

All in all, Caine concluded, the situation could be a lot worse. Given the same circumstances, he would have chosen this cabin, too. The family, or at least Harve Tremayne, knew what he was about.

Not much different from pounding the pavement in the city, after all, he decided. City or country, land records were the same. He couldn't help a smug feeling of accomplishment. Once he'd started thinking, instead of reacting, he'd realized reconnaissance was reconnaissance. Probables were his first concern. Where was the safest, most feasible place for his quarry to hide?

She could be in her Aunt Abigail's home or even at her cousin Harve's quarter-horse farm, although either was unlikely, Caine decided. Too easy. Also too public—employees, friends and any number of regular and occasional visitors. From what he'd heard of Vicki Winslow, he doubted she'd be willing to hide in a closet every time someone rang the doorbell.

She could also be staying with a more distantly related family member, but the fewer people who knew where Vicki Winslow was, or even that she was in town, the safer she'd be. Harve Tremayne would know that; he'd already proved he was no dummy.

So, now that Caine had found Vicki Winslow, all he had to do was plan his approach. His options, unfortunately, were limited to two—a sneak attack or a frontal assault.

The first option had a distinct disadvantage. He was friendly forces. A sneak attack was all but guaranteed not to endear him to his intended target. In addition, there was a problem with the dogs. He suspected they were inside the cabin or they would have sniffed him out by now. He hadn't seen them, but had identified at least two sets of paw prints. Large ones.

Scratch the sneak attack. It was a frontal assault or nothing.

Caine didn't like limited options, but this time, it couldn't be helped. Well, hell. He guessed he'd better get on with it.

He stood up and slipped into the denim jacket he'd purchased a few hours ago in Fayetteville. Not that he needed it for warmth. For a late February afternoon, the air was balmy, comfortable enough for only his jeans and cotton flannel shirt, also newly purchased. The jacket, however, effectively hid his shoulder holster. Experience had taught him that the sight of a gun had a way of making most women a bit hysterical.

He didn't expect to pass as a local. Any spoken word of more than two syllables would brand him as a Yankee. Nor would his hiking boots pass inspection, but even for the sake of disguise, he was unwilling to squeeze his city-bred feet into a pair of those pointy-toed boots the natives seemed to favor. Sacrifice in the line of duty had its limits. Still, his apparel no longer screamed *outsider* as he walked down the street.

He moved out of the shadow of the leafless trees and began walking across the clearing toward the front of the cabin. Should he march up and knock on the door or stop at the edge of the porch? Should he call out as if wondering whether anyone was at home or simply call her by name?

It was a decision he didn't have to make.

He was still several feet from the porch when the cabin door swung open so quickly he had no time to react. His first impression was of long legs clad in ordinary blue denim—and looking anything but ordinary. His second impression was of heat—of fiery red hair tumbling around the lady's face. His third impression was of trouble.

The woman was holding a double-barreled shotgun with twin bores the size of a small cannon.

"Hold it right there, mister. You're close enough. And keep your hands where I can see them."

He froze in midstep. Damn! He'd known it all along. A man could get killed playing hero.

CHAPTER TWO

"HEY, LADY. Don't go waving that thing around. It's dangerous."

Vicki's grip tightened around the shotgun stock as she mentally damned her rubbery knees.

"I'm glad you realize that," she told him, giving thanks that at least her voice sounded calm and steady. Except for his jeans and denim jacket, the man standing in front of her fit Harve's description of the stranger from the Down Home: tall, dark and dangerous-looking. "Who are you and what do you want, mister?"

"The name's Caine, Caine Alexander, Ms. Winslow. I'm a friend."

Caine Alexander? Yes, that was the name Harve said the man had given him. And she'd obviously been correct in assuming he was in town looking for her. He'd called her by name. The thought that she should deny she was Vicki Winslow flickered through her mind and was just as quickly dismissed. It was obvious he knew who she was. But how in the dickens had he found her so quickly?

"Thanks all the same, but we have a quaint custom around here. We usually know the people we claim as friends," she said, not bothering to disguise the bitterness in her voice. "Now why don't you just turn around and go back where you came from. You're trespassing."

"What will you do if I decide I don't want to go?"

"What I have to," Vicki answered with a bravado she didn't feel. It was one thing to declare she could take care of herself and an altogether different matter to be aiming a loaded gun at another human being.

"Do you know what'll happen if you actually pull that trigger?" the man asked casually, as if a double-barreled twelve-gauge pointed at his midsection was an everyday occurrence.

Was he crazy? Vicki studied him for a moment. Outwardly Caine Alexander, if that was really his name, appeared composed and confident. There was an indulgent look about the slight smile on his lips, as if he was humoring a recalcitrant child. Blast it, anyway. Even a semi-intelligent person should be nervous with a loaded shotgun aimed at his guts.

He was bluffing! In spite of his nonchalant posturing, he wasn't able to completely disguise the glint of wariness in his eyes.

Well, she could bluff, too.

"The recoil will probably knock me flat on my ... behind," she told him, congratulating herself when she saw her honest assessment had caught him off guard. Good. At least he now realized she and the shotgun weren't strangers. "That won't matter to you," she added, pressing her advantage. "You won't be paying any attention to what I'm doing. Even if I'd never held a gun before, it would be hard to miss at this distance. So why don't you act smart and just go away."

His expression of amused indulgence was gone now, as was his casual air. If anything, he looked resigned—and even more dangerous than before.

"I can't do that. As I said, I'm a friend, or at least a friend of a friend. I promised him I'd protect you, but I'll admit, I'm glad to see you're not completely helpless. You'll need that against Henderson's confederates."

"Not a good try, mister. Henderson and his associates are the only ones looking for me, which, you must admit, makes your showing up on my doorstep highly suspicious."

"I'm not with Henderson," he protested. "Danny Carelli sent me."

Vicki shivered, fighting down panic. Carelli had made his position clear—the only help he could offer was the witness protection program. In spite of what Harve believed, Carelli would never have sent this man.

She tightened her grip on the shotgun, snuggling it more securely into her shoulder. She couldn't let him get any closer. One barrel at a time, she decided, and if she had to shoot, she'd aim for the legs. But even then, at this distance, she'd do permanent injury. The thought made her sick to her stomach. She swallowed. "You've got to the count of five to get moving, mister. Then I start shooting. One—"

"Hey, what did I say?"

"Mr. Carelli won't be sending anyone, and I know it. Two—"

"Dammit, lady, you could at least look at my identification. I'm not lying. If I were one of Henderson's men, would I have marched up here like this—out in the open and vulnerable?"

He was right, Vicki admitted. Ambush would be more Henderson's style. And Harve claimed that regardless of what she'd been told, authorities wouldn't simply wipe their hands of her. *Careful, Vicki,* she admonished herself. *Don't allow him to convince you just because you want to believe.*

"Look, I'm telling you the truth. I'm here to help. Danny did send me. How the hell do you think I found you, anyway? You pulled one mean getaway from the city. If Danny hadn't known your mother was born in Fayetteville, we'd still be chasing shadows."

Vicki hesitated. True, her mother's birthplace was information anyone could find, but she had to admit Danny Carelli would have easier and faster access to it.

"All right. I'll look at your ID, but you stay where you are."

"It's in my hip pocket."

"Use your left hand. And take it out of your pocket—very slowly."

Was that a glint of admiration in his eyes? Again, Vicki warned herself to be cautious. Just because the man looked like the answer to every maiden's prayer didn't mean he was.

"And what makes you so sure I'm not left-handed?" he asked.

"Less than twenty-five percent of the population is left-handed. That makes the odds in my favor."

"That sounds about right," the man growled in a voice so low Vicki almost didn't hear him. "They sure haven't been in my favor lately." He pulled the wallet from his pocket and held it out in front of him. "Now what?"

Vicki whistled, summoning the two dogs from inside the cabin. They assumed their stances, one on either side of her. Tucker, the spotted shorthaired pointer, looked from Vicki to the man and bared his teeth, a low growl rumbling from his throat. Gourdy, the black and tan, flopped down on the porch, the perfect caricature of a lazy hound.

"Guard," she ordered the dogs, and Gourdy snapped to immediate attention, neck-ruff hair bristling.

"Just drop the wallet on the ground in front of you," she ordered, then addressed the dog on her right. "Fetch, Tucker. Bring it here."

Without a sound, the dog sprang gracefully off the porch, grasped the wallet in his teeth and returned to Vicki.

Vicki shifted the shotgun into the crook of her right arm, careful to keep her finger on the trigger guard and the barrel pointed in man's direction. "Watch him, boys," she ordered. The dogs assumed an alert stance. Hunters made unusual-looking watchdogs, Vicki ad-

mitted, but there could be no mistake in intent. Even
floppy-eared, sleepy-eyed Gourdy looked lethal.

With her left hand, Vicki awkwardly flipped open the
tri-fold wallet. The Maryland driver's license identified
the man as Caine Alexander, six foot three, two hundred and ten pounds pounds. The picture wasn't flat-
tering, but it was him. "I don't see a badge," she said.

"I never claimed a badge. Flip it all the way open.
There's a photograph...."

Vicki saw what he intended—the snapshot of Federal Marshal Danny Carelli, dressed casually in jeans
and a plaid shirt, and a small dark-haired woman in a
maternity smock. Caine Alexander stood between them,
arms around the shoulders of both.

"The lady's name is Maggie, Margaret Alexander
Carelli. She's my little sister. Danny was so worried
about you when you refused to enter the witness protection program he was ready to take leave of absence
and come find you himself. I figured he needed to be
with Maggie. The baby's due in six weeks. So I volunteered to come in his stead."

Vicki's felt her legs go rubbery. Caine Alexander
wasn't from Henderson. She'd trust Carelli with her
life. Had, in fact, on more than one occasion. The sudden relief made her knees wobble. The shotgun barrel
followed suit.

"Hey, careful with that thing."

She eased her finger from the trigger guard, shifted
the shotgun into a more comfortable hold and examined the man more closely. She was ready to admit

Caine Alexander wasn't one of Henderson's men, but that didn't mean he wasn't dangerous, if only to her peace of mind. He reminded her of something ... someone. The impression was faint, smothered in the memories of her days in court, a time she tried not to dwell on. Still, there was something... "Are those sunglasses in your jacket pocket?" she asked suddenly.

"Yeah. But what—"

"Put them on."

"Put on my sunglasses? Why? They don't make a good blindfold, if that's what you're thinking. Oh, why not?"

CAINE REACHED for his glasses with his right hand, hesitating for a fraction of a second when he saw her smile. He shrugged. "As you said, the odds were on your side," he acknowledged with only a little reluctance.

Vicki Winslow was smart, but then, he'd known that already. And pretty. No, pretty was too insipid a description. Striking was more accurate, with that flame red hair and the face of a Botticelli angel. As for the body, well, that was pure twentieth-century modern— slim, trim and curved in all the right places.

Stop it, Alexander, he ordered himself. *That kind of thinking could get you in real trouble.* He jammed the light-sensitive shades on his nose and waited.

"You were wearing the glasses when you were in court. I saw you talking to Marshal Carelli."

Observant, too, Caine realized. He'd stopped by the courtroom only once, simply to see the woman who had Danny so uptight. It had been late in the afternoon and he'd stayed at the back of the room, out of the way—an unobtrusive visit, he'd thought. Obviously he'd been wrong.

"I'm surprised you noticed or remembered," he told her.

"At the time, the trial was an unending blur, but I'm finding, now that it's over, that minute details seem to be imprinted on my mind—like a nightmare you can't shake off. I even remember the sneers and the malice on... on different faces in the courtroom."

She meant on Henderson's face. Caine pushed away his sudden surge of sympathy. Sentiment, emotion of any kind, was a good way to get them both killed. He'd learned that a long time ago.

"The memories—they'll fade in time," he offered brusquely.

She gave him a penetrating look. "Fade, maybe. But they never really go away, do they?"

Intelligent, observant and perceptive. What else made Vicki Winslow tick? Caine wondered. Did she read minds, too? "No," he said, surprising himself at his admission. "No, they never go away completely."

If time could be measured in silence, the next few moments spanned a decade. Caine cleared his throat. "Well, Ms. Winslow," he asked finally, "have you decided to trust me?"

She studied him for another moment, then spoke quietly to the dogs. Both animals sprawled at her feet. "I believe Henderson didn't send you, if that's what you mean," she told him. "But I still don't know why you're here or how that helps anything. The fact that you found me means they now have another trail to follow."

"I didn't leave a trail," Caine found himself protesting. "Besides, I'm not an official player. There's no connection between me and the federal marshal's office, no reason for anyone to suspect I'm here on Danny's behalf."

One-handed, she flipped the wallet closed and tossed it back to him. "It doesn't matter. They either find me or they don't. I'm not running anymore."

"Ms. Winslow—" Caine began.

"Go on back where you came from, Mr. Alexander. Tell Marshal Carelli I'm safe, or as safe as I'm going to be until this is over. Tell him I declined your offer of help, just as I declined his. You do more harm than good here. Until you showed up, only three people knew I was here. Now there are at least four..."

She didn't finish her statement. She didn't have to. By the time Caine gathered his thoughts, she'd signaled the dogs and all three had disappeared behind the firmly closed cabin door.

So that's that, Caine thought, shoving his wallet into his hip pocket. He'd parked his vehicle on the main road, half a mile from the cutoff to Tremayne's hunting cabin. He'd followed Baxter's advice, too, and stored the Mercedes in a garage in Fayetteville. Then he'd acquired a battered-looking pickup that appeared generic to this part of the world. Vicki Winslow had no cause to accuse him of leaving a trail to her doorstep.

Not that it mattered. He'd offered her his help and been firmly refused. As soon as he retrieved his Mercedes, he'd be on his way. He'd go back where he belonged, away from this crazy place where millionaires masqueraded as farmers in down-at-the-heels cowboy boots, and redheads with Botticelli faces wielded double-barreled shotguns.

Ms. Vicki Winslow was a hard lady, and as stubborn as reported. She was independent, determined and very able to take care of herself. If he hadn't been able to convince her he was friend, instead of foe, he had little doubt she'd have pulled the trigger of that shotgun. Probably both barrels.

Ah, hell, who was he trying to kid? Vicki Winslow was scared. Like it or not, admit it or not, the lady was in trouble. He'd seen her vulnerability, the bruised resignation in her eyes. Okay, so maybe she would have pulled the trigger, but it would have been an act of desperation, not malice.

In a perfect world, virtue was rewarded, the good lived forever and the bad died young—but no one knew better than Caine that this was not a perfect world. Certainly he had few illusions left about himself. It was his idealistic kid sister's faith that kept him going through the motions. Maggie was his one slim claim to redemption.

The image of his sister's face as he'd last seen her rose in his mind.

Maggie believed he could slay dragons.

And he, Caine concluded, had no choice but to try.

So, okay, he'd disappear for now, leave Little Falls and stay out of sight, at least out of Vicki Winslow's sight. But he'd be nearby, someplace where he could keep an eye on developments.

When the dragon ventured from his lair, as Caine was sure he would, he would be ready. Like it or not, Vicki Winslow had a champion. He'd never really had a choice.

RAIN PELTED against the tin roof of the cabin, blown by whipping winds that synthesized the staccato sound of individual drops into a continuous reverberating roar. Rafter-shaking cracks of thunder, like crashing cymbals, sharply punctuated the incessant din of the storm. Outside the window, trees, still winter bare, whipped to and fro in the wind, dipping and swaying as if dancing to a frenzied tune.

"Bet you'd forgotten how it feels to be caught in a real Arkansas toad smasher," Harve said from his seat in front of the hearth.

"We have thunderstorms in D.C., too," Vicki told him.

"Yeah, but not many tin roofs."

Vicki made a feeble attempt to laugh and turned to look out the window. "No, not many tin roofs," she admitted. "It's funny. I remember I used to like thunderstorms—the louder and fiercer the better, as long as I was inside. There was a feeling of security—the sound and fury all around, yet knowing it couldn't touch me. Today it sounds like an overture to... I don't know what. I guess I'm a coward, but I'm glad you're here, Harve."

Harve snorted. "A coward, you're not, Victoria Winslow. You're a little edgy. It's the electricity in the air. Look, it's even got Sweetpea upset."

At the sound of her name, Sweetpea let out a squeak and pranced awkwardly from one foot to the other. She'd deserted her usual daytime hiding place under the couch at the first clamorous sounds of the storm, taking up vigilance on the windowsill.

"It's all right, Sweetpea," Vicki assured her. "You're safe and dry."

Sweetpea emitted a series of squeaks, then resumed pacing the windowsill, her black-and-white flag of a tail aloft, her attention riveted on the storm howling outside the glass.

"I hope Tucker and Gourdy are safe. The storm came up the valley so fast it was here before I realized it. I didn't have time to call them in."

"The dogs can take care of themselves," Harve assured her. "They'll be fine, sheltering in a cave somewhere. You'll see them soon as this blows through."

Vicki accepted his assurance, knowing her agitation wasn't about the dogs or the storm.

"Getting cabin fever, cuz?" Harve asked. "You don't have to stay here, you know. You can come over to the farm or go to Grandmother's—"

"No," Vicki said. "I put you in enough danger just by being here. I'm certainly not going to make Aunt Abby or you targets, not any more than I already have. It's the waiting, I guess. I've been here three weeks, and when I think about the weeks, months, maybe even years to come... sitting here... Well, I guess I'm wondering if I was wrong, if I should have listened to Marshal Carelli and got on with my life."

"That would have been a sham, not *your* life at all," Harve said. "You know that. Besides, this is a wait-and-see time. If things stay quiet, I don't think you'll have to keep hiding. The trial's over. There's nothing Henderson can do to change that. I think his talk about revenge was nothing more than talk. He's in enough trouble. He'd be stupid to do anything to make it worse. Roy Henderson is scum, but he isn't stupid."

Vicki bit back a sigh. Harve was being logical, but there was no guarantee Henderson's thinking was as rational. She couldn't shake off the feeling she was in danger, and the fact that the federal marshal's office agreed wasn't reassuring.

"Seen anything else of that man from the Down Home?" she asked, keeping her voice deliberately casual. Her cousin was so convinced no one would be able to find her she hadn't dared mention her encounter with Caine Alexander. She didn't believe Alexander was one of Henderson's men, but if Harve knew her hiding place had been discovered by anyone, he would insist she move to the farm. She was determined not to expose her family to that kind of danger. At least here at the cabin she was reasonably isolated.

"He hasn't been spotted in Little Falls, not since that one day last week," Harve said. "I heard he's staying in Fayetteville. He doesn't seem to be doing anything in particular, just spending time playing tourist."

Vicki's pulse jumped unexpectedly. So, he was still around. She wasn't sure whether to be angry or relieved. True, she'd told him to go back where he came from, but several times she'd regretted that, especially at night when the cabin creaked and groaned in the wind and her imagination ran wild.

Stop it, Victoria, she ordered herself. Harve was right. The storm was preying on her nerves. Caine Alexander appeared as if he could take care of himself, but that didn't mean he could take care of her. Or that he'd want to. He was a hard-looking man, his chiseled features stoic, unrelenting, only his eyes showing an occasional glimpse of emotion. And only, she remembered, when he mentioned his sister.

Vicki could relate to that. Her family was important to her, too, even if none was as closely connected as a sibling. But she had a distinct feeling that Caine Alexander was a cold, distant man. Whatever his qualifications, she wouldn't be comfortable around him.

She remembered the weeks prior to Henderson's trial when she'd been safely hidden away. Protective custody, they called it, but it had felt like confinement.

There'd been a parade of agents through the safe house—most of them hard-edged, detached individuals, just like Caine Alexander.

Intellectually she'd understood that, for the agents, protecting her was only a duty, a job. That hadn't made her stay any easier, or the time pass any more quickly. She'd also chafed at being someone else's responsibility. She was used to taking care of herself. A little assistance from family and friends was one thing, but she wasn't comfortable with the idea of leaving her safety to another person. And whatever else he might be, she was sure Caine Alexander was used to being in charge.

Besides, she'd gotten herself into this mess on her own. There were still times she had difficulty accepting how easily she'd been fooled by Roy Henderson. He'd fooled others, too, but that didn't excuse her stupidity. If there was any consolation, it was that, when she'd learned what he really was, she'd been able to hide her discovery from him.

Perversely her success in deceiving Henderson bothered her as much as her original mistaken belief in the man. Had she appeared so dumb, so gullible, so besotted with him that he'd believed he was safe? Or had he expected her to join in his schemes? Is that how others saw her? Weak and superficial?

"Hey, Vicki. Earth to Vicki..."

Harve's voice pulled her from her thoughts. "Sorry, I was thinking..." She forced a smile.

"About things you can't change, I'll bet."

"Knowing that doesn't make it any easier," she said. "How could I have been so stupid?"

"Lighten up, cuz. Henderson might have misled you in the beginning, but remember, you soon saw through him."

"Still, if I hadn't been such a fool—"

"Stop whipping yourself," Harve ordered. "If it wasn't for you, that scum-ball would still be walking around free. You did good—even if it was a case of fools rushing in where angels fear to tread. Pope said that."

"That's me, all right," Vicki said, acknowledging her cousin's attempt to jolly her out of her self-pity. Harve must be getting desperate to resort to that particular cliché.

It had been years since she and Harve had played their private quotation game, but at one time she'd been able to match him quote for quote. Now she dredged her memory for a comeback, even as she admitted Harve's diversion was working. Then she grinned. "Just be careful with the praise, cousin dear," she countered. "It was Boileau who said, 'A fool always finds some greater fool to admire him.'"

"Touché. A good rebuttal, even if I don't agree. Think you can do as well at poker?"

Now she laughed. Poker had been the main pastime during her safe-house stay. "I think it only fair to warn you I've been practicing," she told him.

As the storm moved slowly eastward, Vicki set out to prove her weeks of confinement had served one purpose, anyway. Rain still lashed the windows and thunder still echoed down the valley, but no longer so close that vibrations shook the cabin.

"See you and raise you two," Harve said, pushing a couple of the acorns they were using as chips into the center of the table.

"Call," Vicki answered, matching his bet, then laying down her hand—three deuces and a pair of tens.

Harve shook his head as he laid down his own hand, two pair, jacks high. "I thought you were bluffing."

Vicki laughed again. "I warned you I'd been practicing."

"Sounds as if the storm's about spent," Harve commented as he shuffled the pack. "Probably too wet for most people to be stirring, though. You want to go to Grandmother's for supper?"

"More than anything," Vicki told him, "but I'm not going to—"

Sweetpea's sudden squeak of agitation startled Vicki into an abrupt silence. She looked around for the skunk, found her halfway between the couch and the front door in attack position, all four feet thumping in a staccato rhythm.

Vicki felt her vocal cords tighten as she fought her panic. "Someone's on the porch," she managed to whisper.

"Take it easy, Vicki," Harve said calmly. "It's probably only the dogs, but just in case, move back so you can't be seen through the door."

If anyone was looking, they could see her through the windows, Vicki thought, but she couldn't make herself say the words. Instead, she did as Harve instructed, trying to ignore the adrenaline rush of fear that made her knees weak. Dammit, anyway. She'd thought she'd conquered at least the paralyzing part of her fear. It appeared she was wrong.

Sweetpea let out another squeak, then disappeared under the couch. Harve looked out the window. "It's only the dogs," he said, opening the door and stepping onto the porch. "Throw me a towel, will you? I'll dry them off some before I let them in."

"Are you all right?" Harve asked once the still-damp dogs were stretched out on the hearth.

"I'm okay now," Vicki told him, knowing it would be futile to deny what had happened. "Sorry I flipped out. Usually I have better control, but occasionally it sneaks up on me. Most of the time, I get mad, instead of frightened."

"Mad's better," Harve agreed, "but I wish you'd move to the farm. There'd be other people around—"

"Which is exactly why I won't come. We've been through this before," Vicki said. "I'm not going to put anyone else in the line of fire."

"All right. I know better than to try arguing with you." He resumed his seat at the table. "I hope you're ready. I'm out for revenge."

"I thought you were going to Aunt Abby's for dinner."

"And leave you here gloating over my pile of my acorns? Not a chance." He grinned. "Grandmother's not expecting me. I simply thought you might want to get out for a bit. I'm not about to show up alone on a Friday night. She'll give me her it's-time-you-found-a-wife lecture. That pot of soup you've got on the stove smells fine."

"Harve—"

"Come on, cousin. Play cards."

An hour later the storm finally cleared the area, leaving water dripping from the cabin eaves. Raindrops on the west window acted as prisms for the late-afternoon sun, sending tiny dots of light dancing across the cabin's wooden floor.

"Leave my acorns alone," Vicki warned Harve when she got up from the table up to stir the soup. "I won every one of them fair and square." She turned from the stove, then froze. Tucker was in front of the door and standing at point.

"Harve," she whispered hoarsely, but her cousin had already seen the dog. He grabbed the shotgun.

"Don't open that door," Vicki cautioned. "You don't know who's out there."

"Just stay out of the way," Harve warned.

"Hello, the cabin," came the sudden voice from somewhere outside.

Vicki gasped.

"Hey, inside the cabin, anybody home?" called the voice again.

"Get back, Vicki," Harve ordered.

"No, it's all right. I recognize the voice," Vicki told him, thankful that this time it was relief making her knees weak. "It's the man from the Down Home. Caine Alexander."

"How do you know?"

"He showed up here last week. He's not one of Henderson's men. Carelli sent him. I told him to go away, and the reason I didn't tell you about it was because I didn't want you to worry."

Harve gave her a disgusted look and, still cradling the shotgun, opened the door. Vicki stood behind him where she could see over his shoulder. Caine Alexander stepped into the clearing, a backpack slung over one shoulder.

"So, we meet again, Mr. Tremayne," he said.

"It would appear so," Harve answered. "What are you doing here, Mr. Alexander?"

Vicki saw Caine's eyes shift from her cousin to her.

"I'm afraid I have some disturbing news," he said without preamble. "Yesterday, Henderson was being transferred from D.C. to Leavenworth. He escaped."

CHAPTER THREE

CAINE OBSERVED Harve Tremayne's reaction to the news of Henderson's escape with an appreciation that bordered on awe. The down-home millionaire's inventive description of Roy Henderson's ancestry and intrinsic value was the most original, caustic and colorfully eloquent he'd ever heard. If speech were visual, as well as audible, the air around the cabin door would, indeed, be blue.

Victoria Winslow, on the other hand, didn't say a word. She went stock-still, her lips compressed into a straight thin line, the color draining from her face like a white drape being pulled across a window. Caine tensed, anticipating her collapse.

She surprised him. Again. Instead of crumbling into a heap at his feet, she stiffened her spine and straightened her shoulders like a general about to enter battle.

"Does he know where I am?" she asked, her voice emotionless. It would have fooled most people, but Caine recognized her careful control.

"Not that we know of," he said, watching her face. "That, however, doesn't mean he isn't looking."

"Oh, yes. I have no doubt he's looking. He swore revenge."

"That makes absolutely no sense," her cousin protested. "Henderson's a wanted man, a man on the run. Surely he realizes you're on guard. Why would he jeopardize his escape by looking for you?"

Caine had tried to tell Danny the same thing, but his brother-in-law insisted Henderson's men were actively hunting Vicki, had never abandoned the search, even after the trial and Henderson's incarceration. He couldn't discount Danny's information, but the revenge scenario didn't fit. Revenge was an act of passion. It was also a useless emotion, not at all Roy Henderson's style. Unless the threats were a smoke screen for—

"Well, that settles it. You're moving to the farm where we can mount a better guard," Tremayne said.

"No."

"Be reasonable, Vicki."

"I am not going to the farm, and that's final. If I'm in danger, it wouldn't be safe for either you or me. I'm safer here."

"She's right," Caine agreed. "If Henderson learns of her ties to this area, the first thing he'll do is check the relatives."

Tremayne gave him a startled look, as if he had just remembered his presence. "Exactly who are you, Mr. Alexander?" he demanded belligerently. "Vicki says you're from the federal marshal's office. Does that mean you're here to take her back into protective custody?"

Caine refused to be intimidated. "It's the witness protection program," he corrected, "and I'm sure she'd be accepted, if that's what she decides to do. But I'm not a federal marshal. I'm not here in any official capacity."

"Then my question stands. Why are you—"

"I am not turning my life back over to a bunch of federal guards, either," Vicki interrupted.

"Wait a minute, Vicki—" Tremayne began.

"No. It's my life and my decision. I'm staying here. Go home, Harve. As for you, Mr. Alexander, you go home, too. Tell Danny Carelli I'm no longer his concern," she said, her eyes flashing green, like light caught in water.

For a moment, as their gazes collided, Caine felt the net closing around him. There was something about this woman. If he wasn't careful, she'd be under his skin.

He also knew, in spite of all logic, that she was in danger. The knowledge was intuitive, but indisputable. *Get used to it, buddy,* he told himself, accepting the inevitable. *You're in Little Falls for the duration.*

She held his gaze for another second, then turned her attention back to her cousin. "I mean it, Harve. Go home. Both of you." With that she disappeared inside the cabin.

Caine eyed Tremayne warily.

The man returned his scrutiny. "You any good at this bodyguard business?" he asked abruptly.

"I'm here, aren't I?"

"Meaning you've survived?"

"Right."

"Okay. Vicki trusts Carelli, and she says you're his man. Guess that'll have to be good enough. I'll hire you to protect Vicki."

"Not necessary. I told Carelli I'd protect her. That's why I'm here. I don't need another boss," he added, deliberately leaving the impression that he was on Danny's payroll.

Tremayne shrugged. "Whatever you say. You might as well come in. Vicki'll be over her snit in a minute. Then we should be able to talk some sense into her. She'll realize she overreacted, that she needs someone. Right now, she's mad—and scared."

Caine nodded. "She has reason to be angry," he growled, "and she'd be stupid if she wasn't scared."

He entered the cabin, dropping his pack by the door, not sure what to expect. As he examined the cozy furnishings of what was essentially one large room, he acknowledged a feeling of calm, one that ignored the chaos of the outside world. Not particularly to his taste, he admitted, but it was certainly more than a primitive hunting cabin.

The place had a museum quality. Inside window shutters, complete with gun slots, told him the cabin had been standing for a long time—perhaps since the days of the Arkansas frontier. The shutters were folded back against thick log walls, although nothing indicated they weren't still serviceable. A thick wooden pole, bearing evidence of its ax-hewed origins, was propped beside the doorframe, ready to be positioned in the iron holders to bar the cabin door. All in all, the cabin looked as if it had been constructed for defense, a quality that might come in handy again, Caine thought.

Modern conveniences had been added, too. An overstuffed couch, designed for comfort rather than style, sat perpendicular to the massive stone hearth, an open book temporarily abandoned on its cushions. Flickering light from burning logs reflected from cast-iron and brass fireplace implements.

The dogs raised their heads from the braided rug in front of the hearth, gave him a cursory glance, then returned to napping.

"The shorthaired pointer is named Tucker. We call the black and tan, Gourdy," Harve told Caine. "They don't look very fierce at the moment, but they make good guard dogs when required."

Caine acknowledged Harve's comment with a wry smile. "We've met," he said, remembering his earlier confrontation with Vicki. It was an image that resurfaced in his mind all too often, the defiant redhead courageously standing her ground, eyes spitting green sparks in spite of the worry and fatigue hidden in their depths.

He made a deliberate effort to banish the memory and returned his attention to his surroundings.

Two unmatched upholstered chairs faced the couch, a piecework quilt draped casually over the back on one. The chairs were separated by a low table, which also showed evidence of its handmade ancestry. A dark wood trestle table, the remains of a card game scattered across its top, and four ladder-back chairs stood on one side of the room. Beyond the table, Caine could see an old-fashioned pump handle positioned over an ancient sink.

Massive log beams, darkened with smoke and age, stretched over the room. On the north end of the cabin, a open-tread wood stairway led to a railed half loft.

Victoria Winslow was nowhere in sight.

"You two still around?" Vicki asked, as if his thoughts had conjured her up from her hiding place. She was peering over the top of the rail.

"Yeah, we're here, cuz," Harve answered. "Come on down. We've got plans to make."

"I already told you, I'm staying right here."

"Vicki, be sensible—"

"It's okay, Ms. Winslow," Caine interrupted. "Staying here's a good idea, at least for now. We can make other plans later if necessary."

"We?" Her voice was almost a squeak.

"That's right. I'm staying, too."

"Now wait a minute," Vicki said, scrambling down the stairway, but Caine ignored her protest and turned to her cousin.

"You have any terrain maps of this area? I need to find a place to conceal the truck, far enough away not to be immediately connected with this cabin, but close enough to reach if we need it. A portable phone wouldn't be a bad idea, either—in case of emergency. And is there any way you can cut off the road into the cabin from the highway—or at least disguise the entrance? It's beginning to look a little too used."

"The maps are no problem," Tremayne told him. "There's a back way into the property from the farm and an old hay barn should hide your truck. It's about half a mile away. Vicki already has a cellular phone. As to disguising the turnoff to the cabin, well, I've been meaning to clear out the brush. The tractor work will hide the entry. The neighbors'll know it's there, of course, but it won't be so obvious. Today's storm should have erased most of the signs of recent use. I'll use the back entry from now on. Is that all?"

"For the moment," Caine said. "Once I take a look at the maps we may want to set up some perimeter security. I'll decide that later."

"He can't stay here," Vicki objected.

"Of course he can," Harve told her. "It's the perfect solution. You know Grandmother and I have been worried about your being here by yourself. You can't be alert all the time. But with two of you and the dogs—"

"No. It won't work. Besides, what'll people say? You know how Aunt Abby hates gossip. She won't agree to this."

"There won't be any gossip. No one knows you're here, remember? And even if they guess, they certainly don't know about Mr. Alexander. Besides, *'Cum finis est licitus, etiam media sunt licita.* The end justifies the means.' Busenbaum said that, as I remember."

"Dammit, Harve, this is no time to be spouting quotations. This is serious. I don't want Mr. Alexander here. I don't want anyone here."

"Will you let me take you back to Danny, Ms. Winslow?" Caine interrupted.

"To enter the witness protection program? No, thanks."

"Then I stay."

"And I have nothing to say about it?"

"That's right. You had two choices. You eliminated one. Unless you'd like to reconsider..."

If the fury in her eyes had substance, he'd be in real danger, Caine thought. Hell, who was he trying to fool?

He was in real danger, anyway, and not only, he suspected, from Henderson and his henchmen.

Caine tried to push the thought away. Vicki Winslow was a fascinating woman. Reluctantly he acknowledged his attraction, knowing he'd be lying to himself if he attempted to deny it. But the acknowledgment was all he would, all he could, allow himself. He had to stay focused. To do otherwise would be courting disaster.

"I don't think I like you very much, Mr. Alexander."

"That's not a prerequisite." Caine deliberately made his voice distant and unconcerned. "Just do what I tell you, and we'll get along fine."

"There, I'm glad that's settled," Harve interjected before Vicki could translate her sputtering outrage into words. "It's almost dark. You need anything else?"

"I'm fine for the night," Caine told him, indicating his pack. "The truck will be okay for now, too. I'll move it tomorrow after I see those maps."

"Okay, then. I'll see you in the morning," Harve said, grabbing his Stetson from the hat peg.

"Harvey Gibson Tremayne III, you come back here. You can't leave like this."

"Gotta go, cuz," Harve told her, stepping out the door. "You're in good hands. I'll see you tomorrow."

"Coward!" Vicki yelled after him.

"Shame on you, Victoria Winslow," Harve called over his shoulder. "Remember Lord Lyttelton's advice—'A woman's noblest station is retreat.'"

"Lord Lyttelton can stick it in his ear. And you, too."

Somehow Caine managed to swallow his laugh. Lord, what a spitfire! It was, he supposed, Danny's stories of

Vicki Winslow's determination, her humor, her refusal to despair that had first captivated his interest. For some unfathomable reason, Caine found himself intrigued, so intrigued he'd been unable to resist the temptation to see the lady for himself.

His visit to the courtroom that one afternoon was the step that had plunged him into this web, he admitted. He swore silently. It was too late to undo. He was committed. He could no more abandon her now than a politician could resist a fund-raiser.

But no more quixotic gestures. He'd keep his distance, do his job, and maybe, just maybe, when this was over, he could return to his own world without new ghosts to haunt him.

He dared a quick glance at the woman who'd been central to his thoughts for the past several weeks. It wasn't like him to let personal interest threaten his focus. Concentrate on the job at hand, not the object, he reminded himself once again. But even as he delivered his silent pep talk, he knew that ignoring Vicki Winslow would be the hardest thing he'd ever done.

HAD IT BEEN only an hour since Harve had left? Vicki wondered as she glanced yet again at her watch. Never had time passed so slowly. And why did the cabin suddenly seem so small, so claustrophobic?

She looked around ruefully. There was nothing different, nothing out of place, nothing except for the man sitting in front of the fire, reading a paperback book he'd dug out of his pack.

"Just do what you usually do, Ms. Winslow," he'd told her shortly after Harve left. "I'll try to stay out of your way. You can even pretend I'm not here."

Sure she could. She could also pretend the moon was made of green cheese.

Oh, she'd tried, all right. She'd dragged out the laptop, set it up on the table and turned diligently to her task of cataloging. Not that she'd accomplished anything. She hadn't even been successful at losing herself in the pages of family history. *He* kept intruding.

It wasn't that he'd done anything to attract her attention. As far as she knew, Caine Alexander hadn't so much as glanced in her direction. He certainly hadn't spoken. He simply sat there reading as if he was completely alone. In fact, during the past hour, other than turning pages of his book, the only time he'd moved was to let the dogs outside. He hadn't said anything then, either, only looked at her questioningly when the dogs stirred from the rug and positioned themselves in front of the cabin door. When she'd nodded, he'd opened the door for them, then returned to his chair.

With a suppressed sigh, Vicki flipped off the switch of the laptop and looked surreptitiously in Caine's direction. He was a big man—the denim jacket, which he hadn't bothered to remove, was stretched taut across wide shoulders. And hard-looking, his face all angles and planes. Even the dimple in his left cheek looked chiseled. She'd bet he rarely smiled, that the faint lines fanning from the corners of his eyes were the result of outdoor exposure, not laughter.

His eyes were brown, a rich chocolate brown, but guarded, not reflecting any emotion. His hair was also

brown, almost black. Her impression was of a totally
closed-off, emotionless man. He was as different from
his friend Danny Carelli as night from day.

Of course, maybe they wouldn't be friends if Carelli
wasn't married to his sister. Or maybe the woman in the
picture wasn't really Carelli's wife. There was no indication of how old the picture was. Maybe Carelli hadn't
sent him, after all.

Ridiculous! Now her imagination was running away
with her. Caine Alexander was exactly who he said he
was. She had to believe that. Besides, even though she
didn't want him here, instinct told her he'd come to
help. For some intangible reason, she wasn't afraid of
him, even if he did scare her half to death.

Not afraid, but scared? *Get a grip! Victoria. You're
thinking crazy*.

What was it about him that intrigued her so? She
found it disturbing that she'd almost recognized him the
first time he'd approached the cabin. And when he'd
donned his sunglasses, it had taken her only a second to
place him.

She even remembered how she'd watched his entry
into the courtroom, an entrance that apparently attracted no notice, raised no eyebrows—except hers.
True, she was on the witness stand facing him, but that
didn't account for her peculiar interest in his arrival.
For a moment, as he stood just inside the door, she
could have sworn he was just as interested in her.

Maybe, she told herself, it was because at that moment, she'd desperately needed something, someone, to
distract her from the other man in the courtroom who
was making her the sole object of his attention. From

his position behind the defendant's table, Roy Henderson hadn't bothered to disguise his malice.

In contrast, the expression on the stranger's face—the man she now knew as Caine Alexander—had been so bland, so nonthreatening, it seemed a calm in the eye of the storm of ill will swirling around her.

Yes, she told herself, that was why she'd watched him, why her subconscious had recorded and retained his image.

Up close and personal, however, Caine Alexander was neither bland nor nonthreatening. She dared another quick look in his direction. One thing was certain. Their present state of silent standoff wasn't going to work. Trying to pretend he wasn't here was as ridiculous as trying to pretend she'd never heard the name Roy Henderson.

She carefully stacked the papers back in Aunt Abby's trunk and replaced the laptop in its carrying case. Then she took a deep breath. "Would you like a bowl of soup, Mr. Alexander?"

"I don't want to be any trouble, Ms. Winslow," he answered. "I said you could pretend I wasn't here."

"It was a ridiculous suggestion and you know it."

He shrugged. "It seemed to be what you wanted."

"What I want is for the last six months never to have happened, but wishing won't make it so," she said, exasperation clear in her voice.

"Does that mean we have a truce, Ms. Winslow?"

"I guess so. I don't want you here. But what I want hasn't seemed to matter much lately, so I'll try to make the best of it. And do you think you could call me

Vicki? Every time you say Ms. Winslow, I want to look over my shoulder to see who you're talking to.''

His brown-eyed gaze captured hers and an almost smile twisted his lips. ''Done, if you agree to call me Caine. The last person I remember calling me Mr. Alexander was my high-school chemistry teacher. And believe me, I don't enjoy being reminded of her.''

Vicki caught her breath. What, she wondered, would it take to make him really smile?

''Okay, Caine. Would you like a bowl of soup?''

He shrugged again. ''I meant it when I said I didn't want to cause you any trouble.''

''Oh, for heaven's sake! The soup's already made. The pot's on the stove. Fill your own bowl. Bowls on are the shelf above the sink.''

''Truce, remember? And thank you very much Ms. Win—I mean, Vicki. A bowl of soup sounds delicious. I'll help myself.''

''Has anyone ever told you you're an exasperating man?'' Vicki asked as he moved past her, his soft footsteps unusual in a man so tall and muscularly built.

''Often,'' he said, reaching for a bowl. ''I'm told it's one of my more endearing traits.'' He gave her another of those almost smiles.

''Bully for you,'' she muttered as she watched him fill the bowl and move to the table. ''I'm afraid to ask about your less endearing qualities.''

''Just as well. I sincerely hope you won't have reason to see them,'' he said, taking a seat.

She couldn't help but notice he'd chosen the chair that placed his back to the wall, giving him a clear view of the front door. Was caution so ingrained in him he'd chosen that position instinctively? She shivered.

"Look, Vicki," he said suddenly, "I'm here to do a job. First names are fine. They're more convenient, but you don't have to worry about playing Southern hostess. I can look after myself."

"In other words, a truce, but keep your distance."

He nodded. "It's best to stay focused on business."

Vicki moved into the kitchen area and poured herself a cup of coffee. Why did he find common courtesy so threatening? He was here on her behalf, even though she'd made it plain she'd rather be left alone. And, she supposed, she'd do as he said, within reason, anyway. He was, after all, the expert. But she wasn't going to let him dictate how she acted in her own home. Southern hostess indeed!

She hesitated, then filled a second mug. She'd pour him a cup of coffee if she wanted to, and if he didn't like it, he could either choke on it or ignore it. She walked to the table and plunked the cup down in front of him.

"Here. And before you say a word, I am not playing Southern hostess. I was pouring myself one, anyway, so it was no trouble. If you don't like it black, sugar and creamer are on the sink cabinct. I'm sure you'd rather get them yourself."

He had the grace to look slightly abashed.

"Black's fine," he said after a moment, "and before...well, I didn't mean to sound unappreciative, but it isn't necessary for you to go to any extra trouble."

"I didn't. I made the coffee for myself, but I wouldn't drink the whole pot, anyway. So you're actually doing me a favor. I don't like waste."

"Look. I've already said I was sorry."

"You did?"

"Well, I tried, but we seem to be having a communication problem."

Vicki studied his face. "Oh, I don't think so, Caine. I understood perfectly what you were trying to say. You're a private person. You don't feel comfortable allowing people too close. It's in the way you move, the way you talk, even the look in your eyes. Keep out. No trespassing."

His face remained impassive, but something flickered in the depths of his eyes. Vicki rushed on before he could interrupt.

"Now I, on the other hand, am usually a more friendly type. I meet people expecting to like them. I think we need to reach some kind of compromise here. If you want to continue your imitation of an agitated porcupine, go right ahead. *I* will continue to act as I usually do, too. And that includes offering a guest in my house a bowl of soup or a cup of coffee. If you don't want it, all you have to do is say so. If, however, you're hungry or thirsty, saying yes isn't a violation of your principles. Nor will I take it as a signal that you wish to become friends."

"Are you through now?"

"For the moment."

His gaze held hers, then to her astonishment, the craggy planes of his face cracked as his mouth curled upward into what she could only describe as a reluctant smile. "I've heard stories of redheads and tempers all my life, but this is the first time I've seen one in action. Lady, you could give cabdrivers lessons."

"Now wait a minute—"

"Hey, truce. White flag. That was a compliment," he said quickly. "I admire people who aren't afraid to speak their mind."

"You . . . you do?"

"I do. As for the porcupine bit, my little sister calls it my grumpy-bear routine. And this time I'll say it very clearly. I'm sorry. As you so adroitly recognized, it's my usual manner. Nothing personal."

The man had actually said he was sorry! In spite of all the reasons why she shouldn't, she found herself liking him—a little.

"Well, I may have been a little prickly too," she admitted.

IT WAS A COMMENT Caine readily agreed with, especially in light of her recent tongue-lashing, but one he decided to let pass. "Let's just agree that circumstances have been somewhat difficult."

She nodded, as if recognizing and accepting his olive branch. "So, what's next?"

What was next? Good question. Problem was, he didn't know the answer. Something still didn't feel right about this. True, Henderson was on the loose, but in spite of the man's ravings, revenge didn't fit the profile. Yet Vicki was definitely in danger. There was too much talk on the street for it to be idle rumor. Caine had the feeling he was missing something somewhere— that they all were—and he suspected it involved the unrecovered money.

"One day at a time," he told her, "at least for now." He picked up his empty soup bowl and deposited it in the sink. "I'll take a look at your cousin's maps tomorrow. Make the cabin and surrounding area as secure as possible. Then we wait."

Vicki sighed. "Sometimes this whole thing seems like a bad dream. Except I can't seem to wake up."

"I know." He worked to keep the sympathy from his voice. "Just remember, it'll end."

Caine turned and stepped from the kitchen area into the main room. Then he froze. He blinked twice, not sure he was actually seeing what he thought he was seeing. Behind him he heard Vicki catch her breath.

"Caine, what's—"

"Shh. Don't move and don't make a sound."

"But what—"

He swallowed against the instinct to yell at her to be still. "Quiet," he whispered desperately, his eyes locked on the furry black-and-white animal emerging from beneath the couch. "There's a skunk in here." He took a step backward, placing himself between Vicki and the animal.

In spite of his caution, the skunk must have sensed his movement, maybe even the desperation in his whisper. It emitted a series of squeaks and flipped around, presenting Caine with a full back view as it raised its tail defensively.

Caine stopped the automatic action of his hand sliding toward his shoulder holster, realizing a gun here would do more damage than good. Besides, the skunk felt as threatened as he did and was only doing what came naturally. He searched his mind for an alternative. He couldn't just stand here. Well, at least Harvey

Tremayne would be happy. There'd be no question of staying in the cabin after this.

Slowly he lowered his hand, reaching for the quilt that lay across the back of the chair. Maybe he could use the quilt like a net. Maybe, if he was quick enough and extremely lucky, he could—

Before he could finish forming the thought, Vicki pushed past him.

"Don't," he managed to gasp, but he was too late. She'd already scooped the creature into her arms. Caine caught his breath and waited for the inevitable, mentally exercising his ability to curse in six languages.

"It's only Sweetpea," Vicki said turning to face him. "She's a pet."

"A pet?" Caine echoed. "But it's a skunk."

"Skunks made good pets. They're clean, intelligent and like being around people."

Her gaze shifted from his face to his right hand, now resting on the quilt.

"What were you going to do? Smother her?"

Caine shrugged. "I thought it was worth a try."

"Sweetpea's been altered, deodorized. But if she was still intact, she'd have been too fast. And you'd have ruined Aunt Abby's quilt."

Caine let his hand fall to his side. "I guess so, but I couldn't think of anything else to do." He sank gratefully into the closest chair.

"In a face-off with a skunk, the best thing to do is nothing. Or back away. Even when threatened, spraying is a skunk's last resort. Unless he's caught by surprise, he'd rather just go away."

"I'll try to remember that," he said, his voice little more than a growl.

Her laughter reverberated through the cabin. "I'm sorry, Caine, but if you could've seen your face... Tell you what, you protect me from the bad guys and I'll protect you from the wildlife."

"You have any more exotic pets around? A wolf? A bear? Maybe a buzzard or two?"

She laughed again and shook her head. Caine found himself enjoying the sound.

"Only the dogs. You've already met them."

"All right, lady. You've got yourself a deal. You protect me from the wildlife, and I'll watch out for the two-legged predators. That should take care of all our problems."

He wished it was that easy, Caine admitted later as he settled into his bedroll in front of the fireplace. But he couldn't shake the feeling that Vicki Winslow herself was more of a threat to him than any skunk—and that included both the two- and four-legged varieties.

CHAPTER FOUR

HOW DID HE DO IT? Vicki wondered. Caine had only arrived three days ago, but to watch him and Harve talking and joking together, you'd think they'd been best buddies since kindergarten.

She'd almost decided that it was a male-bonding thing, that he didn't know how to relate to the female of the species. He certainly ignored her when he could. When he couldn't, he was reserved, distant—about as congenial as a mother possum with a bellyache.

Since that first morning in the cabin when she'd come down from the loft to find him wearing nothing but his B.V.D.s, he'd been extremely circumspect in coping with their forced intimacy. Now she could laugh about it, picturing his frantic dive across the room for his pants. Then she'd been too busy trying to disguise her own embarrassment.

"I made the coffee," he'd offered, hastily pulling on his jeans.

"That sounds good," she'd said, trying to act as if seeing an almost naked man in her living room was an everyday occurrence. Grateful for any excuse to hide the blush she'd felt rising in her cheeks, she'd turned her back to him to pour her coffee.

"I apologize for my lack of...of forethought," he'd said stiffly. "I didn't realize you were awake. It won't happen again."

Damn right, it won't! Vicki vowed. From now on she'd give him adequate warning, even if she had to ring a cowbell before she came downstairs. It wasn't that she was a prude, but the sight of Caine Alexander in the almost altogether was too disturbing for her peace of mind.

He *was* courteous, she'd grant him that. But it was a cold, detached courtesy, as if he found talking to her, being in the same room with her, a chore—necessary but unpleasant, like having your teeth cleaned.

But Harve liked him. And the dogs adored him. After the great skunk stare-down, even Sweetpea had decided Caine Alexander was the best thing since raw hamburger. Vicki tried to convince herself that his aloofness didn't matter, that he was only here to do a job.

Still, it hurt.

She watched as Harve's pickup pulled up in front of the cabin. He wasn't alone this morning. He'd brought the octogenarian family matriarch, who was here, she said, "to get a look at the man who's living with my great-niece."

Aunt Abby made the announcement as she stepped down from Harve's muddy pickup with the aplomb of a visiting duchess and an agility that belied her eight decades. Spine straight, chin tilted arrogantly, makeup flawlessly applied and every strand of her snow-white hair perfectly coiled into a chignon, she confronted Caine with a piercing look from her still-bright blue eyes—a look known to have caused senators and IRS investigators to regress into shuffling schoolboys. It was imperial Abigail Tremayne at her best.

But Aunt Abby hadn't fazed Caine Alexander. Oh, no. He met the woman's gaze without flinching, greeted her with a composure that rivaled an English butler's at high tea and offered her his hand.

"I regret the necessity of impropriety," he said, "but your grand-niece's safety is my first priority."

"That sounds like a speech from a pretentious Victorian novel," Aunt Abby told him, her lips pursed as if she'd taken a bite of a sour green apple. "You, young man, are a fraud."

Caine grinned then, like a schoolboy caught with cookie crumbs on his face. "Only in manner, ma'am, not intent. I assure you, I have your niece's best interests at heart."

"Didn't your mother teach you not to ape your betters?"

"My mother taught me I had no betters."

Aunt Abby's face stilled, then her lips twitched into a smile.

"Well said, Mr. Alexander. You'll do."

"Thank you, Mrs. Tremayne." Then he added in a softer voice, "And I think, perhaps this once, my mother may have been wrong."

Vicki observed the scene like someone watching a stage play. First Harve, then Tucker, Gourdy and

Sweetpea, and now Aunt Abby. Was Vicki the only one not willing to fall victim to Caine's unorthodox brand of careless charm?

She knew it was the wrong question even as she composed the thought. She was as willing to be charmed by Caine Alexander as anyone else. It was Caine who was dictating the terms of their relationship. That he didn't bother to notice her interest, or worse, that he couldn't have cared less, was humiliating.

When Aunt Abby was comfortably settled in the cabin, the two men left, carrying several small boxes of electronic equipment—which was the official reason for Harve's visit.

"I like your Mr. Alexander," Aunt Abby said, turning to her niece.

Vicki managed to stifle a snort. "He's hardly mine, Aunt Abby. In case you haven't noticed, the man scarcely says a word to me."

Aunt Abby's blue eyes twinkled. "He does seem quite determined, doesn't he? Reminds me of your great-uncle. He was prickly as a briar patch when we first met, too. Took me weeks to pull his thorns."

Vicki gave her aunt a bewildered glance. "What do you mean?"

"Simply that a man who fights himself has already lost. Never you mind, dear. Everything will be all right. You'll see."

"Now wait a minute, Aunt Abby. If you've got any matchmaking ideas about Caine Alexander and me, you can forget them," Vicki protested. "The man barely tolerates me. Besides, he's too cold, too hard—"

"Well, of course, dear. I didn't like your great-uncle Harvey much when I first met him, either. Did you know we spent the first two years of our married life in this cabin? It was cozy when there were only the two of us, but when Junior came along, well, thank goodness the big house was finished a short time later. We designed the house for a large family, but as it turned out, young Harvey was our only one."

Aunt Abby sighed. "I've been waiting for that house to be filled with children for over fifty years. It didn't happen for me and my Harvey, didn't happen for Junior and his wife, either. Now my grandson's living there—all alone. I tell you, Vicki, there are times when I despair. All those rooms, just going to waste. I want to see my great-grandchildren. I'm not getting any younger. And neither is Harvey."

Vicki breathed a grateful prayer that Aunt Abby had turned the conversation to Harve's matrimonial prospects. For reasons she couldn't analyze, she didn't want to think about Caine Alexander. Her cousin's love life, or the lack of it, was a topic guaranteed to keep her great-aunt's thoughts occupied and usually did, much to Harve's disgruntlement.

"Harve will find someone to love, Aunt Abby," Vicki tried to assure her aunt. "It's simply taking him a while to get over losing Rosalind. Give him time."

"Time! I'm running out of time. I'm eighty-seven years old. Rosalind died three years ago. She was a sweet girl, but it's time for Harvey to move on."

Vicki wondered if Harve would ever move on. He'd been devastated when his fiancée died in a car accident only weeks before their wedding. The worst of his grief seemed to be behind him now, but if he was dating anyone special, he hadn't mentioned it to her.

"I want him settled before I'm gone, and that may not be too far in the future. I want you settled, too," Aunt Abby continued. "Your mother would have wanted you married, happy, with a family. I don't want to face her up there without being able to report all's well."

Vicki felt creeping anxiety. Aunt Abby never talked this way. Was she ill?

"Are you feeling all right, Aunt Abby?" she asked. "You're not sick and hiding it from us, are you?"

"Bless you, child. I'm fine, or as fine as an any eighty-seven-year-old has a right to be. Better than most, I suspect. But common sense says I'm not going to be around for too many more years. I've outlived my sister, my husband, my son and most of my contemporaries. Still, I'd like to see you and Harve married and happy before the good Lord calls me home."

"Aunt Abby..."

"Now, no call for such a long face, child. It's only the truth and you know it. Never could stand folks who acted as if they were going to live forever. I'm realistic. I know my time's coming, but that doesn't mean I'm just sitting here waiting. I have a few things to do first. I expect you to cooperate, Victoria Abigail Winslow.''

Vicki tried unsuccessfully to laugh. ''Considering the circumstances, that's going to be a little difficult, Aunt Abby. I don't think hiding out in a backwoods hunting cabin is on any of the lists of Best Places to Meet the Man of Your Dreams.''

''Hiding out doesn't mean hiding from yourself, Vicki. You remember that. I'm sorry about the circumstances that brought you here, but I can't say I'm sorry you're here, child. We haven't had much a chance to talk these past few years with your being so busy up there in Washington and all. I figure that now is a good time. I just want you to know that when I'm gone, I'm leaving you my place.''

''Your place!'' Vicki gasped. ''But Harve's your grandson. He should—''

''Harvey has the Tremayne farm. Your grandmother and I were Smiths—we grew up in the *old* house. Of course, there were Smiths living there long before that, back when Arkansas was still a territory. Your grandmother, Laurel, was my older sister and you're her direct descendant. It's only right you should have it.

''And don't you go worrying about your cousin, either,'' she added. ''Harvey knows all about this and he agrees. When the time comes, the Smith place is yours. A person needs roots. Yours are here. Always have been.''

Vicki blinked against sudden tears. ''I...I don't know what to say.''

"Nothing for you to say, child. I wanted you to know so there wouldn't be any misunderstanding when the time comes. But don't you go holding your breath, missy. I've already told you, I'm not ready to go just yet. Not until I see what kind of man you pick. And if you'd hurry up a bit, I might get a glimpse of the next generation of redheaded hellions."

The image of a little girl, with red curls, big chocolate brown eyes and a deep dimple in her left cheek danced into Vicki's mind. For a moment the child was so real it took her breath away. Nonsense, she told herself. It was Aunt Abby's talk of redheads and generations. She shook her head and the image disappeared.

"A woman no longer has to marry and raise a family to be fulfilled," she reminded her aunt gently. "There are other things."

"Of course there are," Aunt Abby returned. "But sharing your life with the right person makes everything brighter, more important, more meaningful. I spent thirty-seven years married to my Harvey. It's been almost that much time since he died. Believe me, together is better."

Vicki sighed. "I know you're right—if you pick the right person—but so far, my track record hasn't been all that good."

"Oh, fiddlesticks," Aunt Abby said. "How do you expect to pick the right one if you haven't had the chance to see a few wrong ones? Your time will come, Vicki. Just be sure you don't waste it. The good Lord provides the opportunities, but don't expect Him to hand them to you on a silver platter. You may have to fight for what you want, although heaven knows why I'm telling you that. You never were one to sit back meekly and wait. Always went after what you wanted. I just thought I'd remind you that now's not the time to change your ways. That's all.''

THE ONLY SIMILARITY between the untamed woodlands surrounding Tremayne's hunting cabin and the landscaped city parks that were Caine's usual habitat was that trees grew in both settings.

Nevertheless, Caine was enjoying his morning excursion with Harve into the woods, even if he found himself hesitant to examine the reason. The air was fresh and brisk, the sun so bright it penetrated the canopy of bare tree limbs to paint abstract patterns of light and shadow on the forest floor. Here and there, a wild crocus had pushed its way through the mat of last year's dead leaves, sprinkling the drab forest floor with exclamation points of purple and buttercup yellow.

Today was the first time since he'd arrived on Tremayne land that he'd ventured farther than the cabin clearing, the first time in three days Vicki Winslow had been out of his sight or hearing for more than a few minutes at a time.

Out of sight or hearing, he admitted reluctantly, but not out of mind. In spite of his efforts to ignore Vicki Winslow except as a job, she refused to get out of his head.

Their enforced togetherness, the almost total lack of privacy in the small cabin, was part of the problem. Neither of them could do anything without the other knowing. The fact that they were strangers made the situation even more awkward.

Yesterday afternoon had been a perfect example. First Vicki had asked him if he was going to Fayetteville. When he'd told her no, she'd suggested that maybe he'd like to take the dogs for a walk.

Since the dogs ran free on demand, the suggestion was not only ridiculous but so patently an attempt to get him out of the way that he'd become immediately suspicious.

"What are you up to?" he'd demanded. "Exactly why are you trying to get rid of me?"

"If you must know, I'd like to take a bath."

The cabin's bathroom consisted only of a toilet and a small washbasin, and for a moment he'd believed she intended to sneak away to use one of her relative's facilities.

"Absolutely not," he'd told her. "The entire object of our being here is for you to remain hidden, out of sight."

"But that's why I want you out of the cabin for a while," she'd said. "It's too hard to carry the water up the stairs. If you'll just go away, I can bathe here, in front of the fire."

Once he'd understood the situation, he'd carried the large galvanized tub in from the shed and even helped her to fill it with water she'd heated on the stove.

Then he'd banished himself to the woodpile and let his imagination play havoc with his hormones. As a result of Vicki's bath and his frustration, he estimated they now had a month's supply of kindling.

Why was he finding it so difficult to separate the woman from the job? He often found himself watching her, waiting for the flash of green fire in her eyes, or studying the way her hair glistened in the sunlight, or the way her hands caressed and soothed Sweetpea when the skunk became agitated. How would it feel, he wondered, if her hands were stroking his skin the way they stroked her pet?

Enough, he told himself. His preoccupation with Vicki Winslow was distracting, something he could ill afford. It was his job to protect her. That was all. Anything else was a danger for both of them.

With a grunt of self-disgust, Caine returned his attention to the job at hand, adjusting the sensitivity setting on the last of the motion detectors he was installing along the trail to the cabin.

Nature, at least, seemed to be cooperating, he thought as he inspected the leafless tree limbs above him. The small but swelling green buds suggested there might be several weeks before it was necessary to devise some other type of early-warning system. The trees in full leaf would render the detectors all but useless anywhere but directly along the trail.

But maybe, if the fates were kind, it would all be over by then, and he'd be gone from this crazy place.

"Okay," he called to Harve, waiting out of sight down the trail, "I think we're ready for a trial run. Send the dogs first."

Moments later both dogs, their tails wagging furiously, were clamoring for his attention. The alarm box remained silent.

He reached down to pet them. "Stay Tucker. Stay Gourdy. Sit," he commanded, when the dogs, in their enthusiastic greeting, threatened to knock him off his feet.

"So far, so good. Now you try it," he called to Harve. This time, the alarm box began its earsplitting squawk even before Harve came into sight on the trail.

Caine gave a grunt of satisfaction. He hadn't been sure he'd be able to adjust the sensors to operate efficiently in this overgrown outdoor environment. It was the first time he'd attempted such a setup, but he'd been unable to think of any other warning system that would work. Security cameras required twenty-four-hour monitoring, and that simply wasn't practical. Mantraps could be dangerous, and there was no guarantee that local wildlife or an area resident wouldn't wander into one.

"I'll be damned," Harve said as he reached Caine's side. "I knew these things worked well in confined spaces, but I never thought you'd get one to work in the woods."

"I'll admit I wasn't certain, either," Caine said, "but the technology's there. The only question was if I'd be able to program it correctly for a wildlife tunnel. As long as your local wildlife aren't much larger than a dog, and if the bad guys aren't midgets, I think we're set."

"Only thing bigger than a dog around here would be deer. A roving buck might wander down this way," Harve warned, "but for the most part, they avoid this area of the woods. They're more likely to be higher in the hills, around the springs, particularly this time of year."

"An occasional false alarm's not a problem," Caine said. "It'll keep me on my toes."

"How large an area are you monitoring? Will it still work if someone isn't on the trail?"

"That could be a problem, Caine admitted, "but if anyone shows up, I figure he's going to be a stranger and not likely to go plunging through unknown woods. Even if he's not on the trail, he'll stay close, and I've calibrated for that."

Caine spoke with more confidence than he felt. It was true the detectors should work, should give him advance warning if anyone was approaching the cabin, but they were only a backup, a little extra protection. No plan was foolproof. He and he alone was Vicki Tremayne's best protection. It was a fact that left him decidedly uncomfortable.

Thankfully Harve didn't appear to have noticed Caine's uneasiness, but Caine sensed the man wasn't completely convinced, either.

"Okay, why don't we put it to the test," Caine said, acknowledging to himself that he welcomed a few more minutes away from the cabin, away from the disturbing presence of Vicki Winslow. "Go back down the trail, then try sneaking past me. But remember, a real intruder isn't going to be looking for security devices, not once he's in the woods."

"It's not that I don't trust—" Harve began.

"Hey, no problem. We need the test, anyway," Caine assured him.

The man was good in the woods, Caine acknowledged five minutes later when the black box once again began its screeching. If he hadn't known Harve was out there, he'd have sworn there was no one but him and the dogs within miles.

Seconds later, Harve stepped out of the underbrush and into sight. "I didn't see or hear you," Caine told him, "but the sensors did. I think we're set."

This time, when Harve nodded, there was no lingering doubt in his eyes. "You're right. I tried my damnedest. If they caught me, they'll sure catch any city hoodlum."

The dogs seemed to sense their excursion was at an end when Caine began collecting his tools to return to the cabin. With a playful woof-woof they disappeared from sight along the trail, leaving Caine and Harve to follow.

When Caine entered the cabin, Vicki was setting a platter of fried chicken on the table. He took an appreciative sniff, then grinned ruefully when he realized she'd caught him in the act.

"I agree," she told him. "There's nothing quite as good as home-fried chicken, especially Aunt Abby's. It's one of the things I missed the most living in Washington."

"Oh, posh," Aunt Abby protested. "I've told you before, child, there's nothing special about my chicken. All you have to do is use buttermilk, instead of sweet milk, in the batter."

"I tell my cooks to use buttermilk," Harve said as he entered the cabin behind Caine, "but their chicken never tastes the way yours does, Grandmother."

"I've told you before, I'll show your wife how to fix it, if you ever decide on one, but I'll not be wasting my time teaching your cooks. They come and go so fast it'd be a full-time job."

"Leave my marital status alone, Grandmother. Please."

Caine coughed to hide his grin. If the look on Harve's face was anything to go by, his marital status was one of Mrs. Abigail Tremayne's favorite topics of conversation. The subject made Caine uncomfortable, too, though that didn't stop Maggie, his sister, from administering her lectures.

Why was it, Caine wondered, that every female in the world, regardless of age, seemed determined to marry off every eligible bachelor they knew? True, there were times when he had to acknowledge the acute loneliness in his life, but he'd decided a long time ago that marriage and family weren't for him.

Frankly, he didn't want to be responsible for another person, not on a full-time basis. Life was too uncertain. What if he had a wife and failed to make her happy or to keep her safe? He wouldn't accept that kind of responsibility, not for a life he couldn't control.

Of course, what woman would put up with him for long, anyway? He was a loner. And he liked it that way. Since Maggie was now Danny's responsibility, the only person he had to worry about was himself.

Caine shot Harve a look of sympathy.

VICKI CAUGHT the look that passed between Caine and her cousin.

Men! It was true Aunt Abby could be a little overwhelming, but it was equally obvious that Caine and Harve were of like mind when it came to discussing marriage.

Not that it should matter to her one way or the other. Of course she hoped that someday Harve would fall in love again and marry—but for *his* sake. Harve was essentially a family man. She suspected he'd never be completely happy alone.

Caine Alexander was another matter. He was so self-contained, so controlled. She couldn't imagine him ever lowering his barriers enough to fall in love. Yet she'd seen that he was certainly capable of opening up—he and Harve had become friends, and Aunt Abby was obviously impressed with him. So maybe he just didn't like her. She was only a job, no more, no less.

The others were already seated around the table when Vicki brought over the pan of biscuits and slid into her chair.

"So tell me, Mr. Alexander—" Aunt Abby passed Caine the chicken "—do you really believe my niece is in danger?"

"It's possible, ma'am. At least Federal Marshal Carelli believes she may be. That's why I'm here."

"And you, Mr. Alexander? What do you think?"

Caine shrugged. "I believe in caution."

"Remember, Grandmother," Harve added, "An ounce of prevention is worth a pound of cure."

"I agree," Aunt Abby said. "And now I want to know what precautions are being taken to protect Vicki."

"We installed electronic sensors along the path up to the cabin this morning. They'll warn Caine and Vicki if someone is coming," Harve explained.

"About all we can do at this point is be vigilant," Caine said. "Precaution is our best defense. And she's reasonably well hidden here." He leaned forward. "I promise you, Ms. Tremayne, I'll keep her safe."

"See that you do, Mr. Alexander, or you will personally answer to me."

"Believe me, ma'am, that thought is a strong incentive to succeed."

Vicki hastily hid her grin behind her napkin. Aunt Abby was one formidable lady, but Caine seemed more than able to hold his own with her.

"Oh, that reminds me, Vicki," Aunt Abby said, turning toward her, "that senator friend of yours called yesterday, wanting to know how to reach you."

"Senator Van Brock?"

"I believe so. At least the man said he was from the senator's office."

"And what did you tell him, Ms. Tremayne?" Caine asked, his voice clipped.

Vicki frowned at Caine, and Aunt Abby gave him an exasperated look. "I told him that I'd be glad to pass on his request that Vicki get in touch with him the next time I talked with her, but that I understood she would be returning to Washington after her vacation and that he'd probably hear from her before I did."

"That was very good, ma'am," Caine said, visibly relaxing. "If you get any more inquires, answer them the same way."

"Hmph." If Aunt Abby's response wasn't enough to convey her disdain, the look in her eyes certainly did. "I may be old, young man, but I am in full possession of my faculties. I might remind you who suggested that my niece leave Washington and come here."

At least he had the decency to look a little chagrined, Vicki thought.

"You're right, Ms. Tremayne," Caine said. "I keep underestimating you. I do apologize."

"Underestimate? I suppose I should consider that a compliment of a sort." Aunt Abby's eyes twinkled. "Very well, Mr. Alexander. I accept your apology."

Caine's lips curved into a slight smile as he nodded. Then he turned his gaze to Vicki. She sat up straighter.

"So why would the senator be looking for you?" he asked in that deceptively casual voice he used so successfully.

"For any of several reasons, I suppose," she said, shrugging. "It's probably something to do with the foundation. He *is* chairman of the board, you know. That makes him my boss of sorts."

"Surely he doesn't expect you to go back to work now," Aunt Abby protested. "He must know that man is on the loose again."

"Besides, I thought you quit that job," Harve added.

"No," she told Harve, grateful for any excuse that allowed her to turn her attention from Caine. "When it became apparent I wasn't going to be able to go back to work for a while, I submitted my resignation, but the board refused to accept it. They told me to take an indefinite leave of absence and think it over. Under the circumstances, I don't think he'd expect me to come back now," she added to reassure her aunt.

"Exactly what is your job with the foundation?" Caine asked.

"Fund-raising. I'm . . . I mean, I *was* in charge of co-ordinating special fund-raising projects for the foundation. I developed money-making ideas, organized and coordinated the events. That's how I discovered the . . . the problem. There were several programs where profits were well below anticipated revenues."

Vicki took a deep breath, remembering her feeling of failure when the corporate field day she'd organized didn't meet expected fund-raising goals, then again when a special concert barely covered expenses.

She also remembered her anger—her rage—when, after analyzing the files, she'd discovered the projects had been more than successful. The problem was, the money had never reached Foundation coffers. Someone was stealing from the children!

It was her rage that had sent her looking for villains and lost money. She'd found the villains, or at least one of them, and some of the money. But the cost had been higher than anticipated—disillusionment, danger, fear and a nightmare that seemed to go on and on.

"I liked my job," she told Caine, then felt the heat in her cheeks when her gaze met his. "I like fund-raising. I'm good at it, too. The foundation's doing important work with children all over the world. But the memories... I'm not sure I'll be able to go back. Besides, it's hard to think of the future when my whole life's on hold."

"This... this waiting won't go on forever, you know," Caine said, and for a moment Vicki could have sworn she saw a look of sympathy in his eyes. "You'll be able to go back to your job sooner or later."

Vicki gazed at him. "Somehow I don't think it'll ever be the same."

"Then you'll find something else you like even better," Harve added reassuringly. "Come on, cuz, buck up. Remember what Virgil said, *'Forsan et haec olim meminisse iuvabit.* Maybe one day we shall be glad to remember even these things.'"

Vicki shook her head. "No, Harve," she said, unable to hide the despair in her voice. "I don't think so. This time I think both you and Virgil are wrong."

CHAPTER FIVE

THAT TEARS IT, Caine thought, his hand clenching the telephone receiver so tightly his knuckles showed white. When Henderson escaped, Caine had anticipated some kind of overt move to indicate that Vicki Winslow was indeed a target. But after a week, with nothing to report on his end and no news from Danny's end, he'd begun to allow himself to relax—to hope that she wasn't a target, that his bodyguard role was nothing more than precaution.

Danny's news had just blown that kind of thinking all to hell.

"You're sure? It wasn't random?" Caine kept his voice expressionless and his features composed. He glanced across the room to where Rodney Baxter sat at his desk and tried to decide if Fayetteville's federal marshal was as involved in his paperwork as he appeared to be.

It wasn't that he didn't trust the man, but he'd learned long ago to limit information to a "needs to know" basis in critical situations. And if what Danny had told him was correct, the Vicki Winslow case had just gone critical.

"It wasn't random," Danny said, confirming Caine's worst fears. "They were in and out clean as a whistle. Vicki's apartment was completely searched. A real professional job. No question about it. Her apartment was the target."

What if she'd been there? A giant fist clutched at Caine's gut. *Don't think about it. She wasn't there,* he told himself. *She's safe.*

But for how long?

"When did they go in?" he asked.

"Two nights ago, about 2:00 a.m.," Danny said, "and we have your surveillance cameras to thank for that information. They disabled the alarm system. We didn't discover the break-in until last night, but the fire-escape camera recorded the time and date. If a neighbor hadn't seen the curtain blowing in the open window, we still might not know about it. They slipped up there. It's the only mistake they've made so far."

"No," Caine growled. "Their first mistake was showing up at all. It tells us they've got no leads."

"There is that," Danny admitted.

Caine forced himself to push back his panic. To think.

Two nights ago. Forty-eight hours. They could be in Little Falls by now.

No, Vicki was safe. Harve was at the cabin with her, and he was no dummy. And Vicki had the dogs. Besides, if there were strangers in Little Falls, Harve would've been warned. Hadn't he been alerted to Caine's arrival within fifteen minutes?

And the cabin didn't have a street address. Professional or not, there was no way anyone could find it without a little preliminary work.

As he reviewed the precautions, Caine's knee-jerk reaction began to recede.

"Was it Henderson? Have you got a description?"

"No, it wasn't Henderson," Danny told him, "but the description's not much help. There were two men. One about five-nine, one hundred and eighty pounds. The other about an inch and a half taller and skinny, maybe one hundred and sixty. Obviously neither of them were our man—he's close to six-two—but I have no doubt they were working for him."

"That's all you've got?"

"That's it. We wouldn't have that much if it wasn't for the cameras. They were both wearing ski masks and gloves. As I said, real pros."

Caine swore softly. "Any idea what they were looking for? What they got?"

"Not a clue, but from the mess in the apartment, it's obvious they were looking for information. Maybe an idea of where she was, maybe something else. They didn't take any of the usual pawn items—camera, microwave, TV, stereo, computer were all left behind. It feels like a fishing expedition to me. You'll have to check with Vicki to see if she left any clues to her whereabouts lying around."

"All right. I'll also see what she wants to do about cleanup. I know you'd rather have her look at the place first, but I'm not bringing her back. Not now."

"You're right, but cleanup's taken care of. She left the name of her attorney with the apartment-house management. A William Ryder. He's some sort of cousin, I think. Whatever, he's already got cleanup under way. What are you going to do, Caine? Move her?"

Caine hesitated. "I don't know. I need to talk to her before I decide. Assess the situation. Can we trust that lawyer? Does he know where she is?"

"I believe so, on both counts," Danny said. "Apparently he made the arrangements on this end to get her out of town."

"If that checks out—and if Vicki didn't leave any clues—then we'll probably stay here for now. Quite frankly, I can't think of anyplace safer. But at the very least, I'll be making some contingency plans. You take care, Danny. I don't like the way this is going down."

"You, too, buddy. You're the one on the firing line," Danny reminded him.

Baxter looked up from his paperwork as Caine ended the call. Had he been able to overhear anything? Caine wondered.

"Everything all right?"

Caine hesitated, debating once again whether or not to confide in him. No, he decided. The new action was in Washington. Nothing Baxter could do about it. No need spreading information around.

"Just more of the same," he said. "It's still a wait-and-see game. Thanks for the use of the phone."

"Anytime," Baxter said. "See you in a couple of days."

Was he being too predictable? Caine wondered as he drove back to Little Falls. For the past two weeks he'd made the same afternoon trip to Fayetteville every third day. If anyone was on to him, it would be the perfect opportunity to take him out, leaving Vicki without his protection.

Exactly what he deserved for not keeping his mind on the job. Only he wouldn't be the only one to pay the price.

Dammit. Now he was being paranoid. Vicki Winslow was going to drive him around the bend.

Still, he'd better vary his routine in the future, maybe take one of Harve's vehicles next trip. And unless something came up, wait an extra day. That is, if he and Vicki were still here . . .

VICKI FOUND HERSELF waiting for Caine's return with both anticipation and dread. She knew he used his trips to Fayetteville to check in with Danny Carelli. Each time he left she hoped he'd have news of some kind when he returned. She almost didn't care if it was good or bad.

She'd never been a placid sort of person, able to sit patiently and wait for something to happen. She was a doer.

Right. And that was what had gotten her into this mess in the first place, she reminded herself. Not that she regretted it. The thought that money donated to help children had been diverted for personal gain still had the power to make her blood boil.

But this living in limbo was driving her crazy. If something didn't happen soon, she was going to go out and find Henderson herself.

"Sit down and relax, cuz," Harve told her. "Remember what Tancred said—'Everything comes if a man will only wait.'"

"That's easy for you to say," she told him crossly. "You're not under house arrest. I'm tired of waiting. I'm tired of this whole mess. I want to get on with my life. I want something to happen."

"Easy, Vicki. There's also an old saw about being careful what you wish for."

Vicki dropped into a chair. "I'm sorry, Harve. I shouldn't take it out on you. It's not your fault. It's just that I'm so...so..."

"Impatient?" he supplied with a grin.

"Yes, impatient," she admitted, and unable to resist, grinned back.

"Actually I think you've been very patient," he told her. "You've changed from the girl who used to spend her summer vacations here. That Vicki would've had an apoplectic fit by now. All that teenage intolerance for the wrongs of the world."

"I should hope I've learned a little patience since then. I grew up, after all."

"And very nicely, too, cousin, dear," he said with a appreciative gleam in his eye. "But what's good is that basically you haven't changed. Not really. You're still ready to take on all comers if you see the need. This latest episode is proof of that. I'm proud of you."

"Thanks, Harve. Sometimes I get so frustrated I forget why I got into this mess."

"You did the right thing, even if it is turning out to be a little inconvenient."

Vicki laughed. "Only you would call it a little inconvenient," she said, shaking her head.

"When weighed against the problems of the world... Besides, if you're making a ledger, you should also list the pluses. What other circumstances can you think of that would have brought you home for such a long visit? Grandmother would never ask, but she's wanted you to come for a long time. And even if she hasn't been able to take you around and show you off as she'd like, she's enjoying the visit. I've liked getting a chance to know my grown-up cousin, too. And then there's Caine. Under other circumstances, we'd probably never have met him."

Oh, yes, and then there was Caine, Vicki thought. Okay. She'd admit it. The man fascinated her. One look from those chocolate brown eyes and her pulse rate went into double time. An accidental touch sent it into overdrive. Still, as much as he fascinated her, he also infuriated her. He was so controlled, so single-minded, so... so hard. Yet under that cool veneer was a vulnerability. And no one had ever made her so angry so quickly or so—

Careful, Vicki, she admonished herself. *Are you interested in the man or in the challenge?* She remembered Aunt Abby's words: "The good Lord provides the opportunities, but don't expect him to hand them to you on a silver platter."

Suddenly the dogs began to bark, a signal that the object of her thoughts had just returned. She jumped to her feet and flung open the door.

Something had happened. Caine's face was completely expressionless, a blank slate, except for his eyes, and those she couldn't read. Was that anger she saw? She couldn't be sure.

"What's happened now?" she asked, unable to keep the apprehension out of her voice.

Caine entered the cabin and cast a quick glance in Harve's direction.

"Shall I leave?" Harve asked.

Caine hesitated a moment, then shook his head. "No. I need you here."

"Good decision," Harve said. "I wasn't going, anyway. Only thought to see how sensible you were. 'Even a sheet of paper is lighter when two lift it.' That's an old Korean proverb."

Caine glared at him for a moment, then his lips twitched into what Vicki could almost describe as a grin. "Do you have a quotation for everything?"

"For most things. Helps keeps the mind focused."

There was a sudden look of comprehension in Caine's eyes. "How did you find out?"

"I have my sources," Harve told him.

"William Ryder? He called you." It was more statement than question. "Why didn't you tell me?"

"Yes, William called," Harve said, nodding. "I didn't say anything because I thought you should hear your report without prejudice. Then we could compile our information."

"Exactly who is he? How much does he know? Are you sure we can trust him?" Caine's questions were rapid-fire.

"Of course we can trust him." Harve's voice held a note of indignation. "He's family."

Vicki looked from Caine to Harve, her patience evaporating. "Why would William call you?" she asked Harve. "Okay, you two. Enough of your games. Will one of you tell me what's going on?"

"Well, cuz," Harve began, then hesitated until Caine nodded his head, "remember how we keep wondering if all this is necessary, if anyone is really after you? Now we know."

Vicki's stomach flipped. She glanced at Caine, who once again was wearing his grim look, then back to Harve. "Just what is it we now know?" she asked carefully.

"That you're definitely a target," Caine said in a flat voice. "Someone broke into your apartment."

"Broke in?" Vicki's voice rose an octave. So much for wanting something to happen! "Someone broke into my apartment?" she repeated. "You mean like a burglary? Was it Henderson?"

Sweetpea emerged from her hiding place under the chair, obviously disturbed by their voices. Chittering, she wrapped herself around Vicki's ankle.

Vicki leaned over to pick her up. Sweetpea curled into a ball, her trembling disappearing as Vicki soothed her with gentle strokes.

"I don't think this was just a burglary," Harve said thoughtfully.

"It wasn't Henderson," Caine said, "and no, it was no ordinary burglary."

He turned to Vicki, his eyes appearing to focus for a moment on Sweetpea.

Vicki saw his jaw clench, then his gaze locked with hers. How had she ever compared his eyes to rich, sweet chocolate? she wondered. They were a hard, dark brown, bleak and bottomless.

"I want you to think very carefully, Vicki," he said in a clipped voice. "When you left Washington, did you leave any clue to where you were going?"

The air in the room suddenly seemed colder. Afraid to trust her voice, Vicki shook her head.

"Anything? Even Harve's address or phone number written on a scrap of paper? Or your aunt Abby's?"

His voice was harsh, unrelenting, reminding her of the time she'd been under cross-examination by Henderson's lawyer. She shivered and again shook her head.

"How about old letters with a Little Falls address?"

"No."

"The name of your travel agent? An address book? Christmas-card list?"

"I've already said no. Nothing."

"How can you be so sure?"

His last question broke her trance. Anger replaced fear. She'd already told him no. What more did he want?

"I'm sure because I double-checked," she said, then seeing the speculation still in his eyes, felt her temper begin to fray. "Dammit it, Caine, it would have been pretty stupid to leave a forwarding address, wouldn't it? Especially after all the trouble Harve and William went through to get me safely out of town."

She forced herself to calm down. After all, he was only doing his job, trying to make sure she was safe. "I was very careful," she explained patiently. "The night before I left, I went through all my drawers, even inspected the books on my shelves to make sure I hadn't overlooked anything. I gave the apartment-house manager William's name and phone number as a local contact in the event anything happened. That's all. I don't keep old letters. I brought my address book with me. There was nothing in the apartment to lead anyone here, if that's what you're concerned about."

"That's my concern all right." Vicki thought she could hear a hint of relief in his voice. "Just how did you get out of town, anyway?" he asked.

She told him about the plane ticket William had given her in her cousin Camille's name. Harve, she said, met her at the airport in Little Rock.

Caine turned toward Harve, a look of respect in his eyes. "I think law enforcement can be glad yours is a law-abiding family."

Harve grinned, and Vicki asked worriedly, "Do...do you think that's what they were looking for? A clue to where I am?"

"Probably. That's why we have to be sure you didn't leave any behind. If you did, it's not safe to stay here."

"If Vicki says she didn't, then she didn't," Harve put in. "She's a very organized person."

"Okay. I'll accept that for now," Caine said. "There's another possibility. They may also have been looking for any evidence you had that would identify Henderson's partner."

"If I had that information, I wouldn't be in this mess now," Vicki protested. "I told the authorities everything I knew, before the trial and again in my testimony."

"It may be something you don't realize you know, something that ties Henderson to someone else," Caine persisted.

"Perception!" Harve said in what Vicki identified as his eureka voice. "It's not what you have, but what they think you have or think you may have." He looked at Vicki. "Now it's beginning to make sense. I never did buy into that revenge idea."

"That's my best theory, too," Caine agreed, "but it's only a theory. The one thing we know for sure is that someone's looking for her. And it's my job to make sure they don't find her."

"So what do we do now?" Harve asked.

Caine gave Vicki a speculative look, his gaze moving across her face, and for a moment it almost felt as if he touched her. Then abruptly, he turned back to Harve.

"For now, we sit tight," Caine told him. "Apparently they have no clue to where she is. If they didn't find anything at the apartment, they must be getting desperate. Desperate men make mistakes."

Vicki sank into a chair. She'd been afraid Caine would say they were going to have to run. Of course, less than an hour ago she'd been wishing for something to happen. But when it came to the crisis point, she was tired of running. Tired of hiding, too, although there wasn't much she could do about that at the moment.

At least the cabin was familiar. She felt safe here.

But maybe she'd feel safe anywhere, as long as she was with Caine.

Now what, she wondered, had prompted that thought?

CHAPTER SIX

CAINE TURNED RESTLESSLY on his pallet. Was he doing the right thing keeping Vicki here in this isolated spot? What if it wasn't as safe as he believed?

The cabin was quiet and dark, the only illumination from the fireplace, the only sound the occasional snort from one of the dogs stretched out beside the hearth. He rolled onto his side, propped his chin on his hand and stared into the dying embers.

What the hell was he doing? Looking for divine inspiration in the shifting patterns of smoke and flame? He'd made his decision, one based on analysis of known facts, years of experience and instinct. Vicki was safer here than anywhere else. So why was he trying to second-guess himself now?

Tucker gave a soft woof and, shadowed by Gourdy, padded across the cabin to the door.

Caine tensed, listening. Had the dogs heard someone outside?

No, he decided seconds later when both dogs sank to their haunches and looked back at him expectantly. They simply wanted to go out.

With a sigh, Caine got up and silently crossed the room to open the door.

He returned to the hearth, shivering, and added a fresh log to the coals. He waited until he saw the telltale fingers of flame wrap around the log before adding a second. It would be enough. Whoever had built this fireplace knew what he was about. The heating system might be primitive, but it warmed the cabin with a minimum amount of fuel.

With a quick glance toward the loft where Vicki slept, he stepped into his jeans and pulled on a shirt. Since sleep seemed to be as elusive as Henderson, he might as well stay up for a while.

Still barefoot, he padded toward the kitchen, adroitly sidestepping Sweetpea as the little animal launched a playful attack at his left ankle. It had taken him several nights to become accustomed to the nocturnal wanderings of Vicki's unusual pet. Sweetpea, who'd apparently become as used to Caine's midnight roaming as he had to hers, scooted around him to wait expectantly in front of the refrigerator.

"Think you have me trained, don't you?" he muttered, then gave in, setting a saucer of milk on the floor for her. He poured himself a cup of coffee and wandered back to the couch.

Inevitably his thoughts turned to the events of the day. After her initial reaction, Vicki had seemed reassured when Harve gave her William Ryder's report of minimum damage in her apartment.

But she'd retired to the sleeping loft shortly after Harve left, and although she'd claimed she was all right, Caine understood how much the news of the burglary disturbed her. Hell, he couldn't blame her. It disturbed him, too. Even more distressing than the actual break-in was the nagging feeling that he was overlooking something important.

His hypothesis that Henderson believed Vicki had information not already known to law-enforcement agencies had crystallized into conviction during the afternoon.

But what did she know, or what did Henderson *think* she knew, that was such a danger?

Caine realized he was a johnny-come-lately on the case. He'd become involved when the trial was well underway, and only then because he'd sensed Danny's concern for his witness.

Now he was going to have to go back to the beginning. He needed to see police reports and trial transcripts. Even newspaper clippings of the breaking story and trial might be useful. He'd already told Harve to get him copies of the transcripts and any other information that lawyer cousin could collect. Once he had those, he could get started.

Most of all, however, he needed to talk to Vicki, to go through the entire sordid mess step-by-step. Somewhere there had to be a clue.

From what he understood from Danny, no one even suspected a crime had been committed until Vicki went to the police with her story. She'd not only given them the crime, but most of the solution. All that had been left for them to do was to confirm the proof she handed them and find the missing money.

Caine allowed himself a wry grin. As an amateur sleuth, Vicki Winslow was one smart lady. If the justice department had been as efficient, he wouldn't be in Little Falls right now. Oh, they'd found enough of the missing funds to make a case against Henderson, but the bulk of the money was still missing.

How had she fingered Henderson, anyway? Had he been her only suspect? If not, who were the others and why had she eliminated them?

Caine wasn't looking forward to tomorrow. Vicki wouldn't be happy when he started probing. Rehashing the investigation and the trial would be like picking at a freshly scabbed wound. But if today's reports had accomplished nothing else, they'd proved the case was far from over.

Sweetpea wandered back toward the hearth, jumped into Caine's lap and nudged his hand with her head. Idly, almost reflexively, he began stroking her. If his colleagues could see him now, he thought, a skunk curled in his lap like a—

"She likes to be scratched under her chin."

Caine uncoiled like a broken spring, dumping Sweetpea from his lap.

"I didn't mean to startle you," Vicki said, one hand clutching the neck of her robe, the other still on the banister, as if she was debating whether to advance or retreat. "I thought you heard me come down the stairs." Her voice sounded tentative, uncertain.

Chittering in protest, Sweetpea flipped her tail and disappeared under the couch.

Caine closed his eyes, relief drawing the adrenaline from his muscles like water through a drain. He should have heard her, he thought. He should have been more alert. If she could catch him unawares, so could someone else. Fine bodyguard he made!

"I'm sorry," he heard her say. "I heard you let the dogs out and I thought... I'll just go back upstairs."

"No." His voice sounded like a growl in his own ears. He swallowed. "No," he said again, this time managing to sound almost normal. "It's all right. The dogs were only restless. What's the matter? Can't you sleep, either?"

She shook her head, light from the hearth reflecting red and gold in her tousled hair. He was uncomfortably aware of how attractive she was.

Enveloped in her oversize robe, she looked small and vulnerable. As his gaze locked with hers, he watched a faint flush creep up her cheeks and felt the fire in his own veins, an unwelcome tightening in his loins.

Tell her to go back to bed, Caine. "There's hot coffee, if you'd like a cup," he said instead.

She grimaced. "I can't sleep now—coffee certainly won't help. I thought I'd make hot chocolate. Would you like a cup?"

Caine flicked on the lamp by the side of the couch, but if he'd hoped the additional light would dispel the sense of intimacy in the cabin, he'd been wrong. He searched for words to break the spell. "I suppose you're going to tell me that it's as easy to make two cups of chocolate as one."

The look of exasperation on her face warred with the impression created by the pulse beating erratically in the hollow at the base of her throat. Caine forced himself to look away.

"As a matter of fact it is, but we've had this conversation before," she said. "If you don't want a cup, just say no."

Hell, what did it matter if she was down here or in the loft? he asked himself. Her physical location didn't seem to determine her place in his thoughts. In spite of all his attempts to deny or ignore it, Vicki was front and center in his mind.

"Hot chocolate sounds good," he said, "as long as you're making it, anyway."

Her sudden smile, slight as it was, lightened her face. "Now see, that wasn't so hard after all, was it?" she asked.

"Women," he growled in mock exasperation. "Happy as long as you get your way."

"I never denied it," she returned sweetly, "but that's not strictly a feminine trait, is it? You like to get your way, too."

"I guess so," he admitted. He had, after all, managed to keep a certain distance between them. That was what he wanted, wasn't it? So he should be happy, right?

Only he wasn't. He was nervy as a rookie on his first stakeout and about as happy as a cabbie with a flat tire in rush hour. Obviously there was a basic flaw in the theory somewhere.

He turned his back, and for want of something better to do, lifted the cast-iron poker to jab unnecessarily at the burning logs.

He'd resumed his seat on the couch, Sweetpea once again curled in his lap, when he heard Vicki approaching. Her hands, fully occupied by the mugs of chocolate, were no longer free to clutch at her neckline. The terry-cloth robe gaped slightly, exposing a hint of soft curves tantalizingly concealed by lace and silk. Terry cloth was supposed to be warm and serviceable and practical—not provocative and alluring and seductive. Caine drew a deep breath.

"I hope you like marshmallows," she said, her fingers brushing against his as she handed him one of the mugs. Then she curled into the chair opposite the couch, tucking her legs under her. The robe's neckline gaped open further.

"Only in hot chocolate," he managed to say above the pulse echoing in his ears. He took another deep breath, diverting his gaze as he sipped at the hot chocolate.

"Not roasted over a campfire?"

"Never had them that way." It was a relief to breathe normally, or almost normally. At least his heartbeat now sounded fainter in his ears. "You make very good hot chocolate."

"You're kidding." There was an incredulous tone in her voice.

"No, honest," Caine said, not understanding. "This is the best I've ever tasted."

Vicki shook her head. "Not that. I was talking about the marshmallows. You really haven't...?"

He frowned. What had he said? Something about never roasting marshmallows? He should have kept his mouth shut. Experience had taught him to guard against such remarks. A seemingly insignificant comment could expose more than intended, but he had difficulty focusing when Vicki was this close, especially clad as she was in that robe.

"Nope," he said, trying to sound casual. "Never did. Why? Is that a crime?"

What did it matter, anyway? He'd bet there were lots of people who'd never roasted marshmallows over a campfire.

"Not even as a boy?" she persisted. "What about backyard camp outs with your friends?"

Caine gave a harsh laugh. "I didn't have a backyard. Neither did my friends. Outside was the front stoop of our tenement house or the alley that ran behind it. Not what you could call prime camp out territory."

He heard Vicki make a sharp inhalation of breath, saw the look on her face. Step one, open mouth; step two, insert foot. Why had he blurted that out? He never talked about his childhood, tried never even to think about it.

"Hey, don't go feeling sorry for me," he said defensively. "I did okay, backyard camp outs or not. They're probably not all they're cracked up to be, anyway."

Now was a fine time to remember how easily she seemed to get inside his head—one reason he avoided talking to her—but it was something akin to slowing to the speed limit after you've seen the cop. Too little too late.

"I didn't mean—"

"Yeah, sure." He shifted uneasily, disturbing Sweet-pea. The skunk gave him a look that could only be described as haughty and, very deliberately, tail up, jumped from the couch.

Sweetpea marched across the floor, then turned to give Caine one last accusing glare from her black button eyes, before hopping onto Vicki's lap and snuggling into a ball. He'd been deserted by a skunk.

"Caine, I'm sorry. I didn't mean to trespass or intrude. I was just interested."

He could hear the embarrassment, the apology in her voice. Ah, hell, he hadn't meant to embarrass her. "No big deal," he said. "It happened a long time ago."

He started to change the subject, then reconsidered, remembering the look of interest, of attraction, they'd shared earlier. He couldn't deny he'd been attracted to her from the start. But it would never work. Vicki Winslow was a forever kind of woman, a lady. He was a child of the tenements, rough, rowdy and with no illusions that the world was a wonderful place.

He'd seen enough and heard enough the past few days to realize that Vicki believed that good prevailed, that truth and justice triumphed over evil, that there was a rainbow after the storm. It wouldn't hurt to let her know just how different they were. Then maybe she'd have enough sense to keep her distance, to stay out of his way.

"Well, you're right," he told her. "The tenements are a horrible place to live." He shrugged. "My mom did the best she could."

"She must be very proud of you."

"Who?"

"Your mother."

"Why should she be? I got out as soon as I could. Left her and Maggie there and joined the army. Went off to see the world. Besides, she's dead."

Silence descended, broken only by the crackle of burning logs in the fireplace.

At last Vicki spoke. "Maggie? Oh, your sister. The one who's married to Marshal Carelli. You're close to her, aren't you? I remember you talking about her the first time you came here. It must be nice having a sister." Her voice sounded wistful.

"Sometimes she can be a pain in the— But yeah, it's nice. And I guess we're close. There's just the two of us. Of course, she's got Danny now. And soon there'll be the baby..."

"And you'll be an uncle."

"Yeah. I'll be an uncle."

"Well, it doesn't sound like she blames you for leaving. Besides, knowing what I do about you, I'll bet you didn't just run off and forget about them."

"You don't know anything about me," Caine said. He bolted from the couch, then, realizing he was telegraphing his inner turmoil, propped one arm on the mantel and deliberately forced his body to relax.

Vicki shook her head. Her eyes confirmed his suspicions. She wasn't buying his nonchalant facade.

"I know you're dependable, that you take on responsibilities that aren't even yours," she said firmly.

"Like what?"

"Like protecting strangers. Like protecting me."

Dear Lord, preserve him from Pollyannas. He'd told her that little bit about his background to point up the differences between them. It was supposed to make her pull back, withdraw. Instead, she was defending him! Trying to absolve him of the misdeeds he'd admitted to. He stared into the fire. "That's my job," he growled.

There was a soft touch on his arm. Her touch. When had she moved? She wasn't supposed to be this close, not so close he could see the tiny hazel flecks in her eyes, not so close that the honeysuckle scent of her hair enveloped him like a cloud. She was supposed to be over there, in the chair, out of reach.

"I don't believe that for a minute," she said, her voice almost caressing. "You may be here because it's your job, but you do that job because you care about what happens to people."

"It's a job. That's all, lady. Why don't you take off those rose-colored glasses?"

Vicki shook her head. "You can deny it all you want, but you'll never convince me it's just a job. I've watched you, Caine Alexander. Don't forget, I spent weeks surrounded by guards 'just doing their jobs.' They were kind enough, I suppose, but detached. You're different.''

Ah, hell, Caine thought. He'd intended to stay detached. He'd tried to stay detached. He'd failed. Bit by bit, he'd allowed himself to fall under her spell, and worse, now he'd allowed her to see his error.

"I would think that by now you'd have realized it's a lousy world," he said, self-disgust making his voice bitter. "People steal from kids. They threaten nice ladies who are only trying to do what's right. They exploit the weak, intimidate anyone who gets in their way, and sometimes they kill. Protecting you is Danny Carelli's job, but Maggie wants her husband by her side when the baby's born, wants her child to grow up knowing a father. I owe Maggie. That's why I'm here. The only reason. And all the rose-colored glasses in the world won't change that. Wake up, Vicki. Don't endow me with altruistic motives. That's a fantasy that exists only in your mind."

She took a step back, her gentle touch on his arm falling away. Funny how he could still feel her hand against his skin. Then he looked into her face, saw the anguish and confusion in her eyes, and felt it echoing in the sudden stab of pain in his gut. Unable to help himself, he reached for her, felt her shiver under his hand. "Ah, Vicki, I'm sorry." He pulled her into his arms. "I'm a cynical bastard."

"I know I'm an optimist." Her voice quivered. She took a deep breath, apparently oblivious that the movement widened the opening V of her robe.

Provocative, tantalizing and oh, so sweet. Caine felt his blood race.

"I always see the cup half-full instead of half-empty." Her voice had gained strength. "And I don't care what you say, you *are* one of the good guys, whether you admit it or not."

She was defending him again! So earnest. So tempting. So close. Caine shook his head, fighting to regain control of his senses, of his sanity.

He lost.

He lowered his head toward her. He'd intended only a gentle caress, a mere nibble from the forbidden apple, but as his lips touched hers, a searing heat seemed to explode from within. With a groan, he pulled her closer and moved his mouth over hers, devouring its softness.

He felt her initial shock as she stiffened against him, then her melting resistance and finally her trembling surrender. A small sigh of wonder came from her throat and then he deepened the kiss, his tongue ravishing the sweetness of her mouth. His hands moved from her shoulders down her back to her waist and pulled her hips tightly against his.

His blood surged, desire twisting in his loins. Dear heaven, what was he doing? All but gasping from the effort, he raised his head, loosened his hold and stepped back.

Vicki swayed and Caine reached to steady her. But when his hand touched her arm, she stiffened and jerked away.

He watched her, fighting to remain stoic, as she raised her eyes to meet his. There was pain there, bewilderment, anger too, and something else.

"Why did you do that?" she asked.

"I told you. I'm a bastard."

"But why—"

"Go to bed, Vicki. Now! Unless you want to join me in mine."

She took a step backward, then whirled and fled.

VICKI HAD NO conscious memory of climbing to the loft. All she could remember, could feel, was the touch of his lips on hers, of the heat, the hunger, the turmoil of emotions that his touch had created.

Be careful what you wish for. Harve had warned her, hadn't he? Cliché or not, she should have heeded his advice.

She'd admitted days ago, at least to herself, that she found the taciturn Caine Alexander fascinating, even if he was the most provoking, irritating man she'd ever met.

Served her right, she told herself. She couldn't leave well enough alone. Had to find out if he was as indifferent to her as he seemed. Well, now she knew. He certainly wasn't indifferent, not if he could kiss her like that. It was a kiss that had curled her toes, straightened her hair and left her feeling as if she'd never been kissed before.

Vicki shivered and burrowed under her blankets, wishing they could protect her from her thoughts as easily as they protected her from the chill night air. She hadn't planned the encounter, she defended herself. All she'd wanted was a cup of hot chocolate to help her sleep.

No, it hadn't been planned, but she couldn't regret it—not all of it, anyway. For the first time she'd seen Caine without his mask—watched as he'd exposed a vulnerability she'd only suspected existed.

What would he do now? How would he treat her after she'd exposed his more human side? Would he allow them to become friends, or would he once again retreat behind his mask? The latter, she guessed.

Maybe it would be better if they both returned to their previous roles. Tonight's episode proved that Caine wasn't as indifferent to her as he pretended to be, but getting involved with him would be crazy. She wasn't a person who enjoyed or engaged in short-term relationships, and Caine wasn't a man who allowed commitment in his life. The fact that he hid behind his mask of cynicism proved that.

She believed him when he said he was only here to do a job. What she disagreed with was his motivation for accepting the job. Whichever, the outcome would be the same. Once the job was finished, he would be gone.

She could still feel his lips on hers, the blistering heat, the explosion of feeling she couldn't describe or explain. And his hands, strong, demanding, yet gentle, as they'd caressed her neck, her back, as they'd rested at her waist, then pulled her toward him until all she could think about was being part of him.

She could feel the heat in her cheeks. She thanked her lucky stars that Caine had retained enough sanity to pull away. At that point, she'd been beyond thinking. She'd been capable only of feeling and reacting.

Could she dismiss her feelings, her reaction, as the result of proximity? she wondered. After all, she'd been on an emotional roller coaster for months. She and Caine were isolated here in the cabin. With the exception of Harve and Aunt Abby, he was the only person she'd seen in weeks.

Proximity. That had to be the reason for her strong reaction to him. Oh, she wouldn't deny he was an appealing, good-looking man, but she'd been around handsome men before. It was the isolation making her vulnerable.

Leave it alone, she told herself. Her life was in turmoil. She didn't need another complication, not now, and certainly not one as potentially powerful and disturbing as Caine Alexander.

Fine. That was settled. Now all she had to do was follow her own counsel.

CHAPTER SEVEN

FROM HIS PALLET on the floor, Caine watched through the cabin window as the night sky slowly changed from black to gray. Sleep had proved not only elusive, but impossible after Vicki had returned to the loft. He'd spent the remaining hours of darkness alternately reliving the few moments he'd held her in his arms and cursing himself for his lack of control.

No doubt about it. He'd messed up. Big time. His question now was what could he do about it?

His gaze swerved toward the loft. There was no light in the cabin: the logs in the fireplace had burned to ashes hours ago and the promise of daybreak was still only that. But he didn't need to see. He knew exactly where she was—in the bed under the eaves of the sloping roof almost directly above him.

Still cursing himself, Caine slipped from his pallet, quietly donning jeans, shirt and boots, then grabbed his jacket from the peg beside the cabin door. One of the dogs brushed silently against his leg as if anticipating his next move. He opened the door and as the dogs darted outside, he followed.

He needed distance. He needed . . . Never mind what he needed; he had to put a brake on such thoughts.

Vicki's being in danger was no longer a question. To protect her, he needed her cooperation. She'd been threatening mutiny ever since he'd arrived. Just how cooperative would she be after last night?

Maybe he should pull out. He could contact Danny, have someone sent to relieve him. Someone official. After the apartment ransacking, Danny should have no problem getting budget approval.

Or, Danny could put her back in protective custody. She wouldn't like it, but with Henderson on the loose, she might be convinced to go along with it.

Caine examined both alternatives and found neither acceptable. He didn't like the idea of turning Vicki's protection over to someone else. He trusted Danny completely, but Danny wouldn't be the only one involved.

The other alternative was to stay and protect her himself, which placed him right back where he'd started. Full circle. Caine sighed. He had to stay. He'd learn to live with it. And so would she.

Could he pretend last night had never happened?

Could she?

Dammit, anyway. How had he let his libido get so out of control? He was a man who enjoyed female companionship—but only on a casual basis. He'd never been a ladies' man or a "love 'em and leave 'em" type. His encounters, infrequent as they were, were always simple: shared company, shared sex, mutual respect, mutual enjoyment, no intensity, no regrets.

He'd known from the beginning that Vicki was the kind of woman who would demand more than he had to give. It wasn't something he was proud of, but wishing he was different didn't change a thing. He'd seen too much, done too much, failed too often to have anything worthwhile to offer a woman like Vicki. And she was too intelligent not to see that.

So why was he worried?

Because he was breaking his own rules. Attraction wasn't allowed on the job. Now that the danger was confirmed, being focused was even more important. Mutual desire was a distraction that could get them both killed.

Caine watched as the eastern light turned from gray to pink. The outline of distant hills, faint at first, sharpened. The stillness of the morning was broken by the wake-up chirping of birds and the rustling of small woodland creatures in the thicket behind the cabin. The day was beginning.

In spite of Vicki's assurances that she'd left no clues, the apartment break-in made him uneasy. He needed to check security around the cabin, maybe investigate the countryside a bit, get the lay of the land in case they had to make a break for it.

Breathing room. That was what he needed. Exploring would keep him out of her way, give her a chance to cool down. It would also give him time to distance himself, recover his equilibrium, regain his focus. Vicki's safety, not to mention his own, depended on it.

Caine continued to sit on the porch, impatient for Vicki to wake up. He couldn't just leave, letting her wonder where he was. He also had to tell her to stay in the cabin out of sight while he was gone.

Although it seemed as if he'd been waiting for hours, the sun was barely over the horizon when he first heard her moving around inside. He hesitated, clamping down on the almost overwhelming urge to see her, to touch her. He was reluctant to put his control to the test, but when the aroma of frying bacon wafted through the air, he knew he couldn't put it off any longer.

Unsure of his reception, he grabbed a load of firewood from the woodpile as an unspoken excuse for being outside and warily entered the cabin.

"There you are," Vicki greeted him. "How do you want your eggs? Over easy?"

Caine swallowed, caught off guard by her nonchalance. He wasn't sure how he'd expected her to act, but certainly not as if nothing had happened. "Over easy is fine," he managed to say.

"I'll have them ready in a minute," she told him. "The coffee's still perking, but there's orange juice on the table."

Caine dumped the firewood on the hearth. Feeling like a general who'd marched off to battle only to find no enemy in sight, he sat down in his usual place at the table—back to the wall in more ways than he cared to examine. In spite of Vicki's apparent composure, his instincts were screaming a warning.

After his behavior last night, he expected her to be angry. Best-case scenario was that she would only be coldly condemning, which would have made it easier for him to reconstruct the barriers between them. But never, even in his wildest imagining, had he expected her to ignore the incident completely. He didn't believe it, couldn't believe it, even if her performance was worthy of an Oscar.

Vicki set the two plates of food and two cups of coffee on the table, then, without saying a word, slid into a chair on the other side of the table.

Still leery, Caine picked up his fork. The eggs were perfect, the bacon crisp, the orange juice cold, and the coffee hot and flavorful. He began to relax. "Breakfast is delicious, Vicki. Thank you."

She sat up straighter, as if his words had triggered some unseen switch. "Caine," she said without preamble, "we need to talk."

Dammit, here it comes, he thought. Worse, she'd caught him by surprise. She'd used the oldest tactic in the book, timing her attack to catch him off guard and vulnerable.

"I owe you an apology," she said without giving him time to agree or disagree. "About last night, I shouldn't have probed into your life. It's none of my business. I'm sorry."

Caine blinked and shifted uncomfortably, too shocked to do more than nod. He'd been prepared for her censure, was ready to admit guilt for his outrageous actions. He certainly wasn't expecting an apology from her. "Vicki—"

"Things got out of hand," she said, ignoring his attempt to speak. "That kiss should never have happened."

All he could do was stare across the table at her, the sound of his heart pounding in his ears. Damn and blast. This was supposed to be his speech. She was taking the words out of his mouth. "Now wait a minute—"

"It's understandable of course," she rushed on, as if trying to get her speech finished before she changed her mind. "Two people, as isolated as we are. We're normal, healthy adults, and emotions were running high. We were both vulnerable. Besides, it was a simple kiss, a very pleasant one of course, but still, only a kiss. In case you're worried that I read too much into it, I know it didn't mean anything."

She was giving him his argument! It had seemed logical when he'd planned to use it, but now, listening to her, it made no sense at all. But he couldn't tell her that. He was caught in his own trap.

"So I think we should just ignore it, pretend it never happened. Don't you?"

The pounding in his ears grew louder. The kiss they'd shared had not been simple, not just pleasant. It had been hot and serious and . . .

"Caine? Say something," Vicki said. "Don't you agree?"

Dammit to hell and back. He had to agree whether he liked it or not. "Yeah. Right," he said, trying to keep the growl out of his voice. *You lie, you lie,* his inner voice chanted.

"Good. I'm glad that's settled," she said. "Now we can decide what we need to do next. Even if they didn't find anything, someone searching my apartment changes things, doesn't it?"

"It might," Caine agreed reluctantly, still mulling over her recent speech. Ignoring last night had been his plan from the beginning. The fact that she'd been the one to present the case shouldn't affect its validity.

"Should I start packing?" Vicki asked. "The family has other places we could go. One of the cousins owns a cabin at a ski resort near Nashville. It'll be almost deserted this late in the season. We could go there."

Caine shook his head, making an effort to catch up with her conversation. "If you're sure you didn't leave behind any clues . . ."

"I didn't."

". . . then here's as good a place as any, unless and until we discover differently."

Vicki nodded, and if he was correctly interpreting the look on her face, she was glad they were staying. He couldn't blame her. He knew the strain of running.

Now seemed like a good time to tell her of his plans for the day. "I thought I'd do a little exploring," he said. "You know, take a look around the countryside as a precaution, just in case we need to hightail it."

The smile that lit her face found him searching for breath.

"That sounds great," she said. "I'll be glad to get out of the cabin, for a while, anyway. I always did love hiking in the woods."

Caine shook his head. "You're not going. I want you to stay in the cabin out of sight."

"What do you mean, I'm not going?" Her voice was only several decibels shy of a shriek. "Of course I'm going. You need me. I know these woods. You don't."

"This isn't a pleasure hike, Vicki." He struggled to keep his voice calm, controlled, reasonable. "I'll be scouting for the best trails between here and help, looking for possible places to hide, identifying places to avoid in case of ambush."

"And I know every one of them. For example, if you want to get from here to Aunt Abby's through the woods, you can't go west. The only trail leads north around a steep ravine, then south. I know the way. If you're looking for a secure hiding place, there's a cave north of here. It was used as a stop on the Underground Railroad in the 1850s. One of my great-great-grandfathers hid out there for several months after he was injured in the battle of Pea Ridge during the War Between the States. You'll never find it on your own, and neither will anyone else. I know the way. Besides, I seem to remember promising to protect you from the wildlife."

Caine cursed mentally. He didn't honestly believe they'd need to escape to the woods. His idea to explore the area was an excuse to put time and distance between himself and Vicki. But what she said made sense. If there was the slightest chance of being forced to take to the woods, it would be stupid not to be as prepared as possible. Stupid, too, for him to stumble around in unfamiliar territory when she was the perfect guide. Besides, if the mutinous look in her eyes was any indication, she'd only follow him if he tried to leave her behind.

"All right," he said, capitulating. "I need to check on the security sensors between here and the road before we leave. Be ready in an hour."

VICKI HADN'T REALIZED exactly how depressing being stuck in the cabin was, not until she felt the sun on her face and the spring breeze in her hair. She stopped on the trail and whirled around, flinging her arms wide, as if she could embrace the whole outdoors. She felt renewed, refreshed, exhilarated.

"Isn't this great?" she asked, giving Caine a look that dared him to disagree.

Caine's only answer was a noncommittal grunt. He shifted the small backpack he'd taken from her before they left the cabin.

She refused to allow his sphinx imitation to intimidate or discourage her. Nothing was going to dull her enthusiasm. How could anyone stay glum on such a glorious day?

The woods behind the cabin were all tangled underbrush and tall trees, still winter bare except for the silver-gray buds swelling on brown branches, a guarantee of new beginnings. Patches of blooming pink redbud and white dogwood dotted the distant hills like puffs of cotton candy. In a few short weeks wild violets would be poking their heads through the carpet of last year's leaves to join the purple and yellow crocuses already heralding the approach of spring. Even the chill wind seemed new and fresh.

Breathing deeply, Vicki continued along the path leading north from the cabin.

"This isn't any good," Caine said from behind her. "The trail's too well-defined. Even a city-bred lowlife would have little trouble following us if we were trying to get away."

"The path leads to a spring-fed pond about half a mile ahead," she said, stopping on the trail to turn and look at him. "It's a good fishing hole. The neighbors use it when they want a mess of bass, which is why the path is cleared like this. We'll only be following it a little longer. Then we have to cut into the woods."

Caine frowned. "Neighbors? There's been no one here since I arrived."

"There's been no one here since *I* arrived," she corrected. "Harve posted the property with No Fishing signs. Surely you saw them?"

"Yeah, I saw them, but I didn't realize they were new. That's all he did? Post signs? No one complained that one of their favorite fishing spots was suddenly off-limits? No one asked why?"

"Of course not," Vicki explained patiently. "Everyone knows he wouldn't have posted the signs without good reason."

Caine fell silent. Vicki could almost hear the wheels turning in his mind. "How many neighbors know you're related to the Tremaynes?"

Vicki shrugged. "Most of them, I guess."

"And how many of them do you think would make the connection between Harve posting his No Fishing signs and the media stories about you suddenly disappearing from Washington?"

"Anyone who thought about it," she admitted.

Caine's forceful and distinctive vocabulary left Vicki in no doubt of his reaction. She waited until he'd run out of breath and words before she spoke again. "There's nothing to get excited about," she told him.

"Nothing to get excited about?" Caine exploded. "Here I thought I had you safe and secure, a place where you couldn't be easily traced. Now you calmly inform me that most of the town's population, three hundred and fifty people, knows where you are? Two people is one too many to trust with a secret."

Vicki couldn't resist a grin. "The population is three hundred and fifty-two. Martha Jean Cogsdale delivered twins last week. And I did not tell you that the entire town knew where I was. I only said they could make the connection. But they won't, because they don't want to know. That way, if anyone comes around asking questions, they don't have to lie."

"If you believe that, lady, you're a—"

"Tremayne," Vicki said firmly. "At least, I'm a shirttail Tremayne, and so is everyone in town. Look, Caine, Little Falls is an old community. The history of the town and the families who live here are all entwined—a large extended family, even in cases where blood ties are thin. Sure they feud and fuss among themselves, but they also band together when one of their own is under attack. No one questioned Harve when he posted the property because they knew he had good reason, just as they knew he had good reason not to explain why, or else he would have. I'm safe here because I'm family."

"We can't take that kind of chance, can't take the chance that someone might slip."

"There's no chance of that. In fact, I think I'm safer here than anywhere else because no stranger can get anywhere near town without some kind of alert. When you parked your Mercedes on Main Street, no less than three people contacted Harve, and that was before you ordered your first cup of coffee at the Down Home. Believe me, if word of my presence gets out, it won't come from anyone in Little Falls."

"You'd better be right," Caine muttered. "You may be betting your life on it."

As well as yours, Vicki thought silently, and for a fleeting moment wondered if she had the right to risk his life on her beliefs. But she had complete faith that no one in the community would betray her, just as she had faith in Caine to protect her, if necessary. No, if betrayal came, it wouldn't be from anyone in Little Falls.

Vicki turned her attention back to the trail, aware that she hadn't totally convinced him. She could understand his caution, particularly after his revelations last night. It sounded as if he'd grown up in a dog-eat-dog world, his only support a struggling mother and a younger sister. In fact, he'd probably been *their* support, a heavy responsibility for someone who was only a kid himself. No wonder he was so angry and isolated.

Her present crisis, although more critical than any of her previous ones, wasn't the first time she'd been thankful for her family and their support. Her grandmother, Aunt Abby, Harve's parents and the other more distantly related relatives and residents of Little Falls had been surrogate parents for a lonely child who'd lost both mother and father before she reached her teens. These past weeks had given her a new appreciation of how lucky she'd been.

She stopped on the rise and waited for Caine to join her. "The fishing pond is down there," she told him, pointing into a ravine. "This is where we leave the trail. If we want to explore the path to Aunt Abby's, we need to cut north through the woods to the next ridge, then head southwest. If we go southeast we can backtrack to Harve's place. Or we can go on north toward the cave I told you about."

"If we're being chased, I can't see us putting your great-aunt in harm's way," Caine said. "And the trail from the cabin clearing to your cousin's farm would be closer and faster. Why don't we scout out that cave you were talking about? If nothing else, it'll give me a feel for the terrain.''

Vicki felt a surge of happiness at Caine's reluctance to place Aunt Abby in danger. Aunt Abby would be incensed at the idea that she couldn't take care of herself, but the fact that Caine was unwilling to put her in jeopardy only confirmed Vicki's belief that he was a natural protector, even though he was loath to admit it.

"The cave's a good hour's hike from here unless we're really hurrying," she warned.

"I won't starve if we get back late for lunch."

"Neither of us will starve," Vicki said with a grin. "That's our lunch you so gallantly insisted on carrying. When you finally agreed to let me out of the cabin, I wasn't about to give you an excuse like missing lunch to cut our time short. There's a small spring at the cave. We can eat before we begin the trip back."

"Why do I get the idea you've manipulated me?"

"Come on, Caine. Lighten up. We're as safe here as we'd be sitting around the cabin. Tucker and Gourdy are around somewhere. They'd let us know if anyone else was in the woods. It's a beautiful, warm spring day. Relax. Stop and smell the roses."

"Roses belong in flower beds," he growled.

The look on his face told Vicki that once again he'd spoken without thinking and now regretted it. The contradictions in the man intrigued her. She couldn't help pushing for more information, even as she realized he'd resent it.

"Why do I get the notion you're not particularly fond of the great outdoors?" she asked, her voice slightly teasing. "It was your idea to do some exploring."

"At the time, I thought it might be a good idea."

"And now?"

"It's still a good idea. A part of the job."

"I can hear the 'but' at the end of that sentence," she said.

Caine shrugged. "Look, Vicki. We're here to scout out the area. It's preparation, precaution. View it as a fun kind of picnic if you like, but it's not a crime that I don't see it the same way."

"But that's exactly what it's supposed to be, a picnic," Vicki protested. "Besides, I don't see why one has to preclude the other. Can't we do the 'Be Prepared' thing and have fun, too? Aren't you as tired of those four walls of the cabin as I am?"

"The cabin's contained. I know the territory, know what I need to defend."

"But wasn't that the reason for this excursion? To become more familiar with this territory?"

"Isn't that exactly what I said?"

A sound of exasperation escaped her. "Yes, it is, but you also indicated we couldn't enjoy ourselves at the same time. I don't understand your reasoning. It's not as if you're unacquainted with this type of territory. You're no novice. I've watched how you move, how you walk—quietly, like a hunter. You know your way around the woods, which means you've spent more than a little time in them, even if you were raised in the city.''

Caine shot her a look she couldn't interpret. "Yeah, you're right. I'm a hunter—only my prey is the two-legged variety. I know this kind of terrain, or at least something similar. Most of the time I spent in the wilds, the birds didn't sing and a rustle in the leaves probably meant a sniper, not a squirrel. I don't have cherished memories of picnics under spreading chestnut trees or walks beside pristine mountain streams. Sorry, but I can't buy into your nostalgia for the great outdoors."

Vicki felt the color drain from her face. She turned away. "I've done it again, haven't I? I'm sorry," she muttered. "I didn't—"

"You didn't know. No reason you should." Caine's voice sounded of carefully controlled indifference. She was beginning to recognize the nuances.

"Now, which way to the cave? Let's get on with this if we're going. Unless you insist on some kind of happy bucolic companion, you can have your hours on the outside. Or we can go back to the cabin. Your choice."

She didn't dare speak again, couldn't risk the chance she'd be unable to control her voice. Had his entire life been so bleak, so devoid of the simple day-to-day pleasures she'd always taken for granted? Silent, she pushed her way through a thicket of redbud, not even stopping to admire the ruffled pink petals that lay along whip-thin branches, and began climbing the ridge.

CHAPTER EIGHT

DAMMIT, CAINE BERATED himself. He'd done it again—blasted away at her illusions. It seemed he was determined to destroy her picture-pretty view of the world. He was supposed to be protecting her. Shouldn't that include shielding her from life's ugliness?

Silently he followed her through the woods, angry with himself, angry with her, because for some reason she seemed to bring out the worst in him. It wasn't her fault their outlooks were so different, wasn't her fault that his world was most often cold, dark and dangerous while hers was warm, bright and secure—until this episode with Henderson, at least. So why was he acting like the neighborhood bully who enjoyed pulling the wings off butterflies?

It was self-defense, he decided. He was using his anger as a way to keep his emotional barriers in place. She made him want too much, hope too much.

"Hey, Vicki, wait up," he called, hurrying after her. "I know I warned you I'm a bastard, but I'm sorry I blasted you. You caught me at a bad time. I was remembering . . . something else. You got the fallout."

She gave him a wary look, as if trying to decide whether to believe him or not.

"Remembering what?" she asked.

Stubborn woman. She wasn't willing to simply accept his apology and let it go. "Nothing important. Nothing to do with you."

"Apparently it does," she told him. "I don't understand you."

"Sometimes I don't understand myself."

She shook her head. "I always seem to catch you at a bad time. We can't even talk. You build fences and post them with No Trespassing signs. Only, the warnings are invisible. I don't mean to irritate you, but I can't seem to avoid stumbling into forbidden territory. And when I ask, you say it doesn't matter."

Oh, hell. He'd spent more time examining his past and his motives in the short while he'd been around her than he had in the last ten years. Now she was doing it to him again. He'd have to give her some kind of explanation or she'd keep asking. "I was in the military, a Special Forces unit," he explained reluctantly. "One of my last assignments was a jungle operation. It went bad."

"And the countryside around here reminds you of that?"

"Yeah. The jungle was greener, of course, denser, hotter. But it had the same kind of feeling—fresh, natural, innocent, just as God made it. Unspoiled by man's evil. Only, the innocence was a deception. A lot of good men died."

"Oh, Caine, I'm sorry."

"Yeah, well . . . I shouldn't let my bad memories affect you."

For a moment, she didn't say anything, and when she finally spoke her voice was low and concerned. "You know what I think? I think you need some new memories."

"You might be right," he told her. But new memories wouldn't change the past, he reminded himself.

They began a gradual climb up the next ridge, stopping occasionally as Vicki pointed out various items of interest. The poison ivy, she said, identifying a clump of vines that had all but covered a dead tree, was still potent, even if it hadn't yet leafed out. A large slab of granite precariously balanced on the edge of a rock outcropping was, according to local legend, the site of a shoot-out between lawmen and a group of desperadoes in the 1880s. It was called, appropriately, Deadman's Ledge.

It was only as they stopped for a moment's rest halfway up a steep rock-strewn hillside that Caine realized the wind was chill against his skin. Anxious, he looked around and drew a sharp breath at the sight of dark, churning clouds on the western horizon.

"Uh-oh . . ." Vicki had apparently seen the same thing.

"How much longer to that cave?" he asked.

"About twenty minutes if we hurry." An ominous clap of thunder echoed off the hills around them. "Come on. We'll have to run for it."

They almost made it. Vicki had just pointed out the narrow, naturally disguised opening of the cave a couple of hundred feet above them when the rain began pelting down.

Caine, scrambling through the narrow opening behind Vicki, couldn't hide his exclamation of surprise when the short tunnel-like entrance opened into a large cavern. Stalactites, shaped like free-form sculptures, hung from the ceiling. Embedded crystals twinkled in the dim light.

He was barely aware of Vicki stretching on tiptoe to reach a small rock ledge to the left of the opening and registered her action only when she gave a small cry of success. Soon, the cavern was bathed in the soft golden glow of an old-fashioned lantern, its flickering flame casting dancing shadows along the cavern walls.

For a moment, wonder and awe held him speechless.

"Beautiful, isn't it?" she said. "I haven't been up here in several years, but this was always one of my favorite places. Every summer when I came to visit, Harve and I and some of the other cousins would camp out here for a night."

Caine smiled. "And roast marshmallows?"

She nodded. "Roast marshmallows, tell ghost stories and dream about all the things we would do and the fantastic places we'd go when we grew up." She seemed pensive. "It's funny. I've traveled a lot of places and seen a lot of sights since then but none of them have been more impressive than this."

"I can believe that." His gaze met hers and for a moment, his thoughts whirled into a free-fall. Heat coursed through his veins; his pulse pounded in his ears.

She was the first to look away. With a visible shiver, she wrapped her arms around herself, glancing toward the cave opening.

"You're cold," he said.

"The cave has a natural fifty-eight-degree temperature the year around. It's great in the summer, but now—especially with wet clothes—well, I'm sure you're cold, too."

Caine shrugged. If truth be told, he hadn't noticed, not with those inner fires of want and need playing havoc with his thermostat.

"How long can we expect the rain to last?"

Vicki shook her head. "It looked like a fast-moving weather cell. Maybe a couple of hours?"

"Then we'll have time to get back to the cabin before dark."

"We should, unless there's another storm chasing this one." She shivered again.

Caine dropped the backpack and stripped off his denim jacket. Then he removed his shoulder holster, laying it out of the way against the cavern wall, and began unbuttoning his shirt.

Vicki took a step backward. "What...are you doing?"

"You're freezing. Get your wet shirt off and put on mine. It's damp, but not as wet as yours. The jacket gave me some protection."

"But . . . but you'll freeze."

"I'll be fine." He moved toward the cave entrance.

"Caine? Wait. Where are you going?"

"To find a couple of dead limbs. It hasn't been raining long. I should be able to find some that aren't wet through. If we're going to be here for a couple of hours, we need heat. I saw the fire ring just inside the entrance, so it's been done before. I guess the smoke funnels out through the entrance.

"But the lightning. You shouldn't be outside. It's dangerous."

There were all kinds of danger, Caine thought, and right now a cold bath was exactly what he needed, even if it was accompanied by electrical fireworks. "I'll be careful and I won't be gone long."

"Wait a minute. Won't you at least take your shirt back?"

"Why? To protect me from the lightning?" Seeing the look of concern in her eyes, he regretted his sarcasm. "I'll be all right, Vicki. Honest. Skin drys more quickly than clothes. And I'll be moving—exertion produces body heat. Now stop arguing and get changed. You can also look around a little, see if you and your cousins left anything besides that lantern behind. A little dry kindling would be nice." Before she could think up another argument, he ducked out the cave entrance.

Obstinate man, Vicki thought, staring at the cave opening. As if he could dodge lightning bolts. Well, maybe. If anyone could, she'd bet it would be Caine.

She shivered, remembering his instructions to put on his shirt. If she wasn't so cold, she might be tempted...but perhaps this wasn't the time to bait the bull. He was so sure of himself, so determined to take care of her. If she didn't follow orders, he'd probably undress her and put it on her himself.

That thought sent a wave of heat through her body, and she shucked off her wet shirt and slipped into Caine's. She hugged the shirt against her. It was almost as if she could still feel him, feel his strong arms holding her close.

Not the right time for such thoughts, she told herself, and holding the lantern high, began a careful search of the cavern.

By the time Caine returned, dragging a good-size tree limb behind him, she had a small blaze going in the fire ring, a neat stack of kindling beside it and her shirt and Caine's denim jacket stretched out to dry on nearby rocks.

"Here," she said, handing him a napkin she'd retrieved from the backpack. "It's not much of a towel, but better than nothing."

"It'll sluice most of the water off. The fire'll do the rest. I see you found some dry wood." He took the napkin, rubbed it across his face and over his head, then began to wipe down his chest.

Vicki's breath caught. "I see you did, too," she managed to say, then ducked around him to pull the tree limb farther inside the cavern.

"There's two more limbs at the entrance. I'll drag them inside in a minute. I called the dogs, but it's raining so hard I doubt they heard me."

"Don't worry about Gourdy or Tucker. They'll hole up somewhere until the rain slacks, then head back to the cabin," Vicki said. She propped the end of the tree limb between two rocks, then stomped down with her foot. The limb splintered under her boot heel, but didn't completely break. She turned it over and brought her foot down again.

"Here, I'll do that," Caine said.

"I can do it."

"I can do it easier. Wipe off my back, will you?" He offered her the now wet napkin.

She hoped he didn't notice the slight tremor in her hand as she took it. "All right. Turn around." Even through the clammy cloth she could feel the warmth of his smooth, muscular back. She heard him give a slight gasp.

"What's the matter? Are you hurt?"

"No. Nothing's wrong," he said in a tight voice. "You almost done?"

With brisk, efficient strokes, Vicki finished wiping his back. "There. Now for heavens's sake, get over by the fire before you turn into an icicle."

"Stop fussing, Vicki. It's nowhere near freezing in here. Too cool for comfort, but certainly bearable—as long as we aren't here too long. Now, as I recall, you said something about a picnic..."

Vicki moved back to the fire and delved into the backpack. Caine had every right to be annoyed with her. She'd talked him into coming up here, knowing how far it was and how difficult it would be to get help if anything went wrong. She'd had no way of predicting the thunderstorm, of course, but she should have considered the possibility. It was that time of year.

Caine repositioned the tree limb between the rocks and stomped, cleanly breaking off a length in one try. He repeated the process until the entire limb was in lengths short enough to fit into the fire ring.

Ducking back through the tunnel-like entryway, he pulled another couple of branches farther into the cavern, then picked up several of the short pieces and walked to the fire.

"If I'd been smart, I've had brought something like hot dogs," Vicki said. "Hot food would be—"

"It doesn't matter. I'm sure whatever you brought will be fine." Caine carefully laid a couple of the small logs on the fire and sat down next to it. "Good oak. It makes a nice hot blaze."

Vicki handed him an apple and one of thick roast-beef sandwiches she'd made—had it been only a few hours ago?—then watched as he took half of the sandwich from its wrapping and carefully laid the other half aside.

"I thought you'd be hungry."

"You make a mean sandwich. This is fine."

What he was doing? she wondered. Saving food for later?

She shouldn't have been so pigheaded. Now they were stuck here. "Caine, I'm sorry I insisted on coming with you. And I certainly shouldn't have dragged you all the way up here. I can't imagine that we'll ever need to use the cave. I was selfish. I just wanted to get away for a while. If I'd stayed in the cabin like you wanted me to, you could have explored the area nearby, then been back warm and dry before this deluge started."

He shrugged. "I could have refused to let you come. A little wet never hurt anybody. Besides, I'd hate to think I missed a chance at seeing this place."

"What if we have to stay the night?"

"What if we do? It's certainly safe enough. I can see why that ancestor of yours was able to hide here. Besides, we could get back to the cabin if we really needed to. We'd get wet, but the front has moved east. No thunder and lightning out there now. Just rain."

"But if Harve comes by the cabin and doesn't find us..."

"He'll know you're safe with me. There's nothing at the cabin—no indication of trouble—to cause him to worry."

"Other than the fact that we're not there."

"Other than that," he agreed. "Don't borrow trouble, Vicki. Chances are we'll get back before we're even missed. The rain shouldn't last much longer."

They finished the meal in silence. Caine rewrapped his remaining half sandwich, then dragged one of the tree limbs over to the side of the fire ring. He hung her shirt and his jacket on its branches.

Vicki moved closer to the fire ring, savoring the heat on the front of her body. But her icy back made her even more aware of the chill in the cave. She looked across the fire at Caine, still stripped bare to the waist, and knew, regardless of what he said, he had to be cold.

He was staring moodily into the flames, apparently unaware of her scrutiny. Her gaze lingered for a moment on his face, then dropped to the muscular planes of his chest.

Caine's body was magnificent—a perfect blend of form and function. She jerked her gaze away, raising her eyes to his face, and found him watching her, a frown on his forehead and a knowing look in his eyes. He blinked and the look disappeared.

She dropped her gaze to her lap, then with a spurt of courage she hadn't known she possessed, raised her head again, certain she wasn't the first woman who'd found him attractive, or the first one to let him know it.

She wasn't, however, quite brave enough to say it out loud. "I was looking for goose bumps," she said defensively. "You have to be cold. I should give you back your shirt. Mine must be practically dry by now."

"I'm in no danger of hypothermia. Are you still cold?"

"Not the parts of me facing the fire."

He laughed, the sound a low rumble that echoed through the cavern. It was a warm, comforting sound, a sound she wished she could capture and replay.

"I could build a second fire and sit you between them. Instant Vicki toast. Warm on both sides."

"Caine—"

"Or you could come over here and sit by me. I'll keep your back warm."

"You can tease—"

"I'm not teasing, Vicki. I was trying to figure out how to suggest it without offending you. Shared body warmth is one of the first rules of wilderness survival. I'm sure you know that."

Not sharing body warmth was one of the first rules of fantasy control, Vicki reminded herself.

"I'll even admit I'm beginning to feel chilled," he went on, "but I don't want to put on still damp clothes. I don't want you to, either."

She had to admit his idea had a certain appeal.

"It's warmer over here," he said. "The heat reflects off the rock wall behind me. Right now your back is to the open cavern."

She knew that, too. Anticipating that he'd opt to sit as far away from her as possible, she'd deliberately chosen the open side of the fire ring. After all, Caine was the one who was half-naked. He needed the extra heat more than she did. But now it seemed she'd suffered needlessly.

"All right, all right. I'm convinced," she said, managing to swallow a groan when she stood, her muscles protesting the cold and their cramped position.

VICKI'S CAPITULATION took Caine by surprise. He'd expected to have to argue a lot longer and harder before she finally agreed. He scooped out a shallow indention in the dirt of the cave floor next to him. "Sit here," he told her. "Now stretch your legs out straight, angling them to the side of the fire, and lean back against me."

He put his arm around her shoulders and pulled her against his chest. It felt right, exactly right, as if she'd been made to fit there. Dangerous thoughts, he warned himself, but was unable to control the impulse to give her shoulder a gentle squeeze.

She stiffened. "Caine—"

"Relax, Vicki. The idea was to share body warmth, remember? I promise not to repeat last night's episode."

She went still. "You weren't the only participant last night," she told him. "Don't be so quick to assume responsibility."

Now, what had he said? All he'd been trying to do was reassure her. He should've known he couldn't win with this woman. Hell, he couldn't even figure out the rules of the game.

"You said it yourself. Last night was a mistake, a natural consequence of our situation. Since I suggested you move over here by me, I didn't want you to feel threatened. I was simply trying to assure you that you're safe with me."

"How noble," she said, not bothering to disguise the sarcasm in her voice. "If I remember last night correctly, I was the one who precipitated our kiss. I was the one who approached you. I never felt threatened—at least not by you."

"Yeah, sure. You scampered up those stairs like a mugger was chasing you. Someone certainly had you scared, and since I was the only one there, I think it's safe to assume it was me."

"Not someone, something," she protested. "That kiss . . . well, it surprised me. It was more than a simple kiss, and you know it, Caine Alexander."

"This morning you suggested we should ignore it, forget it." His strained to keep his voice natural. "And I agreed."

"Well, I've had time to think about it some more. I don't think we *should* forget it. I don't think we can."

Now was a fine time for her to change her mind! "Lady, are you always this perverse?"

"I'm not being perverse. I'm being realistic," she protested. "We both agreed to forget it, right? But then neither of us did. I certainly haven't forgotten it, and obviously neither have you, or you wouldn't have brought it up again."

"I didn't—"

"Of course you did. You're the one who said you wouldn't repeat last night's episode. Episode? If it was just a simple kiss, how did it escalate into an episode?"

How could he have been so stupid? He never should've started this. He should have left her to freeze on her side of the fire while he froze on his. He'd known it would be torture to hold her in his arms, but he'd convinced himself he'd be able to handle it. She wasn't making it easy.

"Dammit, Vicki, give me a break here. I'm not the one who called it a simple kiss. *You* did."

"Well, I was wrong. I admit it."

Caine groaned. "This isn't the time—"

"I can't think of a better time. We've got nothing special we have to do."

His breathing stopped. "What are you suggesting?"

"The thing is, it *should* have been just a simple kiss, considering the circumstances. We both know that. So the reason we think it was *more* than a simple kiss, even when we know it was *only* a simple kiss, is that we both overreacted."

Caine shook his head. "Your logic escapes me. I think we should change the subject."

"I don't. I think we should try it again."

"Try what?"

"Kissing, of course. I think we should try it again."

"You're crazy. And you're making me crazy, too."

"It's the logical thing to do. Think about it, Caine. Last night... the circumstances... it caught us by surprise and we overreacted. But this time we know what we're doing. It won't be surprise. It'll only be a simple kiss. And then we'll be able to put last night's kiss into perspective."

Caine realized he was fighting a losing battle. With both himself and her. Hell, he'd lost the entire war the minute he'd pulled her into his arms. He might, just might, have been able to hang on to his resolve to keep his hands off her—figuratively speaking at least—if she hadn't initiated this discussion.

"Let me get this straight. You think we should try kissing again to prove that last night's kiss was nothing special?"

"That's right."

"Have you thought about what happens if you're wrong?"

"Then we'll know."

He already knew—Vicki Winslow was the kind of woman who could make him want, make him need, make him dream of things he could never have. She was as dangerous to him as a terrorist with a secret cache of explosives. And there wasn't a damn thing he could do about it. Neither could he resist the temptation she offered.

"All right, Vicki," he growled. "Just remember, this was all your idea."

CHAPTER NINE

IN THE SPLIT SECOND before Caine's mouth closed over hers, Vicki fought a sudden sense of panic. Then it was too late. Soft as a whisper, his lips touched hers, and fear evaporated into a whirling vortex of sensation. An enticing, delicious heat uncoiled deep inside her.

She trembled, shocked at her eager response to his lips. Dear heaven, she'd done it now—gone and tweaked the tail of the tiger. She should have left well enough alone!

But desire defeated logic. She turned in his arms, returning his kiss with reckless abandon. It felt so good, so right. Her hand moved against his chest, tingling at the warmth of his skin under her fingertips.

When Caine lifted his head, her sense of desertion, of deprivation, was almost overwhelming. Then he gave a soft moan and swooped to recapture her lips in a kiss more demanding this time, a kiss that seemed to draw from a bottomless pool of need.

He pulled her closer until she could feel the trembling of his arms, could feel her own desire pulsing painfully through her veins. Her hand moved up his chest, around his shoulders and twisted in the dark hair at the nape of his neck. Her heart beat wildly.

Shivering in his arms, she wondered how she could have been have stupid enough to believe that anything about Caine was simple.

He lifted his mouth from hers and cradled her head against his shoulder. She could feel his chest heaving, as if he'd just finished running a marathon. There was comfort in the sound of his racing heart beneath her ear, comfort in the knowledge that she was not the only one so affected. She wanted more, but for this moment she was willing to enjoy the sensation of being so close.

"Vicki..."

The sound of her name on his lips was a combination of caress and plea, as if it had escaped him inadvertently. She clung to him, still lost in a turbulence of sensation, unable to speak.

"Vicki," he said again, his breathing as ragged as her own, "are you all right?"

Was she all right? Would she ever be all right again? Desperately she tried to gather her scattered wits. Finally she nodded.

"I didn't mean..."

"I know," she said. "I remember. This was my idea."

"That wasn't what I was going to say."

"It doesn't matter." She tried to move out of his embrace. His arms tightened around her.

"Let me go, Caine."

"I don't want to."

Heaven help her, she didn't want him to, either. It was madness. Vicki took a deep breath. "I was wrong. This wasn't a good idea."

"No," he said, "I was the one who was wrong. It was a very good idea."

"Caine, please. Let me—"

"Quiet," he whispered harshly, and before she realized what was happening, she was flat on her back, under him, his left hand firmly over her mouth. Raw fear washed over her as he reached out with his right hand and grabbed the gun and holster he'd left lying by the wall.

Then she heard it—the sound of someone at the cave entrance—and went perfectly still. *This can't be happening. It's a nightmare.* Caine gave her a warning look before lifting his hand from her mouth.

Vicki was afraid to move, almost afraid to breathe, as Caine slid off her, placing himself between her and the cave entrance, gun in hand.

The sound of a familiar "woof-woof," followed immediately by Tucker and Gourdy's scrambling entrance into the cave left Vicki giddy with relief. Head swimming, she gasped for breath, but the roaring in her ears couldn't drown out Caine's fluent string of expletives.

Tucker barked again as, tails wagging, both dogs bounded across the cave toward them. The feel of the dog's tongue against her cheek had the effect of a bucket of ice water. Vicki pushed Tucker away and struggled into a sitting position, while Caine fended off Gourdy's enthusiastic greeting, dumping the black-and-tan hound from his lap.

"If the dogs are moving around, the weather's probably settled down enough to get out of here," he said.

His voice was bland again, the look in his eyes guarded, as if the past few minutes had never happened.

What kind of man was he? He seemed to simply flip a switch and turn off all emotion. Although her own heart rate had finally slowed to normal, she was still trying to come to grips with the experience of his kiss—a kiss that redefined her perception of the act.

Caine's attempt to ignore what had happened between them was not going to make it go away, but for the moment she'd follow his lead. She brushed at the dirt clinging to her jeans. Caine moved to the other side of the fire and began tucking the remnants of their lunch into her backpack.

"I'll be ready in a minute," she told him, grabbing her shirt from the limb where he'd hung it to dry. She walked deeper into the cave and stepped behind a stalactite to change, hoping the moments alone would also give her a chance to collect her wits.

Caine had smothered the fire by the time Vicki finished buttoning her shirt. He pulled on his shirt, then handed her his jacket. Vicki started to protest.

"Don't argue. Put it on," he demanded in a clipped voice, "and let's get out of here."

Vicki took one last look around the cave. With the exception of new ashes in the fire ring, there was no evidence she and Caine had been here. Yet it was different. The cave had always been one of her favorite places—a place of natural beauty and the innocent dreams and memories of childhood. From this day forward, her memories and dreams would be different.

Caine, she realized intuitively, would try to forget the kiss, the feelings it had aroused. That was all right—for now. He was used to being alone, and it would be difficult for him to accept what was happening between them. But accept it he would. She was, above all, tenacious.

She was also falling in love with Caine Alexander.

With an inner sigh, she turned and followed Caine and the dogs.

THE RAIN HAD STOPPED but the woods were wet, and although she hadn't complained, Caine knew Vicki was both damp and cold when they finally reached the cabin. He was relieved when she didn't protest his order for her to remain outside with the dogs while he inspected the premises, although the look on her face clearly reflected her displeasure. As he entered the main room, Sweetpea emerged from her usual place under the couch, chittering as if disapproving of being left alone most of the day.

He quickly scanned the room, looking for anything out of place, anything to indicate someone might have entered the cabin during their absence. He found his evidence in a stack of papers piled conspicuously in the center of the trestle table, then relaxed when he realized they'd been left by Harve.

He laid the papers aside and continued his inspection. Tail high and still complaining, Sweetpea followed him around the cabin. "It's all right, girl. No one deserted you. We're back," he told her, then found himself grinning at the idea that he was actually trying to reassure a skunk.

Sweetpea waited at the foot of the stairs while he made a quick visual inspection of the loft area. Finally satisfied no unwelcome visitors had invaded the cabin during their absence, Caine moved to the door and motioned to Vicki that it was safe for her to enter.

She entered, the dogs at her heels. "Find anything?" she asked, clearly exasperated.

"Nothing dangerous, but it's better to be sure," he answered. It was all he could do to keep from smiling at the look of mutiny on her face.

Vicki let out a long sigh, acknowledging the correctness of his position with a slight nod. "I guess so," she said. Sweetpea chittered again and twisted herself around Vicki's ankles. She bent to give the skunk a pat and a scratch behind the ears. "I'm going to change into dry clothes," she told Caine. "You should, too."

As Vicki disappeared into the loft, Sweetpea, finally quiet, jumped onto the couch, stretching herself across the armrest. Caine shook his head. Obviously the animal had wanted more than company. It had taken Vicki's touch to comfort and quiet her.

He and the skunk had a lot in common, Caine realized, although quiet was not exactly *his* reaction to Vicki's touch. Dangerous thoughts, he reminded himself again, and pushing them to the back of his mind, he lifted a log onto the bed of coals still glowing in the fireplace. The dogs flopped down on the hearth.

Caine stripped out of his damp clothes, quickly redressed and was sitting at the table examining the papers Harve had left when Vicki came down from the loft. She was dressed in a light blue sweatshirt and matching jogging pants, which covered her from neck to ankle—a warm, comfortable and utilitarian outfit. Except on her it looked anything but utilitarian.

The soft knit material draped loosely over her slim figure, hinting at the tantalizing curves it concealed. The blue color seemed to intensify the green of her eyes. Her hair, obviously freshly brushed and left loose to finish drying, framed her face in a cloud of burnished fire. Caine allowed himself only a second to look, then swallowed and dropped his gaze back to the papers.

"What's that?" Vicki asked.

"Transcripts of the trial and some other files I requested. Harve must have left them while we were gone."

"Find anything?"

"Not yet," he told her, "but then, I've barely started." Not that he was likely to accomplish much, he acknowledged. He could only hope that Vicki decided to retire early in the evening. After she was tucked safely in the loft out of sight, maybe he'd be able to concentrate enough to get some work done.

"Well, I'll see what I can find for supper. Is stew okay? It's quick and easy."

"Sounds good to me," he said when it became apparent she was waiting for him to answer. Stew? Bread and water? He doubted if he'd know the difference.

Once again he turned his attention back to the papers and once again found Vicki's presence a distraction. Finally he laid aside the papers and retrieved his jacket from the hook by the door. "I'm going to take a look around," he told her, escaping outside.

Caine walked far enough down the trail to be out of sight of the cabin. Automatically his eyes scanned the scene, all senses on alert. He stepped off the trail, moving through the woods behind the motion detectors, checking each for signs of malfunction or tampering. There weren't any—but he was well aware there was a problem. It wasn't, however, in the motion detectors or any of his other security precautions. The problem was himself.

He'd experienced a sense of attraction the first time he'd laid eyes on Victoria Winslow, but he'd been sure he could handle it. A lady like that would have nothing in common with, and no interest in, a loner like him.

He'd been wrong. He was neither as strong nor as immune as he'd believed. Each day, each hour he was around her, confirmed that finding. He was growing more and more involved. If he'd ever been so closely attuned to another person, he couldn't remember it, not even with his sister.

You didn't have to guess with Maggie. If she was happy or sad or disappointed or enthusiastic, she let you know. Vicki was more complex. She guarded her feelings, protecting both herself and those she cared about—letting those around her see what she thought they wanted to see.

Yet he seemed to be able to sense her moods. He knew instinctively how hard he could press, knew when she was becoming irritated with him—a state of affairs that was more or less ongoing. He was able to read her, regardless of her public face, and that knowledge scared him half to death.

He'd lost his edge, his sense of detachment, and both experience and knowledge told him it was time to get out.

But his inner voice whispered no.

One thing for sure, he decided, he could not repeat last night's or today's activities. Maybe in another life, or if he were another man... Hell, he was who he was, and nothing, neither dreams nor regrets, was going to change that.

Somehow he had to regain his equilibrium—and his objectivity. He couldn't allow this distraction to continue. His job was to protect her. It was a job that could at any moment require cold, hard and instant decisions. Both her life and his might depend on his ability to make those decisions on the basis of instinct and logic—not emotion.

The dogs had saved him this afternoon. He couldn't risk depending on such a rescue again. He was going to have to draw away, to rebuild the wall between them, brick by brick if necessary. Vicki would be hurt. She wouldn't understand.

Better a little pain now than a lot later, he reminded himself, and knew he was thinking about his own pain, as well as hers. In the end, when this was all over, she'd realize it was for the best. She'd be more than happy to see the back of him.

Caine was so preoccupied, he didn't notice Harve's truck until he was nearly to the cabin. He shouldn't be surprised, he told himself. It made sense that after Harve had found the cabin empty earlier, he'd check back to make sure everything was okay.

Silence fell between the two cousins as he entered the cabin, and one look at Harve's face told him all was not well. "What's going on?" he demanded.

"The Fayetteville marshal paid me a visit awhile ago," Harve said without preamble. "Left a fax for you." He shoved the paper at him.

Caine's hand closed around it. He scanned the top of the sheet, confirming the fax was from Danny to the Fayetteville office. The fact that Danny had sent Baxter after him was another indication that the news wasn't good. He looked across the room to where Vicki was standing behind the couch, her face white, her expression pinched, and knew that, whatever the news was, it was very, very bad.

He scanned the message quickly, his gut knotting as he read. "Return Victoria Winslow to protective custody. Henderson's body discovered this a.m. Preliminary reports indicate death occurred a week ago."

Caine did a quick mental calculation. If Henderson had been dead a week, then he'd already been out of the picture when Vicki's apartment was broken into. The implications made Caine's blood run cold. Whoever was behind Henderson's death wanted Vicki, and he was both clever and ruthless. Embezzlement was essentially a nonviolent crime, but now murder had been added to the mix.

Caine scanned the rest of the message. He was to use his own judgment about whether to turn her over to authorities in Fayetteville or escort her back to Washington himself.

It was the last line, however, that set all his nerves screaming. "See you at Loch Lomond."

Caine laid the paper aside and looked up to see both Harve and Vicki watching him intently. "You read this?" he asked Harve.

"Of course I read it," Harve said without apology. "What I want to know is what you're going to do about it."

"I am not going back into protective custody," Vicki interjected, her voice adamant.

Caine tried to ignore her. "When did Baxter deliver it?"

"About half an hour ago. I told him I'd be unable to reach you until tomorrow. Of course he might not've believed me."

"Did you hear me?" Vicki said again. "I am not going back to be locked up again."

"You might as well know," Harve said somewhat belligerently, "that I agree with Vicki. I don't think she should go back into protective custody. And by law, there's no way you can force her."

"I know that. So does Danny."

The belligerence on Harve's face disappeared. "Ah. That last line. I thought it was a little cryptic. What's it mean?"

"Danny's on the high road. I'm on the low. He's cutting me loose." Caine's gaze locked with Harve's. "Let's hope Baxter isn't as perceptive."

"You suspect Baxter?"

"Let's just say the fewer people who know anything, the better off we'll be."

"Ah, yes," Harve said. "'Distrust and caution are the parents of security.' That's from *Poor Richard's Almanac*. Franklin was an astute man."

Caine felt some of his tension drain away. He shook his head and grinned. "Never at a loss, are you?"

"Rarely," Harve said, returning his grin.

Vicki stamped her foot. "Will you stop discussing this as if I'm not even here? I don't find it the least bit amusing."

"Sorry, cuz," Harve said. "We didn't mean to ignore you, but Caine and I needed to understand each other. Is that stew I smell? Why don't we eat? Then we can talk."

If anything, the look on her face grew more mutinous. "If you think you can send the little woman to the kitchen while you two continue your cryptic verbal shorthand, you're wrong. This concerns me."

Caine sighed. She was right. She needed to understand what was at stake. Even if he and Harve agreed, it wasn't their decision to make. It was Vicki's.

"Henderson's associates killed him," he told her bluntly. "And they're still looking for you. Remember, embezzlement is a white-collar crime. Murder isn't. Danny's officially authorized to take you back into protective custody."

"And if I don't want to go?" Her voice was firm and steady. The trembling of her clasped hands, however, gave away her tension. Caine wanted to gather her in his arms, assure her everything would be all right. But he couldn't. He wasn't God, he reminded himself. All he could do was accurately describe her alternatives. The choice ultimately was hers.

"It's your call. You can go back under federal protection and wait it out, or you can fend for yourself."

"What did you mean when you said Danny had cut you loose."

"No contact. Official or otherwise. You're back to your original proposition. If you stay out, you're in the cold—you're on your own. No official help. Although your cousin and I believe you're safer outside the system, it has to be your decision."

Vicki's face blanched even more, her eyes darkening to jade. "They're going to find me here, aren't they?"

Caine nodded.

"Then I have no choice. I can't put Harve and Aunt Abby at risk." Her shoulders slumped. "When can you take me to Fayetteville?"

"Dammit, Vicki," Harve roared, "I'm not going to let you do this! This is the same situation as before. You were right to say no then. Nothing's changed."

"Yes, it has, Harve. A man's been killed. It was a gamble before. Now we know for sure how dangerous they can be. I cannot, will not, sit here and wait for them to show up. I told you from the first I wouldn't put you, Aunt Abby or anyone else at risk. I have to go in."

"We wouldn't have to be here when they showed up," Caine told her. "That would reduce the danger to Harve. But it means going on the run. If, that is, you decide not to go back to Danny."

"We? But I thought you said..." Her voice trembled. "You mean you... you'd come with me?"

It was the rising note of incredulous hope in her voice that got to him. His rage was sudden and searing, making his senses spin. After everything that had happened between them, she thought he'd desert her now? He shoved his hands into his pockets, clenching his fists in an effort to rein in his anger. "Of course I'm coming with you," he snapped. "What do you think—that I'd just walk away?"

"But...but Marshal Carelli ordered you to bring me in."

"I don't work for Danny, and you know it. I told you that the first day I arrived." He struggled to bring himself under control.

Vicki drew an audible breath. "I'm sorry, Caine. I didn't understand."

Her voice was soft, pleading; he felt his anger, his rage, drain away. Why had he expected her to understand? He hadn't understood either. Until now. Regardless of his debate with himself before Harve arrived, he'd had the same chance as a snowball's in hell of walking away from her. He'd been whistling in the dark. Deluding himself. Running scared.

"My fault," he told her. "I didn't explain myself well."

"No. It was my fault. I should have realized... should have known—"

"Enough of that," Harve interrupted, giving them both a piercing look. "Now that we've decided Vicki's not going in, we have to decide what she *is* going to do. We've got plans to make. But first we eat. 'An army marches on its stomach.' Napoleon said that."

"Does he always get the last word?" Caine asked Vicki.

Vicki sighed. "Most of the time," she admitted, "but that's only because I let him."

CHAPTER TEN

THE STEW, Vicki decided, might as well have been a bowl of cornmeal mush for all the attention Caine and Harve were paying to it. Debate on where she and Caine should go began even before the two men sat down at the table.

"You could use Cousin George's ski cabin north of Nashville," Harve suggested.

"If we stayed isolated in that type of resort area, we'd attract attention," Caine said.

"Then how about a hunting lodge in Montana? I've got a standing offer to use one anytime. No questions asked."

"Too isolated," Caine vetoed again. "We'd have no way of staying in touch with what's happening—not without breaking cover."

As Vicki listened to Caine and Harve, her sense of depression seemed almost to smother her. When would this all end? During her stay here, she'd at least been on familiar ground. The cabin held memories of family and childhood. Dammit, she refused to go hide in Nashville or Montana or anywhere else and simply wait for them to find her. It was time to stop being a victim. A vague plan began to form in her mind.

"Wait a minute," she protested, "we're going about this all wrong. Exactly why am I in hiding, anyway?"

Caine exchanged a look with Harve, an exasperated expression on his face.

"Because, cousin dear," Harve said bluntly, "the bad guys are looking for you. You're hiding because they've killed one man, and you may be next on their list."

"Don't patronize me, Harve. I'm trying to put things into perspective here. Tell me why you think I'm on their list?"

Caine straightened in his chair and turned to study her. "Because they believe you're a danger to them."

"Exactly. They think I know something that could identify them, right?"

Both Caine and Harve nodded.

"So it stands to reason that if they think I know something, then I do, or at least I should."

"What are you trying to say, Vicki?" Harve asked.

"It's perfectly clear to me. He or she, the person who was behind Henderson, thinks I can identify him, so I'm in danger until he's caught. Only, no one can catch him because no one knows who he is. So if I'm the only one who is supposed to be able to identify him, then I'd better start doing something about it. And I can't do that in Nashville or stuck in some hunting lodge in Montana. I need to go back to Washington. That's where the answers are."

"Dammit, no, Vicki!" Caine exploded. "It's too dangerous."

There was a reflective look on Harve's face. "There is that old saw that the safest place to hide is in plain sight," he said calmly.

Vicki turned her attention to Caine. It was obvious he was the one she had to convince. "Harve's right. Washington is the last place he'd expect me to be," she said. "If we could sneak back into the city, maybe I could find out what it is I'm supposed to already know."

Caine shook his head. "Even if, as you suggest, we could sneak back into the city, we'd have to stay in hiding. As soon as you poked your nose out the door, you'd be vulnerable. He might not be expecting you to be there, but that sure won't make you invisible."

Although he was still arguing, his voice, Vicki, noticed, was not quite as adamant.

"I don't plan to go marching around in broad daylight," she said, "but if no one knew I was there, we could get into the foundation offices at night. I still have my keys. The answers have to be in the files somewhere."

"I don't like it. You'd be in constant danger."

Although he was not yet convinced, Vicki thought she could detect a slight wavering in his position. "Tell me, Caine, honestly, if it was you in this situation, would you go into hiding, or would you go looking for answers?"

"I'd go looking for answers," he admitted gruffly, "but it's not the same thing. I know the risks and I can take care of myself."

"I know the risks, too. I knew them when I started this. And I'm not completely helpless," she told him. "Besides, I have you to look after me."

Caine's face expressed caution, as well as calculation and concern. But she sensed he was at least considering the idea. For a moment there was silence around the table.

She held her breath. Would he agree? He had to, because although she'd never admit it, her plan scared her to death. She knew she'd never be able to do it on her own, not if Caine didn't agree to help. He was her protection, her strength.

"Will you promise me you'll do what I say?"

Vicki's fists were clenched in her lap. She knew Caine's agreement to take her back to Washington depended on her answer, but she didn't want to make a promise she couldn't keep. Why was it so difficult for Caine to accept that she had a mind of her own, or that sometimes her ideas were good ones? She suspected it was all part of the male-protector syndrome.

"You're the expert at this," she said carefully. "I'd be stupid not to follow your advice. I promise I won't do anything without your knowledge."

Although she knew it fell short of Caine's demand for complete obedience, she hoped it was enough. With her gaze on his face, she twisted her hands and waited for his decision. Finally he gave an almost imperceptible nod. It was enough. Vicki couldn't hold back her grin.

"All right," Harve said after a moment. "Now we need a safe house for you to stay."

"We can probably hide out at my place," Caine said finally, his voice still reluctant. "There's no indication that anyone's connected me to the case. At least not yet. That's why Danny warned me not to get in touch. Apparently he believes I'm still clean."

Caine turned to Harve. "Can you get over here early in the morning?" he asked. "I don't want to leave Vicki alone, but I need to retrieve my car from storage. We're going to need some cash, too. I don't want to leave a trail of credit-card slips from here back to Washington. It's only a matter of time until they trace you through the lawyer cousin. I don't want a trail leading from here back to Washington."

"William's been very careful about contacting me."

"Obviously, or we would already have had visitors. But they'll make the connection sooner or later. Vicki left his name as official contact, remember? They'll have tagged him by now and will eventually follow the trail from her to him to you."

Vicki shifted uneasily. It was something she hadn't thought about, and she found the knowledge of how vulnerable she was, even here, frightening. Apparently Harve hadn't thought of it, either. What would they have done if Caine hadn't shown up?

"You're assuming they have a lot of resources at their disposal," Harve said.

"Yes. We don't dare assume otherwise. Whoever was behind Henderson's death is intelligent, well connected and resourceful. Or we'd have him by now."

After a moment's contemplation, Harve nodded. "I can manage the cash," he said. "And I'll be here in the morning early enough for you to be at the storage garage when it opens. Are you going to check in with Baxter?"

Caine shook his head. "The fewer people who know where we're going, the less chance for leaks. Let's keep it to three."

"Four," Vicki protested. "I can't leave without saying goodbye to Aunt Abby."

"All right, four," Caine agreed. "You can get in touch with her right before we leave."

Although Harve left a short time later, promising again to be back early, it was hours before Vicki was able to climb into the loft. Caine had spent the evening going through the files and trial transcripts, stopping often to ask Vicki for additional information. She was sure he'd been hoping they'd solve their problem before they left for Washington. All of his careful questioning, however, had not produced the answers they needed.

Henderson, Caine claimed, had been the front man in the foundation, the one who actually manipulated the funds, but it was obvious now that he was taking instructions from someone else. That someone didn't have to be directly involved in the foundation, but there had to be a trail, a link between them, or whoever it was wouldn't see Vicki as a danger. It was that link they had to find.

Vicki knew sleep was impossible. She tried to put the problem of who was looking for her out of her mind. For the moment, she'd done all she could do. She was satisfied that if she did indeed have the answer, it was so nebulous a tie or hidden so deeply in her subconscious she had no chance of making the connection without new information. She had also given up the idea that the authorities would be able to find the culprit. She suspected Caine had, too. The law was apparently no closer to answers then they'd been when she'd first fled to Little Falls. At least now, returning to Washington, she and Caine had a chance of identifying who was after her.

The rest of the day's activities were even harder to dismiss. In the cave she'd finally admitted, at least to herself, that she was falling in love with Caine. She was willing to consider that part of the attraction might be simple proximity. There was also the chance that dependency—his determination to protect her and her belief that he would and could—was playing a part. But neither of those possibilities explained the flaring need between them, her certainty that without Caine, her life would be cold and incomplete.

Her intuitive knowledge of their attraction had been present from the beginning, which was why she'd sent him away the first time he'd come to the cabin. She'd been afraid then. She was still afraid, but now her fear was that, when this was all over, he'd leave her.

Caine had been up-front with her from the start. He avoided serious relationships. She understood his reluctance. The kind of magic she'd found in his arms, in his kisses, made a person vulnerable, and she suspected vulnerability was a feeling Caine had problems acknowledging. But the magic couldn't all be her own wishful thinking. It took two, whether he wanted to admit it or not.

Before the dogs found them this afternoon, he'd been as deeply involved as she, although he wasn't ready to admit it. Harve's news about Henderson's death gave Caine another reason to retreat behind his professional mask, to begin rebuilding the barriers that had fallen during their visit to the cave.

But what if he really didn't care for her? What if all he felt was sexual attraction? That thought was more frightening than the physical danger that threatened her.

No, she refused to believe it. He did care, or he couldn't have responded the way he had. Lust was one thing, love another. Although she'd never felt the latter before, she knew she'd given it the correct name. She remembered her great-aunt's advice on the subject: "Sharing your life with the right person makes everything brighter, more important, more meaningful." Now she knew what Aunt Abby meant.

There was a chance that Caine would never acknowledge his feelings, would never admit he loved her, either to himself or to her, but that was a chance she'd have to take. Time and circumstances were on her side. Caine was determined to find and expose the threat to her. He worried about her safety. That was a kind of caring.

And they had time. It was, for example, a long way from Little Falls to Washington. With that thought, she snuggled more deeply into the covers and closed her eyes. Tomorrow, as Scarlett O'Hara had announced, was another day.

CAINE CAME AWAKE with a start, an electronic beeping sounding in his ear. He muttered a string of curses that would have done the boys of his old neighborhood proud, then punched the button on the signal box to cut off the sound even though the tiny electronic lights continued to blink.

It could be a false alarm, he reasoned, perhaps a deer who'd wandered in front of the sensors. But he doubted it. The signal box showed a slow but steady progress past the pairs of motion detectors he'd placed along the path.

A glance at the cabin window as he hurriedly pulled on his clothes told him it was just past dawn. They were lucky. A few minutes earlier and there probably wouldn't have been enough light for the sensors to detect motion on the path.

The dogs, awake since he'd begun stirring, weren't sounding an alarm. That meant whoever was approaching the cabin was still too far away for them to hear.

Good. It gave them a little time.

Caine climbed to the loft and, placing a hand over Vicki's mouth to prevent her from crying out, shook her gently.

Even in the dim light, he saw the fear shining in her eyes as she awoke, then watched it fade as she recognized him.

"Someone's coming," he warned, speaking quietly. "Get dressed and hurry. We need to get out of here, and we don't have much time."

Her eyes grew wide, but he had to give her credit. She neither protested nor questioned. She was out of bed and reaching for her clothes by the time he started back down the stairs.

As Caine waited for Vicki to join him, he began closing the shutters over the windows. No point in making things easy for the intruders. He had no way of knowing if whoever was approaching the cabin was working on probabilities as he had when he first found the cabin, or if they had definite information. He'd assume the worst until he learned otherwise. At least the fire on the hearth had burned to mere coals. There would be no smoke coming from the chimney to verify anyone's presence.

He was both impressed and relieved when she joined him only moments later, dressed in jeans and a dark jacket, a stocking cap hiding her bright hair.

"What can I do?" she asked.

"If you order the dogs to find Harve, will they go to him? Without sounding an alarm?"

"I think so, but—"

"We're getting out of here. I don't want the dogs following and I don't want to leave them here. They might get hurt."

Vicki nodded and quietly opened the door, signaling the dogs to follow. "Find Harve," she ordered. "Go Tucker. Go Gourdy. Go home. Find Harve."

Gourdy made a whining sound, as if reluctant to leave, then as Tucker took off around the back of the cabin, he followed.

Caine handed her a pair of binoculars. "Let's go," he said securing the cabin door behind him. "I want us in the woods out of sight, but close enough to be able to see our visitor. Maybe we'll finally get some answers."

Caine left Vicki behind a small boulder on the hill overlooking the cabin with a warning not to move, and took his own position only a few feet away. If one looked closely enough, he supposed they would be visible, at least from the back of the cabin clearing, but as long as there was no movement to attract attention, they should be safe enough. Their hiding place had the added advantage of being only a few feet from a shallow gully that cut across the hill. And the boulder gave Vicki good protection in the case of gunfire.

Once he was able to make out who and how many were approaching the cabin, he and Vicki could use the gully to hide their movement back to the trail. From there it would be only a short distance to where he'd hidden the pickup.

He wondered briefly if he was making a mistake in not simply running. That would be safer. But then they'd be no closer to answers then they were now. Vicki had made a lot of sense last night. She was at risk until the culprit was identified. He suspected whoever was approaching the cabin was hired help, but couldn't ignore the possibility that it might be the big man himself. Everything would be easier if they knew who the enemy was.

As the sun peeked over the eastern ridge, he glanced at Vicki and saw her looking back at him, apparently calm. She was some woman, beautiful, intelligent, courageous—

A faint rustle jerked his attention back to the clearing. He watched tensely as two men stepped furtively from the shadows. He didn't recognize either of them, but their drawn guns guaranteed they meant business.

He glanced over at Vicki and motioned for her to use the binoculars. When the men moved onto the porch and out of sight, he joined her by the boulder.

"Did you recognize them?" he asked softly, knowing how easily sound carried in the quiet of early morning.

Vicki shook her head. "No, I've never seen either of them before, but I'll know them if I see them again."

"Good girl. Okay, let's go."

Caine slipped into the gully, then turned to assist Vicki. "If they break into the cabin, and I'm sure they will, they're going to realize someone's been using it. They'll be searching the woods in a few minutes. We're heading down the gully, then we'll cut across the trail to Harve's barn where I've hidden the truck. With a little luck, they may think we're still hiding in the woods. Move as quickly and as quietly as you can."

Vicki nodded. "It's our turn for some luck," she said. "Let's go."

It took them less than two minutes to reach the end of the gully. Ordering Vicki to wait, Caine cautiously climbed to the trail, checking to make sure their early-morning visitors were still out of sight before motioning for Vicki to join him.

"We've got to cross about fifteen yards of fairly open ground before we hit the dense woods," he told her. "Stay low and use the brush as cover. Once you make it to the big trees, wait for me. I'll cover you from here, then be right behind you."

She looked as if she wanted to protest, but apparently thought better of it. "Be careful," she whispered. She took off in a zigzagging path that had him wondering if she'd been a commando in some earlier life.

Caine breathed a sigh of relief when he saw her disappear into the edge of the woods.

"Where'd you learn to run like that?" he asked when he joined her moments later.

"Summer nights playing King of the Hill with the cousins."

Caine grinned. "I'll bet you were the champion."

"The only one who could beat me was Harve." She grinned. "And then only occasionally."

"Well, the hard part's over, but we still have a ways to go. You take point and I'll be rear guard. Let's get moving."

As Vicki started down the trail, Caine saw the two men move into sight. Damn, he'd hoped for a few minutes' head start. Although he didn't think he could be seen, he stepped behind a tree for additional protection. He watched until Vicki was out of sight, debating whether to follow or wait here. He was almost sure he could take them out.

But as soon as Vicki realized he wasn't behind her, she'd probably come back looking for him. Probably? Who was he trying to kid? She could walk right into the showdown.

He saw the men enter the woods on the main trail, the one that led to the fish pond, and knew they'd soon realize it was the wrong direction. With the trail so damp from yesterday's storm, there'd be footprints if he and Vicki had gone that way, which meant the men would spread out to search the woods. He started after Vicki. Protecting her was his first priority.

As Caine rounded a bend in the path, the last thing he expected to see was Vicki standing apparently frozen in the middle of the trail. "What the—"

Vicki's frantic hand signal behind her back cut his expletive off. He, too, froze in place, unable to see the problem but having no difficulty reading her body language.

In excruciatingly slow motion, Vicki took a step backward, then another and another until she was close enough for him to peer over her shoulder. Under other circumstances, he might have been inclined to laugh at the slightly larger, slightly fatter version of Sweetpea now holding Vicki hostage. But today, with two hood-lums behind them, the black-and-white creature bar-ring their way was no laughing matter.

The skunk was posed in a familiar-looking stance, tail first and at full mast, its paws dancing in the dirt—only unlike Sweetpea, this skunk's indignation was more than bluff.

"Move back—slowly," Vicki hissed.

Caine obeyed, withdrawing two careful steps. When Vicki mimicked his retreat, the skunk slowed its frantic dance, but the tail stayed up.

"Another couple of steps ought to do it," Vicki whispered.

Caine wasn't about to argue and again moved slowly backward until he was almost at the bend of the trail. He heard Vicki exhale with relief when the creature fi-nally dropped its tail.

"I thought you said a skunk would rather run than confront," he said, once the immediate danger was past.

"Not when she's protecting her young," Vicki said. "She's probably got them hidden by the side of the trail. We're going to have to go around."

"We don't have time," he said catching the sounds of pursuit behind him. "Quick. Off the trail. Hide be-hind anything that will give you cover and freeze."

The frantic seconds that followed seemed all too short, but somehow both he and Vicki were prone on the ground behind a fallen log a dozen yards off the trail when the first of their pursuers came into view.

Caine motioned for Vicki to keep her head down as he peered around the edge of the log.

City hoods, he decided, as the two men trotted, huffing and puffing along the trail. One was about five-nine, dressed in jeans, baseball jacket, running shoes and a black T-shirt that bulged over his belt. The other, maybe an inch taller and similarly dressed, was thinner, but apparently in no better shape for a run through the countryside. Although neither wore ski masks today, Caine would bet they were the same two caught by the surveillance cameras during the break-in at Vicki's apartment.

The two men spotted the skunk at the same moment. Faced with this new threat, mama skunk again went into her defense stance—tail raised, feet beating a tattoo in the dirt.

"Holy Jeez..." the heavyset one sputtered, grabbing for the automatic now tucked in his belt.

"Don't be dumb," the other man said, grabbing his arm. "We can't risk gunfire. Someone might hear. Besides, it can't hurt us."

"I don't know," the first man protested, retreating a step backward. "It looks pretty mad."

"It's the dame's pet. It's been fixed, I tell you. Go on, grab it."

The second man gave the fat one a shove forward, propelling him straight into the path of the skunk's first shot. The man fell to the ground, writhing in pain as his hands clawed at his eyes. The other hoodlum was already bent double and gagging when the skunk's second shot performed the coup de grace.

Although far enough off to be protected from actual contact with the acrid spray, Caine and Vicki were close enough to suffer the residual effects of the skunk's attack. Both staggered to their feet, gagging. "Shallow breaths through your mouth," Vicki managed to gasp. "Let's get out of here before she has time to rearm."

Fighting nausea, Caine managed to nod his agreement. "Go on. I'll follow in a minute."

"What are you going to do?"

"Get their guns and make sure they stay where they are for a while. Go on. There's no danger now. Both of them are too sick to lift their heads."

"Don't get the spray on your hands," Vicki warned.

Caine wasn't sure how he survived the next few minutes, but between bouts of dry heaves, he managed to disarm the two men, bind their arms behind them with their own belts and prop them up by the side of the trail so they wouldn't choke to death on their own vomit. By the time he was ready to follow Vicki, he had his own gagging almost under control, although he didn't know if it was because the odor was dissipating or because his olfactory senses were becoming numb.

"Numb," Vicki told him, inspecting his hands. "It appears you got some spray on you. We're going to have to go to Harve's for help. And I imagine we're not going to be welcomed with open arms."

"As I remember, you were supposed to protect me from the wildlife," he accused weakly, surprising himself at how light-spirited he felt now that the immediate danger was over.

"It's a matter of degree," Vicki protested. "You're in better shape than those two back on the trail. A little tomato juice on your hands and you'll be good as new. I'll drive. Stuff your hands in your pockets and don't touch anything or we'll never get the aroma out of the truck."

Caine sighed. He wasn't sure what tomato juice had to do with the situation, but he suspected he would soon find out. With Vicki's assistance, he managed to climb into the pickup cab without touching anything.

It was a bit of luck that their two pursuers had mistaken that skunk for Sweetpea, he thought, although he wished he and Vicki had been a little farther away when the animal had attacked.

The implications of that piece of information suddenly hit him. How the hell had they known Vicki had a pet skunk?

Caine was afraid he knew the answer to his question—and he didn't like it. Not one little bit.

CHAPTER ELEVEN

EVEN AFTER FORTY-FIVE minutes of soaking in a lavender scented bubble bath, compliments of Harve's current cook, Vicki could still smell and taste *le parfum de skunk*. Although she knew the lingering stench was more imagination and memory than fact, she also knew it would be hours, maybe even days, before her sense of smell returned to normal.

But she was the lucky one. Caine hadn't fared as well. In spite of her warning, he'd been unable to avoid getting spray on himself when he'd secured the two men. The fluid the skunk releases contains a heavy oil that clings to its target and is easily transferred by touch. Although Caine had escaped skin burns when he'd tied up the two men, there'd been no way for him to escape some contamination.

Alerted by the dogs that something was wrong, Harve had met them en route to the farm and immediately taken charge of the situation. He'd bundled Vicki off to the big house and sent Caine to clean up in a washroom in one of the barns. He'd also contacted authorities to take the hapless thugs into custody.

Vicki could imagine the ensuing debate between county law enforcement and medical personnel about which service would take charge of the two. Winner of the debate was undoubtedly the one who lost temporary custody. Jail or hospital, it was certain that wherever the men were being held, they'd be extremely unpopular.

Although the decision had already been made for Vicki and Caine to leave Little Falls, the confirmation that her hiding place had been discovered removed any lingering doubts that the move was necessary. Even with the two attackers out of commission, it was only a matter of time before they reported to someone that she was here.

Vicki wondered if this morning's activities would give Caine second thoughts about taking her to Washington. If so, she'd simply have to convince him all over again. If anything, it seemed even more urgent then ever that they discover who was behind this. She wanted her life back!

She stepped out of the tub and was wrapping herself in a large bath towel when she heard someone enter the bedroom suite.

Carefully she opened the bathroom door a crack and was surprised to see her great-aunt's smiling face.

"Wondered if you were trying to turn into a prune," Aunt Abby said. "Here. Harvey brought you a change of clothes from the cabin."

"What are you doing here?" Vicki asked, accepting the bundle gratefully.

"Harvey sent out an SOS for some of my canned tomatoes for your Mr. Alexander." She laughed. "Almost didn't convince him to use them. I thought every one knew that the only way to neutralize the smell of skunk was with tomatoes or tomato juice. Fresh would have been better of course, but it's the wrong time of year."

"Caine's a city boy," Vicki explained. "I suspect he'd never even seen a live skunk until he met Sweetpea."

"Well, it's an experience he isn't likely to forget," Aunt Abby said with a grin. "Sweetpea's fine, by the way. Harvey found her hiding under the couch at the cabin. She's in the kitchen now harassing the dogs. I'm supposed to tell you to come down for breakfast soon as you're dressed."

A short time later Vicki entered the farmhouse's big country kitchen two steps behind her great-aunt, her eyes unerringly seeking Caine. He was hard to miss at any time, Vicki knew, but now he was dressed in a bright red jogging suit, its "Go Hog. Soo... ie" slogan and the depiction of the University of Arkansas's snarling razorback mascot clearly proclaiming Harve's ownership. Seated on the far side of the table, Caine had tipped his chair against the wall and was apparently completely relaxed. His dark hair, still wet from a shower, was brushed casually back from his forehead except for one lock that fell defiantly forward over his left eyebrow.

As Vicki gave the air a delicate sniff, Caine's dark gaze caught hers, humor bubbling in his eyes.

"I'm presentable," he told her. "Been sluiced, scrubbed, rubbed down with burned cork, smeared with lard and washed with tomato juice."

"Those are all tried-and-true folklore remedies for neutralizing skunk spray," Vicki told him with a grin. "Don't complain. They worked, didn't they?"

"They did, but I tell you, if I'd had any idea of what I was doing that first night in the cabin, I would never have stepped between you and Sweetpea. There are some things no one, not even a bodyguard, can be expected to do."

Sweetpea looked up from her saucer of milk, chittered briefly, then returned her attention to her breakfast.

"I thought it was quite heroic of you," she said.

"'Where ignorance is bliss,/'Tis folly to be wise'— Thomas Gray," Harve intoned in a dramatically solemn voice. "Anyway, 'All's well that ends well.'"

"Even I know that last's a quote from Shakespeare," Caine said, "but somehow I doubt Willie-boy ever tangled with a skunk."

"Pancakes? Scrambled eggs? Or both?" Harve asked as Vicki seated herself at the table. "I'm cooking."

"Pancakes," said Vicki. "Where's Mrs. Martin?"

"I gave her the day off after I borrowed her bubble bath. It seemed to me that the fewer witnesses around here, the better off we'd be," Harve said, turning back to the stove. "Since I filed the police report on our two skunk victims, there's no longer any question that I've been hiding you, but it was that or let those two off on a simple trespassing charge. Now we've got them for breaking and entering, threat to commit bodily harm, maybe even attempted murder. We're going to have to get you out of here and on your way to Washington quickly.''

"We've got a new problem with that," Caine said, leaning forward to rest his elbows on the table.

Vicki lifted her chin, telling herself she shouldn't be surprised he'd changed his mind. Hadn't she been expecting it? "I don't see why," she said. "We'd already decided it was only a matter of time until they traced me to Little Falls. So what if they caught up with me a little sooner than we'd expected? It docsn't change the reason for going back to Washington."

"The reasons for going haven't changed," Caine agreed, "but now the question is how to get there and what we're going to do once we arrive."

Vicki didn't understand, but was relieved that apparently Caine hadn't changed his mind about taking her to Washington. He was worried about something else, although she couldn't imagine what.

"Our two uninvited visitors are out of commission for at least twenty-four hours," Harve told Caine. "They're too sick to worry about anything else right now. Once they start thinking again, you two will be long gone. I don't see a problem."

"Tell him why the skunk attacked," Caine instructed Vicki quietly.

She shifted uneasily. "Because they thought she was Sweetpea and couldn't hurt them," she said.

"And how did they know you had a pet skunk?" Caine said. "You didn't have her with you in Washington, did you?"

Vicki shook her head. "No. Sweetpea belongs to Harve. He thought she'd be company for me at the cabin."

"Hellfire and damnation!" Harve exploded. "There's no way they could have known about Sweetpea unless—"

"Exactly," Caine said. "We've got a leak. If they know about Sweetpea, then we have to assume they also know about me."

"But how?" Vicki turned to Caine. "I know you were afraid someone in town would be careless, but even if they guessed I was here, they wouldn't know about Sweetpea."

"I'm not blaming anyone in Little Falls," Caine said in a voice tinged with resignation. "This one's all mine. I told Danny about my face-off with Sweetpea the first time I checked in with him."

"That means the marshal's office has a stoolie," Harve said.

"It looks that way," Caine agreed, "although we don't know if it's Danny's office or Fayetteville. Danny must have at least suspected the possibility. That's why he cut me loose. But neither of us figured I'd been identified, or he'd have warned me."

Vicki drew a deep breath. "I'm afraid I still don't—"

"It means we don't go to Washington in my car. It also means we can't stay at my place once we get there. They'll be watching. I was your ace in the hole. No one should have known anything about me—that I was with you. Now we no longer have that advantage. If the leak is in the federal marshal's office, it means we're completely on our own."

"Not exactly," interrupted Harve. "Vicki has her family. You do, too. I can come up with another vehicle, but a place to stay that isn't traceable is going to be harder."

"Vicki has a another choice," Caine said. "I can take her into the marshal's office—either to Danny or to Baxter in Fayetteville. Even if there is a leak, it's undoubtedly only one person feeding information to the other side. She'd have more than one guard. With the force of the marshal's office behind her, she should be safe enough."

"That's the stupidest suggestion I've ever heard!" Harve declared.

Vicki ignored him. She was looking at Caine. "Why would you suggest such a thing? Is that what you want me to do? Do you want out?" she asked quietly.

Caine shook his head. "I'm in as long as you want me. But you have to consider your alternatives. I'm only one man. As far as that goes, I could be the one who leaked your whereabouts. Pretending to protect you makes a good cover."

What was Caine up to now? She knew he'd never betray her. Maybe that was the problem, though. Maybe he needed to know that she trusted him completely.

"I don't know what you're trying to pull, Caine Alexander, but if you want to make me believe you'd betray me, I can tell you now it's not going to work. If, on the other hand, you want to turn me over to official protection and go back to doing what you usually do, all you have to do is say so. Henderson's dead. This is getting dangerous. I can't expect you to stay when it's really not your job."

"I finish what I start," he told her, "if you're sure that's what you want."

"I trust you with my life, Caine. I'd rather have you than any three other men. Is that what you want to hear?"

"I want you to be sure." There was a peculiar look in his eyes.

"I'm sure," she said firmly.

"Fine," Harve said, looking from one to the other. "Now that you've got that settled, we're back to where we started. Ways and means of getting you to Washington and keeping you safely hidden after you get there. Anybody got any ideas?"

"What about a nice, anonymous camper van?" Aunt Abby said, speaking up for the first time. She looked like a magician who'd just pulled a rabbit out of a hat.

"Your cousin Henry's youngest wants to follow the summer rodeo circuit, and Henry figured the boy would have a better chance of making expenses if he didn't have to worry about lodging costs. It's even got one of those racks on the back so he can carry his Harley around with him."

"You're a genius, Grandmother!" Harve exclaimed. "Henry's a Smith. Nice anonymous name, that. Transportation and lodging all in one. And the Harley will give you mobility in the city—that is, if you can ride a bike?"

Caine nodded. "I can," he affirmed. "But will Cousin Henry be willing to loan it out no questions asked?"

"Of course he will," Aunt Abby said. "Henry's family. All Harvey has to do is ask."

Harve nodded. "I've seen it," he added. "Top of the line. Even has a CB built in."

"This just might work," Caine said thoughtfully.

"Of course it'll work," Aunt Abby said. "Why wouldn't it? I only wish I knew how we could do more to help. It sounds as if you're going to be on your own."

"Don't worry, Grandmother." Harve tried to reassure her. "Vicki and Caine will do just fine. And we'll be here if they need us. Remember Milton. 'They also serve who only stand and wait.'"

Aunt Abby rolled her eyes. "Don't you start again. Come on, Victoria. Now that I've solved the major problem, we'll leave the men to work out the details. You need to pack your toothbrush."

Vicki would rather have stayed in the kitchen, but knew better than to ignore her great-aunt's summons. Aunt Abby was wearing her Grand Inquisitor face. She wanted a private discussion, and Vicki strongly suspected it wasn't about her toothbrush.

"Vicki, are you sure you're comfortable with this?" Aunt Abby asked as soon as they entered the bedroom.

"Comfortable?"

"Traveling with Mr. Alexander to Washington."

"Of course I am," Vicki told her. "It was my idea in the first place. And if you mean do I trust him, well, I've already answered that."

"That's not what I meant, young lady, and you know it. I trust him to take care of you, but I saw the way he was watching you. The man's in love with you."

Vicki felt her pulse accelerate. She ducked her head, not wanting Aunt Abby to see the blush she could feel in her cheeks. Caine in love with her? Wishful thinking. "Caine's not in love with me, Aunt Abby. I think he likes me a little—some of the time, anyway. But he sees himself as my protector. I'm a responsibility, nothing more."

"Maybe these old eyes see better than yours, child. Believe me or not, I say the man's in love with you. He may not know it yet, but in time he'll realize it. What I want to know is how you feel about him. There's not much room for privacy in a camper. And it's a long way to Washington. Things could get awkward, especially if he realizes his feelings and more especially if you don't feel the same way."

Vicki swallowed. "I . . . I like Caine," she finally admitted.

"You're sure?" There was a twinkle in her aunt's eyes that contradicted the solemn look on her face.

"Well, of course I like him. I mean..." Vicki sighed. "It's all so confusing, Aunt Abby. Sometimes I think... and then... he's so determined not to treat me as anything but a job. He's a hard man to get to know."

"Hmph. The best ones always are. The man's smitten, I tell you. But honorable, too. If you want him, you may have to have to reel him in."

This time Vicki laughed. She couldn't help it. "Reel him in, Aunt Abby?"

"You know what I mean. A lot of things have changed since my generation was your age, but not everything. Men, most of them, anyway, still haven't a clue when it comes to picking out a soul mate. It's always the woman who recognizes it first. And does something about it, too. You want him, girl, you go after him. And that's all I've got to say."

"I love you, Aunt Abby."

"And I love you, too, child. Better go pack your toothbrush. If I know Harve, he'll be yelling for you any minute."

CAINE WAS FEELING GOOD. No, he was feeling better than good—more like euphoric. He loved it when a plan came together, and this one certainly had.

It was, he'd admitted a couple of hundred miles ago, a perfect getaway, as expertly conceived and executed as a strategy that had taken weeks of planning, instead of only a few hours. He was in awe. He'd met few men as creative, as organized, as meticulous as Harve Tremayne. That the man had the resources to put it together, had efficiently bridged the stages of planning and execution; but then, if the man hadn't been so smart, he wouldn't have been so successful.

Within half an hour of discussing their plans around the kitchen table, a panel truck pulling a horse trailer—both clearly marked Tremayne Farms—had headed west out of Little Falls toward Tulsa. That the truck and trailer would arrive two days early to pick up the mare Harve was transporting back to Little Falls would cause little or no comment, Harve had assured Caine. The important thing was that the closed panel truck and trailer made a perfect hiding place for two travelers who didn't want to be seen.

Red herring number one.

Then Harve, piloting his own plane, had taken off for Little Rock after filing a flight plan that indicated he'd be carrying two passengers. No biggie, he told Caine, if he forgot to mention that his two passengers had decided at the last minute not to come. The FAA would be concerned only if he didn't complete the flight successfully. After a quick turnaround, he'd be back in Little Falls before nightfall.

Red herring number two.

At about the same time Aunt Abby had announced to family members that she was going to visit Cousin Bea in Springfield for a few days of shopping. Only someone following very closely would have noticed the short diversion she made from Highway 65 to rendezvous with Cousin Henry and his camper. After that, Aunt Abby would be very visible on her Springfield shopping spree for the next few days.

Red herring number three.

Cousin Henry's out-of-state residency was an added bonus. The camper Caine was now driving east carried Missouri license plates—no easy way to make a connection between it and Little Falls, Arkansas.

Caine couldn't restrain a smug smile. Vicki's pursuers would be chasing themselves in circles for days, and that suited him just fine.

He glanced at Vicki, saw her apparently sleeping comfortably in the passenger seat. Good. She needed the rest. He suspected she had no idea of how dicey things might become in the near future.

Caine flexed his shoulders, trying to relax his tired muscles. A sign announcing a rest stop in five miles caught his eye, and he made the decision to stop for a few minutes. If Vicki awoke, maybe she'd like to take the wheel for a while. He'd already driven nearly three hundred miles, but before stopping for the night, he'd be happier with still more distance between them and the point where they'd picked up the van.

Tomorrow, once they were out of Missouri, they'd travel at a more leisurely pace. Let their pursuers stew a little. The longer he and Vicki stayed out of sight, the more confused the opposition would become.

He returned his attention to the highway, but his thoughts strayed inevitably back to the woman at his side. He'd never forget the expression on her face, the look of complete faith in her eyes, when she'd told him she trusted him. It had shaken him to the bone. In that moment he'd known he'd never be free of Vicki Winslow, even after he was no longer a part of her life.

He'd never meant to become so involved, never meant to allow himself to care so much. But there it was. Harve would probably have an apt quote for the occasion, something along the lines of the road to hell being paved with good intentions. Oh, Lord, the man had him doing it now, spouting quotations like some damned storefront philosopher. The trouble was he not only liked Vicki, he liked her whole family—the country-bumpkin, near-genius millionaire cousin, the bossy, down-to-earth grand-dame great-aunt, even the once-and twice-removed cousins he'd never met. God help him, he actually liked those two mangy hounds and that chittering skunk.

Interacting with so large a family was a completely new experience. Not that such a situation would ever work for him. He'd never been much good at relationships, anyway. He operated best alone.

And that, he told himself, was something he'd better keep in mind.

CHAPTER TWELVE

WHILE PRETENDING to study road maps, Vicki sneaked a look at Caine. He drove with the precision and expertise of one used to traveling long distances. Even after two days on the road, he appeared rested and relaxed.

She suspected it was a pose he'd adopted to hide behind just as he hid the expression in his eyes behind mirrored sunglasses.

Two days. No, it had been two and a half days since they'd said goodbye to Aunt Abby and headed cross-country. Only the two of them living, eating, sleeping in the camper van.

Not that time or lack of privacy had mattered, Vicki thought. Aunt Abby had been wrong in anticipating awkwardness between them. Caine was the perfect traveling companion, courteous but distant, as if they'd only just met, as if they had no history, shared no knowledge of each other before the trip began. Once again Vicki wondered at his ability to turn off his emotions.

She didn't believe his pose, at least not completely, although he certainly put on a good act. He was trying to convince himself, as well as her, she realized. What had Aunt Abby called him—"a man who fights himself"? Or was that wishful thinking? Still, the idea that he wasn't as completely indifferent as he appeared encouraged her.

She wished she knew his secret. If she appeared as disinterested in Caine, would it affect him the same way his manner affected her? Make him mad enough to spit nails?

She kept watching for his facade to slip. But since they'd left Little Falls, he'd managed to stay safely behind his mask of indifference.

It was high time the status quo changed, Vicki decided. Each day, every passing hour, brought them closer to their destination. And some intuitive knowledge told her if she hadn't made him acknowledge, at least to himself, that she was something more than just a job, events would take the future out of their hands and it would be too late. Besides, she wasn't sure how much longer she could continue like this. The closer they came to Washington, the more agitated she became.

She sighed, laid aside the road maps and fidgeted in her seat, trying to deal with her ambiguous feelings of anticipation and anxiety.

"Tired?" Caine asked.

"More restless than anything," she told him. "How much farther are we going today?"

"We'll stop in about an hour. We should be in Washington the day after tomorrow. I'm trying to plan our arrival for early afternoon, time to get settled somewhere inconspicuous and make our plans."

They'd be in Washington the day after tomorrow? So soon? Vicki drew a deep breath. Sometimes it seemed that her future was rushing toward her; at other times it crawled on snail's feet.

"I'm also going to contact a friend of mine tonight to do a little advance scouting," Caine said before she could comment. "I want dossiers on the foundation's board of directors. It might give us a place to start." He glanced at toward her, his sunglasses effectively hiding any expression.

"They're mostly figureheads, selected because of their healthy contributions to the cause and the prestige of their names," Vicki said. "They don't have much to do with the foundation. It's the staff who actually runs the foundation. Roy always—" She stopped abruptly.

"Roy? You mean Henderson?"

Vicki nodded.

"Henderson always what?"

"He always said the board would approve any plans he presented."

"And did they?" Caine asked softly.

Vicki nodded again. "Most of the time, but there's nothing wrong with that," she said defensively. "Proposals put before the board were well planned and within the polices and intent of the foundation charter."

"What about that senator, the one who called your aunt?

"Senator Van Brock? He's the current chairman of the board."

"Did he always go along with Henderson's ideas?"

Vicki frowned. What was Caine getting at? "As far as I know," she said stiffly. "He always approved of the ideas I presented to him, too."

"So the great and powerful Senator Van Brock is just a rubber stamp?" Caine said, the sarcasm evident in his voice.

"I didn't say that," Vicki protested. "Senator Van Brock always studied the projects carefully. But you have to understand, plans are never taken to the board unless they're ready for final approval."

"And who develops the plans before they go to the board?"

"The entire staff. I'm in charge of fund-raising, and Mark Gleason is assistant director of aid projects. There're also several organizers and facilitators working for the foundation, as well as support staff—secretaries, accountants and the like. Mostly we all work together when we start on a project. We're a small foundation, and by combining duties and support personnel we keep administrative expenses low."

"Danny said you had most of the evidence in hand when you went to the police about the embezzlement," Caine said. "How closely did you check out your fellow assistant director?"

"You mean Mark Gleason?"

Caine nodded. "It seems to me he would be in the perfect position to play with the funds. Didn't you say he was in charge of planning the aid projects?"

"Yes, but don't forget, it wasn't Mark's funds that were being stolen. It was mine."

Caine whistled softly. "That's right. It was the money from your fund-raising projects that was being pilfered, wasn't it? Someone may have been trying to set you up for the fall. No wonder you wanted to nail the bastard."

The idea that anyone might believe that she was the thief had never occurred to Vicki until after she'd spoken to the police. "I didn't think about it at the time. All I knew was that someone was stealing from the foundation. I wanted it to stop. Then I found out I was the cops' number-one suspect," she said bitterly. "And it made absolutely no more sense to me then than it does now. Why would I blow the whistle if I was the guilty one?"

Vicki stopped to draw a few breaths. She knew she'd raised her voice, but she couldn't help it. The memory of her original interrogation still made her furious. "Now it seems as if that thought occurred to you, too. Tell me, Caine, is it some idiosyncrasy of the male mind to always suspect the woman?"

"Pax, Vicki. I didn't say I suspected you. And no, it is not a quirk of the male mind to always suspect the woman. It is, however, a trait of detectives to be suspicious. The first details a detective considers are ability, opportunity and motive. You obviously had the ability and the opportunity. As for motive, well, greed is a powerful one. You will also recall that I said pretending to be on the side of the righteous makes a good cover."

"I find your reasoning completely illogical," Vicki said, "exactly the same as when you suggested you might be only pretending to protect me."

"I remember," Caine said softly. He cleared his throat. "We've strayed away from the main question. I was asking if you'd checked out your fellow assistant director. Even if it was the funds from your projects and not his that were disappearing, he, like you, would have had the ability and the opportunity. He could also have been greedy."

"When I discovered the missing funds, he was my first suspect," she said reluctantly, "but I couldn't find a thing wrong with Mark's records. I doubt if the man ever took a paper clip for his own use. Although the rest of the staff weren't quite as rigid as Mark, they were all clean, too."

"You saved Henderson until last?"

"Yes. No. I mean, I did some preliminary scanning of the records on him at the time I ran the accounts for the whole staff, but I didn't see anything wrong," Vicki said. "Afterward, I went through them more carefully and..."

"And?" Caine prompted.

"I found a dummy account." Vicki turned her head away to look out the side window.

"You didn't want it to be Henderson, did you?"

Vicki didn't answer.

"Were you in love with him, Vicki?"

Oh, Lord, why did he need to ask that? She wasn't sure she knew how to answer.

"Vicki?" This time he spoke more softly.

She leaned her head against the window. Had she been in love with Roy? Was that why she was so bitter, why she'd felt so betrayed when she realized he was the one behind the theft? With a sudden clarity, she knew the answer.

"No," she told Caine, surprising even herself with how definite she sounded. "I wasn't in love with Roy. I think that, when I first started working with him, I was intrigued. Maybe it was even a slight case of hero worship. He was so charismatic, you see, a sincere, dedicated, concerned and caring director. The foundation's work was a cause he sincerely believed in.

"Except it was all an act. He could have treated the directorship of the foundation as a purely professional position. But he didn't. He pretended to really care. And I think that was the biggest betrayal of all."

"You saw what he intended you to see. From what I've heard, he was a master at it. There's no shame in that."

"I was duped."

"So were a thousand other people. Are you supposed to be smarter than all of them? Don't blame yourself for seeing what everyone else saw, for seeing what he intended you to see. If anything, you should take comfort in the fact that in the face of everything and everybody telling you how great he was, you were the one to see behind the mask.''

"Ben said almost the same thing, but it's still hard to accept."

"Ben? Who's he? One of the support staff?"

"Ben Sinclair. He's an attorney who does volunteer work for the foundation. He's not really involved very much, because several of the board members are attorneys, too, and they do most of our legal work. But occasionally legal papers need to be filed, and Ben's law firm acts as a neutral third party. It's convenient, because his law offices are in the same building as the foundation."

"Lawyers are suspicious people. Apparently Henderson fooled him just as he fooled everyone else. Like I said, you've got nothing to be ashamed of."

"You'd have seen through Henderson."

Caine grimaced. "Maybe, but then, I'd never have believed in the foundation in the first place, or you, either. And that would've been wrong."

"You, forever the pessimist, and me, the eternal optimist—we're quite a pair, aren't we?"

"Yeah, but maybe between the two of us we can see the cup as it really is—exactly half-full."

Vicki straightened. "I still don't understand why you want to know about the board of directors. As I said, they really have little to do with the foundations's day-to-day work."

"We're still looking for the connection between Henderson and whoever is calling the shots now. From the files Danny sent and what you said, it seems clear that our man isn't one of the staff. That leaves the next step up—the board of directors."

"I can't believe that Senator Van Brock or any of the others would be a party to—"

"That's where we differ, Vicki. Unlike you, I never trust a politician."

CAINE SECURED his purchases in the saddlebags of the Harley, settled himself onto the elongated seat of the bike, adjusted his goggles and glanced at the sun still hanging above the western horizon. His errands had taken no longer than planned. He and Vicki should have time for a short spin before dark—assuming, of course, he could get her to speak to him.

She'd been furious when he'd insisted she stay at the campground while he ran his errands in town, but Cousin Henry had provided only one helmet, and Caine wasn't going to risk either her safety or the possibility of being stopped for a equipment violation.

It wasn't that he didn't sympathize with her wanting to get away from the camper for a while. A second helmet and a good leather jacket, both her size, were his first purchases when he'd arrived in town. He was sure that by now, with time to calm down, Vicki would've accepted the reasons for his refusal and forgiven him. Or almost sure, anyway. As he'd observed early in their acquaintance, she was an intelligent woman.

She was also very independent and very determined, he remembered with sudden misgiving.

She wouldn't dare.

Oh, yes, she would.

Goaded by a fear he didn't want to identify, Caine forced himself to remain under the speed limit as he drove to the campground.

He found the camper empty. Dammit, he should have expected this, should have learned by now. Vicki Winslow wasn't a woman who easily accepted orders—not even when the orders were for her own good.

Where was she? Where could she have gone? And how?

What if she hadn't simply taken off on her own? What if someone had grabbed her?

Don't be stupid, he told himself. *She's gone off by herself.* It was just like her. Besides, there was nothing in the van, no indications of a struggle, to suggest she hadn't left willingly.

Stupid little— No, he was the stupid one. He should have made her promise. She wouldn't break a promise. She'd done exactly what he should've known she'd do the minute his back was turned. Taken off in a snit. Well, she couldn't have gone far, but when he found her, he was going to... He wasn't sure what he was going to do, but he'd think of something.

Still muttering curses, Caine reached for the van door, only to find the lever pulled from his hand.

"Caine! I didn't know you were back. I didn't see the bike."

Caine felt his jaw move, but no sound came from his mouth as he stared at Vicki. She was dressed in snug-fitting jeans and a white T-shirt, and her hair was lying in wet burnished-copper ringlets against her head. A damp towel was draped casually over her shoulder, and she carried a small plastic bag in one hand. His hot gaze recorded the image, seeing but not comprehending.

Anger, anxiety, relief roiled in his belly. He reached for her arm, all but dragging her into the van. "Where the hell have you been?" he demanded, making no attempt to disguise his anger.

"I took a shower at the bathhouse—a long shower— one that didn't require water rationing. Where'd you think I was?"

Caine unclenched his fingers from around her arm and shoved his trembling hands into his pockets, fighting to regain his control. His breath came in short desperate gasps; his knees felt like rubber. His head was swimming, an adrenaline overload caused by anger, relief and several unnamed emotions. She hadn't taken off, after all. She'd simply gone to have a shower.

"What the hell was I supposed to think when I got back here to find the van empty?" he demanded, his voice still loud enough to be identified as a yell. "I told you to stay put."

She raised her chin defiantly, her green eyes sparkling. "I assumed you meant I was supposed to stay in the campground, as if I could do anything else. Honestly, Caine, I'm not stupid enough to go wandering down the road."

He moved back, hoping the space would serve as a damper on his emotions. He couldn't decide whether to shake her or kiss her. "I didn't think you were," he admitted, his voice still rough, "but when I couldn't find you..."

"I didn't expect you back so quickly. I only went to the bathhouse. Don't you trust me to have any sense?"

Oh, Lord, now she was getting mad. Pound for pound, TNT was less explosive than redheaded Vicki Winslow when her temper was hot.

"Okay, I admit it," he told her in what he hoped was a conciliatory voice. "I overreacted, but don't you dare do that to me again."

"Caine, we're going to have problems when we get to Washington if you don't trust me to do what I say I will."

Yeah, he thought. He was going to have problems. He'd been knee-deep in alligators since the first time he'd seen her. So what else was new? "Look, I've already admitted I overreacted. I'm the guy who always thinks the worst, remember?" he added in what he hoped was a lighter tone. "Next time, leave a note, okay?"

He heard her sigh as she moved toward the back of the van. "All right, I promise to leave a note. I didn't deliberately set out to upset you. I really didn't expect you back so quickly. Did you get all your business finished?"

"All done. Wait here a minute. I bought something for you, too. It's in the saddlebags." He ducked out the van door, thankful for a moment alone. *Way to go, buddy,* he thought in disgust. He couldn't remember another time when he'd lost it so completely, but when he'd found the van empty... What the hell was happening to him? he asked himself as he pulled the bundle from the back of the bike.

"Here," he said, pushing the package into her hands.

The look of delight on Vicki's face sent Caine's heart into double time.

She set aside the helmet to pull the leather jacket from the package. "For me? Oh, Caine, thank you."

"Telling you that you couldn't ride the bike was not pure obstinacy on my part," Caine said. "We didn't have the right equipment."

"I know, and I'm sorry about what I said. I was just so... so frustrated."

"Cabin fever. I know the feeling," he told her. "Here, let's see if I got the right size helmet." He placed the helmet on her head, removed it to make a small adjustment to the interior headband, then replaced it, fastening the chin strap securely. "About perfect, I'd say."

"It feels great. Can I take the bike for a spin now?"

Caine groaned. "Don't tell me. You ride a Harley, too."

"I've ridden trail bikes. Surely it isn't so different."

"Not a lot," he admitted, "but it's more powerful. That takes getting used to, and it'll be dark soon. I was going to suggest I take you for a ride. We can check you out on the bike in the morning if you like. It's probably a good idea, in case you need to use it later."

"Okay," Vicki said, pulling on the leather jacket. "Let's go."

"What? No argument?"

"Of course not. What you said makes sense. I'm not an argumentative person, Caine. I only disagree with you when you're wrong."

"Yeah," Caine muttered under his breath, "and Genghis Khan was a pacifist."

Caine seated himself forward on the bike seat and lifted his helmet off the handlebars. He felt the bike rock gently as Vicki settled herself behind him.

He could feel her closeness, the tingling sensation where their bodies touched. His gut tightened into a knot.

Damn. He didn't need this. He'd forgotten the intimacy inherent in riding double. He'd also forgotten how physical contact with Vicki affected him. All he had to do was touch her and he was as horny as a sixteen-year-old.

Oh, hell. He hadn't forgotten. It was denial, pure and simple. The only one he was kidding was himself. He kicked the starter petal and the motor roared to life.

He realized Vicki was scooting backward to the very edge of the bike seat. Did touching him affect her the same way? If she was trying to avoid contact, she was doomed to failure.

"Hang on to me," he said over his shoulder. "The bike's not equipped with handholds."

Even though he'd braced himself, he gave an involuntary jerk as her arms closed around his waist. His sudden movement send the bike jumping forward. Her arms clutched more tightly, and he felt her shift position to regain her balance. Feeling like an idiot, he eased off on the throttle.

"Sorry," he said, almost shouting to be heard above the roar of the motor. If she answered, he didn't hear her.

As they rolled onto the highway, he increased the speed. Vicki tucked in her chin and burrowed her head against his back to protect herself from the wind. It was one more tantalizing torment he didn't need.

They rode for several miles, following the twisting Appalachian highway through the rolling hills. At last Caine pulled off at a place that provided a view of the surrounding landscape.

"That was fantastic," Vicki said, climbing off the bike. "I'll never be satisfied with a trail bike again."

"Trail bikes are for trails. This is a road bike. Never use the one where you should be using the other."

"I hear and obey, Oh, Great One," Vicki said, a teasing smile on her face. She removed her helmet and shook her head. Caine caught his breath as the rays of the late-afternoon sun shot flashes of fire through her hair.

"I saw this spot on the way to town earlier," he said, pulling his gaze away from her as he turned to look at the valley spread out below. "I thought we could watch the sunset, then drive back to camp before dark. We need to get an early start in the morning."

"You promised to let me try out the bike by myself in the morning."

"If you don't do it before we leave, you can do it at our midmorning stop."

"You won't forget?"

"Fat chance of that," Caine said, "and if I do, I'm sure you'll remind me."

CHAPTER THIRTEEN

THE INCESSANT DRUMMING of rain on the metal roof of the van was hypnotic. Cocooned comfortably inside the van, Vicki welcomed the illusion of isolation from the rest of the world.

Tonight was their last night on the road. Tomorrow they would be in Washington where events might well be taken out of her control. It was now or never. If she was going to seduce Caine, it would have to be tonight.

Oh, Lord, she wasn't sure she could do this.

Pollyanna, he'd called her. Nice, sweet, wholesome. Not exactly a siren image, but then no one, especially Caine, was likely to mistake her for a scarlet lady.

On the other hand, desire led to a certain desperation. She wanted Caine, wanted him and needed him with an intensity that shocked her. She'd always considered herself a normal woman with normal needs and desires, but this craving, this insatiable yearning, was something new. And scary.

Caine was a loner, but she couldn't believe that this attraction was all on her side. Neither would she accept it was only physical. No one could kiss her the way he did without feeling some strong emotion.

Even if he didn't know it.

Even if he wouldn't admit it to himself.

She had to believe that, or she'd never be able to go through with this. She kept remembering Aunt Abby's observation that a man who fights himself has already lost.

Would Aunt Abby approve of what she was about to do? Vicki wasn't sure. At eighty-seven, Abigail Tremayne was of a different generation. But she was still young at heart and a very savvy person, Vicki reminded herself. She might not approve of her great-niece's methods, but Vicki suspected she would approve of her intentions.

From her position in the van's over-the-cab sleeping quarters, Vicki watched as Caine converted the table booth into a second bed. When he'd insisted she use the upper bed, she hadn't argued, because she'd known she'd lose. It was that protection thing again. Tucked away up here, she was out of the line of fire if anyone broke through the door.

One thing was certain, though. It would be easier for her to crawl into his bed than coax him into climbing into hers.

She examined her bedtime attire and gave a snort of irritation. Not exactly seduction rags. The terry-cloth robe was warm and practical. Wholesome. It was a sensible choice for travel, not that she'd had much in the way of options. She'd fled Washington with only the clothes on her back. Her hideout wardrobe consisted of a few items donated by various family members and a collection of knock-around vacation apparel left at the cabin over the years and faithfully preserved in Aunt Abby's might-come-in-handy-someday storage trunk.

Her blue nylon pajamas, trimmed in lace, were a little improvement over the sensible robe, but still not the right costume for seduction. Her only other choice was a high-necked, long-sleeved, ankle-length red flannel gown. "The sleeping loft gets cool at night," Aunt Abby had told her when she'd pulled the old-fashioned garment from her storage trunk.

Forget it! She couldn't do this.

She wasn't dressed right.

She didn't know the right moves. She'd make a fool of herself. Instead of going to bed with her, Caine would probably laugh and she'd die of mortification.

Besides, the man was supposed to be the seducer. He'd think she was crazy. He'd think she was brazen. He'd think she was desperate.

She was. She needed Caine.

"Ready to call it a night?"

Caine's voice brought her should-I-or-shouldn't-I debate to a screeching halt.

Now or never. Time to make up her mind. What was she? Woman or wimp?

"I think I'll make a cup of hot chocolate first," she heard herself saying as she slipped off the bed. "Want one?"

Caine backed out of her way. "I don't think so. Not tonight."

"Not even with marshmallows?"

"No. No thanks."

Caine sat down at the far end of the table-bed.

"Well, if you're sure…" Vicki reached into the small cabinet above the sink for a packet of instant cocoa. Fixing hot chocolate had given her an excuse to climb out of her bed and get close to him. Now what did she do?

"It shouldn't take more than a minute, then I'll be out of your way," she said.

"That's all right."

With the table-bed already let down for the night, she had the choice of standing by the stove, climbing into the driving cab or taking a seat on Caine's bed. She chose the last. The bed springs shifted slightly as she sat down next to him.

Caine picked up a magazine.

Vicki took a breath. Now or never, she reminded herself again. "Caine, can I ask you a personal question?"

He looked at her over the top of the magazine. "You can ask. I don't promise to answer."

"Do you have a fiancée, or a girlfriend or anything like that?"

His face settled into immobile planes and angles. "No," he said, his voice flat, without inflection.

"Can I ask another question?"

"Could I stop you?"

Oh, Lord, if only he knew how close she was to stopping. A quick glance revealed his brown eyes flint hard. Courage, she told herself. She couldn't back down now.

She sat up a little straighter, as if the act of physically stiffening her spine would also fortify her mentally.

"Do you find me attractive?"

"What the hell kind of question is that?"

"A relatively simple one," she said, feigning nonchalance. "All it requires is a simple yes or no."

"It's not the kind of question a woman should go around asking a man."

"I don't see why not. Not if she wants to know the answer."

"She shouldn't ask because he might not be comfortable answering."

"Well, that's plain enough," she said, her voice trailing off into a soft sigh. "I guess that means you don't."

"Dammit, that's not what I said."

"You mean you do?"

"You are the most stubborn, exasperating woman I've ever known." He raked his hand through his hair. "Of course I find you attractive. You have to know that."

Eyes lowered, afraid of what she'd see in his expression, she twisted her hands in her lap, then forced them to be still.

"So, are you attracted to me?"

Caine bolted from the bed. "Vicki, we shouldn't be talking about this—not here, not now. I mean in the circumstances—"

"What do circumstances have to do with it? Either you are or you aren't."

"I think your hot chocolate's boiling."

"You're trying to change the subject." Vicki stood to turn off the stove, pushing the pan aside.

"Aren't you going to drink it?"

"It's too hot. I have to wait until it cools. Aren't you going to answer my question?"

"What kind of game are you playing?"

"I'm not playing a game," she said, her voice little more than a whisper. "I'm very attracted to you, Caine."

"Vicki, for God's sake, give me a break here."

She moved closer to him, raising her gaze to search his face. "All you have to do is say yes or no. If you're not, then you're not. And I'll leave you alone."

Caine closed his eyes, as if trying to shut out the sight of her. "And if I said I was . . ." he began raggedly.

She laid her hand on his arm. "If you said you were attracted to me, then I think we should do something about it."

"Oh, God!"

"Caine, I want you."

IT WAS THE SOUND of hope and hopelessness in her voice that got to him.

She wanted him! Her words reverberated in his head like the Hallelujah Chorus.

She wanted him! Wanted him enough to risk her pride to ask.

She wanted him! And had the courage to tell him so.

He was no good for her. He was supposed to protect her, not seduce her. She was infuriating, aggravating and opinionated. She was soft and vulnerable and oh, so tempting. She was driving him crazy.

He needed her like he needed a hole in the head. He needed her like a politician needed a conscience. He needed her like he needed food and drink and air.

He groaned.

"Caine?"

He grasped her shoulders, holding her in front of him. "Be very sure, Vicki," he said, a note of desperation in his voice. "The first time I kissed you I managed to find the strength and decency to send you away. The second time, in the cave, Tucker and Gourdy saved you. This time...this time I'm not strong enough. This time I wouldn't be able to stop."

"Third time's a charm," she whispered as she lifted her face to his.

Her whispered words broke his last claim to reason. He had to hold her, to feel her mouth under his, to taste and touch her. Just this once, he told himself, just for a little while.

He pulled her tight against him and bent to claim her lips, his mouth covering hers, hard and hungry and desperate. His tongue joined hers in a kiss he wished would last forever.

With a sudden shock he realized he wanted to hold and cherish her every bit as much as he wanted to possess her. He'd never thought, never allowed himself to think, of a woman in such terms before. His previous relationships had always been mutually satisfying sexual encounters, diversions without significance or importance played with women who knew the rules. Neither he nor they had been interested in anything other than the fulfillment of the moment. But Vicki was infinitely precious to him in ways that went beyond mere sex, and the knowledge terrified him.

He made a low, rough sound in his throat and rocked her against him, letting her feel his need. The delicate aroma of honeysuckle teased his senses. His hands slipped down her back, caressing her through the silky material of her pajamas.

"We shouldn't be doing this," he whispered, making one last bid for sanity. "I'm the wrong man for you."

"You are not the wrong man," she answered breathlessly. "I want you."

Her need and honesty sent a wave of tenderness through him. "And God knows I want you."

He lifted his mouth from hers, his lips sliding along her collarbone, nuzzling aside the lace of her pajama top,

Her hands tugged at his shirttail. "Take it off," she murmured, her voice both pleading and compelling. She stepped back as he pulled the shirt over his head, watching him with eyes that reflected a hunger as fierce as his own. Then she was back in his arms, her arms encircling his neck, as if she was afraid he'd change his mind. She pressed closer to him, her soft breasts flattening against the harder planes of his chest, and gave a soft moan of pleasure.

CRAZY MAN, thought Vicki. Couldn't he sense, couldn't he feel how much she wanted him, needed him? How could he believe he was wrong for her? He was exactly right. He was the man she'd been waiting for all her life. He was the other half of herself, the one man who could make her complete. And if she couldn't have him, she realized with a certain desperate clarity, she would spend the rest of her life alone.

Her hands tangled in his dark hair, pulling him closer, and her lips parted under his. She wanted to go on kissing him forever.

Outside, the storm, fueled by gusting winds, pelted the van with furious rain. Inside, the storm was an emotional tempest, kindled by weeks of frustration and the twined demands of want and need.

Caine lifted her onto the bed, stopping for a moment to shed his jeans and briefs, the rasp of his zipper echoing the sound of his harsh breathing. He captured her mouth again as he lowered himself to the bed beside her, his hands resting for a moment at her waist, then moving upward to cup her breasts.

As his fingers caressed her nipples through the thin material, Vicki jerked, her body reacting to the feeling of pleasure dancing along her nerve endings. His fingers fumbled with the tiny pearl buttons of her pajamas, and need, like a fine wire spring, coiled tighter and tighter, wild and wonderful and deliciously sweet.

She felt the cool air caress her skin as the pajamas parted, then gasped as his mouth, wet and warm, closed over her nipple. Heat spiraled from deep within, a river of pleasure. Caught in the storm of sensation he had unleashed within her, she moved restlessly against him.

"Caine," she breathed urgently, pulling him closer.

He answered by kissing her deeply, his hands as gentle as a whispered promise as they moved down to her waist. Tugging her pajama bottoms over her hips, he let his mouth follow his hands.

Impatience flared through her, and a desire to know all of him instantly almost overwhelmed her. She arched silently beneath him, afraid to break the spell. His hands moved again to her breasts, then down her body, touching, caressing, teasing, until the sensation of his touch became indistinguishable from the desire curling through her.

She let her hands and lips roam, exploring the different textures of his body, the smooth, heated flesh, the roughness of his cheek and chin, the soft sprinkling of hair on his chest. She breathed deeply, savoring the musky aroma of arousal.

CAINE STROKED HER SLOWLY, savoring her response to his touch, delighting in the tactile sensations of her satin-soft skin under his fingertips.

He raised himself above her, for a long moment touching her only with his eyes, then lowered himself gently. As he settled himself between her thighs, she arched to meet him. Calling on his last reserves of restraint, he entered her slowly.

Her eyes widened. But as he began to move within her, she arched against him again, tossing her head back and forth on the pillow. She twisted wildly and pulled him deeper into her, meeting his thrusts eagerly. His muscles strained against the relentless surge propelling him to climax. And then she stiffened and cried his name.

Caine gave an urgent answering cry and felt his own body dissolve in a series of mind-shattering explosions. Trembling, he rolled to his side, still cradling her in his arms.

VICKI LAY IN THE CROOK of Caine's arm, her head on his shoulder, her heartbeat gradually regaining its natural rhythm, her breathing returning to normal. The perfection of their lovemaking still vibrated between them, and nothing, not even the knowledge that she had deliberately seduced him, could diminish her overwhelming sense of wonder. Never before could she remember feeling so completely alive, so blissfully happy. Outside, a last booming clap of thunder echoed in the distance.

Even as a child, she remembered feeling alone. Her parents, when they were alive, seemed more closely involved with each other than with her; she'd been an extension of their love, not a focus. After their deaths, she'd felt even more isolated.

Her large extended family had tried to replace what she'd lost, not realizing that it had been missing all along. She loved them and knew they loved her in return, but it was a love and an association she shared with many—not one special relationship exclusively hers. And so she'd taught herself to be independent, to rely on her own resources.

Aunt Abby had told her that sharing a life with a special person made every thing brighter, more important, more meaningful. Vicki hadn't really believed her...until tonight.

She heard Caine whisper her name and, reluctant to answer, snuggled more closely into his side. She wasn't ready to talk, wasn't ready to destroy this sense of complete contentment.

"Vicki," she heard him say again. "Are you all right?"

There was no help for it. She had to answer. "I'm perfectly all right. In fact, I feel wonderful, fantastic," she said softly. "How could you doubt it?"

He would, she suspected, try to deny the magic between them, try to shut her out again. He guarded his emotions carefully, hiding them behind an armor of cynicism he'd spent years constructing.

In a way she could understand that. Before she met him, hadn't she done the same? She'd pretended that she was fine alone, that she didn't need anyone.

Tonight had taught her differently. Now that she'd found Caine, she wasn't willing to let him go—not without a fight. Maybe she wouldn't win, but at least she'd know she tried.

"Vicki, we need to talk."

His voice sent a shiver of dread through her. Wouldn't he let her have tonight? She wanted to remember, to savor. Besides, she could predict what he was about to say. He'd claim the magic they'd created together was wrong and he'd blame himself.

"Not tonight," she said. "We can talk tomorrow."

"Vicki..."

It wasn't fair. He'd loved her so perfectly, so completely. Now he seemed determined to spoil it. "Caine, if you're going to tell me tonight was a mistake, I don't want to hear it. In fact, if you said it, I'd probably hit you. And that would be an awful ending to a perfect night."

"I wasn't going to say—"

"Good."

She heard him give a long sigh and held her breath.

"I thought it was fantastic, too," he said, pulling her closer against him. He raised his head and dropped a kiss on her brow. "You're right," he added softly. "Go to sleep. We'll talk tomorrow."

Vicki doubted if she'd sleep, didn't want to sleep. She was more than content lying in Caine's arms. She wished she could stay here forever.

Tomorrow, she knew, would come, and with it tomorrow's problems. Caine's talk. Washington and whatever awaited them there. Mystery. Danger.

Finding the answers had seemed so important a few days ago. No longer. Not now. Not when she was here with Caine.

If she had a choice, if she could forget Washington and simply walk away, she would. She couldn't of course. She'd started this, and now she'd have to see it through to the end.

Caine would be with her, she reminded herself with a spurt of optimism. And until they found the answers, he would stay with her. She couldn't help hoping that it would give him time to realize how perfect they were for each other.

Life didn't come with guarantees, she knew that. After this was over, he might still choose to leave. If he did, if she couldn't convince him they belonged together, then she would have to let him go. But it certainly wouldn't be because she hadn't tried. And at least she would have tonight to remember.

CHAPTER FOURTEEN

CAINE FORCED HIMSELF to lie still, afraid to disturb the woman who lay sleeping in his arms. Never could he remember feeling so confused.

He was a cautious man. He'd spent most of his life convinced that alone was better. As long as he trusted no one, he couldn't be betrayed. As long as he allowed no one close, he could neither disappoint nor fail them. It was a sterile life—no commitments, no responsibilities except to himself, no setting himself up for failure.

His sanitized, protected world was gone now. Falling in love, making love, with Vicki was the most extraordinary, most agonizing experience of his life.

His gaze rested on her gorgeous fall of flame-bright hair, which had tumbled across his chest. Branded, he thought. Her hair would leave no visible mark on his skin, but his heart would forever bear her imprint.

He wanted to care for her, to protect her, to shield her. She was willing to share his kisses, to share his bed, but she would never agree to share his life, he realized.

Despite her courage, she would, if given a choice, prefer a life of calm, supported and surrounded by her large and loving family. There was no place in that life for him, a hard cynical warrior who lived with demons of guilt and debts of atonement, even if she was willing to try.

The faint fragrance of honeysuckle, as delicate and elusive as the woman herself, infused the air. He knew she cared about him. Her response to him, to his love-making, had been unguarded, complete. Once committed, she had held nothing back. And so she would believe she was in love with him.

But she didn't know the real Caine Alexander, didn't know about the blood on his hands or the dark places in his soul.

The best thing he could do for her was secure her safety, then get out of her life. It would be the hardest thing he'd ever attempted, but still far easier than sticking around to see the disillusionment in her eyes when she learned the truth about him.

Through the small window above the bed, Caine watched as the dark night began its slow fade to gray. Memories of another gray morning pushed into his mind.

It had rained that night, too, a usual occurrence in the South American jungle. He remembered the damp, the pressing humidity, remembered wondering if he would ever again feel completely dry, as he led his patrol through the lush green wilderness. After two weeks of searching for hidden rebel outposts, he and his men had been anxious to return to the small village they'd adopted as home away from home.

But even as they approached, he'd known something was wrong. It was gray and damp and quiet—too quiet.

There were no sounds, no movements, not even the village dogs running to greet them, only the smell of wet charred wood and the sweet-sour cloying scent of decay.

They were dead, all dead, the entire village destroyed. Six-year-old Francisco with his liquid brown eyes and gap-toothed smile; Consuela, the dark-haired two-year-old who toddled after him on chubby, unsteady legs; old Miguel, whose carving knife and gnarled fingers fashioned Madonnas and monkeys from scraps of wood; Serafina, the ancient grandmother, who dispensed corn tortillas and wisdom with equal aplomb. All slaughtered like a flock of chickens and left in the dirt as they fell, prey to rot and jungle scavengers.

He and his men had buried the villagers in a mass grave and set one of Miguel's Madonnas—scorched by smoke and fire, but still intact—over the final resting place.

He'd gone a little crazy then, his anger and need for vengeance allowing him to hide from the truth. Although the carnage was the handiwork of the rebels, he was the one responsible for the villagers' deaths. If he'd never come here, never led his men into the remote village, never allowed the villagers to befriend them, this would never have happened. He carried their blood on his hands and on his soul.

Tormented by the images, Caine was no longer able to lie quietly by Vicki's side. Carefully he eased her head from his shoulder and rolled out of the bed.

He needed air, space, distance. Moving cautiously, he pulled on a jogging suit and, shoes in hand, slipped silently outside for a quick run.

VICKI FEIGNED SLEEP as Caine moved silently around the trailer. She didn't want to intrude on his thoughts. As he crept from the trailer, she had no fear that he was about to leave her, but she also knew he would try to put distance between himself and the passion they'd shared last night.

Now was not the right time to confront him, she told herself, not with their arrival in Washington so imminent. When he'd wanted to talk last night, she'd forestalled him, afraid to hear what he wanted to say. Would she be able to deter him again? Would she have to? He might choose to let the impending events distract him, hoping they would distract her, too.

Probably, she decided. She was coming to know him well. Caine was something of a coward when it came to facing his emotions. He would justify his decision by reasoning that their immediate danger had first priority.

And wasn't she doing the same thing?

But not for the same reasons, she realized. She wanted time. The longer she could delay their discussion, the longer Caine would have to come to his senses, to realize that the two of them belonged together.

She waited until Caine left before moving from the bed. First she folded down the table and started a pot of coffee, then she made quick use of the van's shower. By the time she heard Caine coming back, she was dressed and seated at the table, a steaming cup of coffee in front of her.

If he was surprised to see her awake and dressed, he made no comment. Instead, he poured himself a coffee and slid into the seat facing her.

"We should be in Washington in about five hours," he told her. "I need to check in with my colleague sometime in the afternoon. He's making arrangements for a rental car, too."

She raised her cup to her lips, relieved to see her hand was steady. Well, she'd been right—he *was* trying to ignore what had happened between them. Unaccountably she felt hurt.

"I thought we'd be using the Harley for transportation," she said, breaking the silence that stretched between them.

"A motorcycle tends to be more memorable than a car, especially in certain parts of town. Besides, we both might need to have our own transportation."

"Then I guess we'd better get on the road. I'll be ready as soon as I pour the coffee into the thermos."

Caine stretched his hand across the table to touch her arm. "Vicki, I know we need to talk about last night..."

"But now's not the time," she finished for him. "Don't worry, Caine. There's nothing to discuss. Last night was wonderful. It was my decision and I don't regret it. I'm not going to send Harve or Aunt Abby after you with a shotgun, if that's what you're worried about. If you want to hold a moratorium, we can do it later.''

"I didn't mean . . ."

She slid out of the seat and turned away, not wanting him to see her cry. "Later," she repeated as she emptied the remaining coffee into the thermos. "Let's get this show on the road. We've got appointments to keep."

They stopped for breakfast an hour later, then again a hundred miles outside the city for Caine to make a phone call.

"We'll be picking up the car at a truck stop a few miles from the trailer camp where we have reservations," he told her when he returned to the van. "I want you to stay out of sight while I'm picking up the keys. I don't want anyone to see you. After my contact's gone, you can follow me in the car."

"You don't trust your friend?"

"I trust him as much as I trust anyone—this is for his protection as much as yours. The less he knows the safer both of you will be."

When they pulled into the busy truck stop, Vicki slipped out of the passenger seat and into the back part of the van. She was tempted to sneak a peek at Caine's friend through one of the van's windows. After all, Caine hadn't forbidden her to see him, but in the end, discretion won. No need to take chances, she told herself. And so she waited, perhaps not exactly patiently, but at least calmly, until Caine returned.

"Here," he said, thrusting a tall, sweating glass at her. "I thought you might like something cold to drink. We'll give Charlie a few minutes head start before we leave."

"Your friend's name is Charlie?"

"Charlie Abbott. He runs a private-investigation company. Strictly first-rate. I've worked on a project or two with him before."

It was one of the few mentions she could remember Caine making of his work. "Is that what you usually do?" she couldn't help asking. "Are you a private detective, too?"

From the look Caine gave her, he, too, apparently realized he'd been more forthcoming than usual, but for once he didn't close up.

He shrugged. "Not exactly," he told her, "although I'm licensed as a P.I. in Delaware, Virginia, Maryland and D.C. I own a consultation company. We're more into security systems. Prevention before the need for protection."

The memory of several of their previous conversations suddenly made more sense to Vicki. "You usually don't do bodyguard jobs, do you? You're only here with me because Marshal Carelli asked you to come."

"I told you in the beginning I owed Danny," Caine said, then sighed. "That was the truth, but maybe not the entire truth. That day I came to court, I was impressed. I admired you, admired what you were doing. There aren't many people willing to take on somebody like Henderson, regardless of personal cost."

Vicki's heart gave a small jump. If he'd admired her even before he met her, maybe she *was* more to him than just a job. Her world seemed suddenly brighter.

"To be honest," she said, "I didn't know what I was getting into."

"But you didn't back off when you found out, either. Vicki, I . . ." His voice trailed into silence.

"You what?"

"Nothing. Never mind. It isn't important." He shook his head, as if to deny his thoughts. "I think we've been here long enough. Let's get you in the car and get back on the road."

Although Caine had given her specific instructions to the trailer park in case they got separated, Vicki was able to keep the van in sight. Part of her mind kept replaying their conversation. What had Caine been about to say? Something personal? Like maybe he cared for her?

"Hope springs eternal," Vicki quoted to herself.

By four o'clock they'd checked into the park, leveled the van, hooked into the power and water, and Caine was seated at the eating nook, busy studying the reports he'd picked up from Charlie.

He flipped over one paper, gave a little grunt, inspected the next, then returned to the first.

Vicki told herself to be patient, but curiosity finally won. She slipped into the booth seat opposite him. "What are those?" she asked.

"Background reports on your board of directors, such as they are."

"Find anything suspicious?"

"Not a damn thing, but I'm betting it's Senator Van Brock."

"Why?"

"Ability, opportunity and motive, remember?" he asked. "A politician can always use a secret kitty, and as chairman of the board, it'd be easier for him than any of the other directors."

"No. I can't believe that," Vicki protested. "I worked for Senator Van Brock before I went to work for the foundation. He's an honest man. He ran an honest campaign, and I should know—I was in charge of fund-raising. I knew exactly how much money he raised and how much the campaign cost. Besides, he was the main reason I got the job at the foundation. It was his recommendation that put me in front of the other candidates."

Caine seemed thoughtful for a moment. "He knew you, knew you were one of his supporters. Maybe he thought he could pull the wool over your eyes more easily than a stranger's."

"I don't believe that, either," she told him, shaking her head. "You're saying Senator Van Brock was willing to use me, set me up."

"Someone sure was," Caine countered, "and in my experience, politicians will use anyone, even their own mothers, to stay on top."

"You're a cynic, Caine Alexander," she charged.

"Right. And proud of it. Expect the worst and you're not disappointed."

Vicki sighed. There seemed to be no reasoning with him. "This is getting us nowhere. You think Senator Van Brock's guilty. I believe he's innocent. The lack of evidence against him should speak in his favor."

"We don't have evidence against anyone, Vicki," Caine reminded her, "but someone sure as hell is guilty. Henderson didn't set this up by himself. He must have trusted his partner, too. And paid for it with his life. I want to make sure you don't make the same mistake."

She closed her eyes. At times it all seemed so futile. The thought that they might never know, that she might have to keep on looking over her shoulder forever, was almost paralyzing. She opened her eyes and fought to appear calm, but her despair must have been evident in her voice.

"What if we can't find any evidence? How are we going to discover who it is?"

"We'll find him," Caine assured her, his face set in determined lines. "Just because we haven't found anything yet doesn't mean it's not there. Remember, until now, we've only been waiting, not looking. There has to be a connection somewhere. We simply haven't looked in the right place."

She wanted to believe him, was desperate to believe him. And what he'd said did make sense. Besides, wasn't it the same argument she'd used to convince Caine to bring her to Washington? That it was time to stop waiting around for something to happen and take matters into their own hands?

So why was she so discouraged now? He was right— they hadn't really had time to start looking. If the connection was an easy one to find, something so simple that it would show up in a background check on the board of directors, then the police would have discovered it long ago.

Caine frowned as he rustled the papers. "Was Henderson the director when you started working for the foundation?" he asked abruptly.

"No," Vicki said. "The previous director left, taking the assistant director in charge of fund-raising with him. Mark Gleason was acting as interim foundation director when I started work for the foundation."

"Did he want the job permanently?"

"Heavens no, although he would have been qualified. But Mark made no secret of the fact he was happier running aid projects than playing foundation director. He used to complain it was all politicking and glad-handing. He wanted to be working with the people who needed help. He didn't even apply for the position."

Caine paused for a moment. "How long had you been working for the foundation when Henderson was hired?"

"About six months."

"And during that time did any money disappear?"

"No."

"Had any money gone missing before you started to work for the foundation?"

She'd answered these questions before, although Caine's voice didn't hold the accusatory tone that her earlier inquisitors had. "Not that I know of," she told him. "The books balanced for at least two years back. I checked that out when I first discovered the missing funds."

"Okay, that means whoever was working the scam had to wait until he had a confederate in place. Do you remember how many people applied for the director's position?"

"I don't know for sure, but personnel narrowed it to three before they took the candidates to the board."

"Do you know who recommended Henderson? Why he was picked over the other two? Who supported him?"

Vicki was beginning to see where his questions were leading. "All we heard was that he had an impressive record."

"Is there any way to find out? Are there minutes of the board meetings?"

"No," she said, her enthusiasm fading. "The foundation is a nonprofit organization. Official minutes and open meetings are required, but staffing decisions are made in executive session. All that'll be in the official minutes is a motion to hire. And approval was unanimous."

"Damn," Caine said. "I can't help thinking that we'd have our man, or at least a darn good lead, if we knew who recommended Henderson for the job."

"Roy could've planned it all *after* he started working for the foundation."

"You mean he might have seen opportunity and grabbed it?" Caine shook his head. "I might buy that if Henderson was the only one involved. But everything points to him simply being the errand boy. No, someone else was pulling the strings, and there has to be a previous connection between him and Henderson. If only we could find it."

Another dead end. Vicki slumped in her seat. If only there was a way. "I could contact Senator Van Brock and ask," she said. "I'm sure he would tell—"

"Unless he's our man. And then you'd have tipped him off that you're here and still looking," Caine said. "No. I absolutely forbid it."

Vicki glared at him mutinously.

"I mean it, Vicki. I want your unqualified promise that you will not contact Senator Van Brock, that you will not speak to him and that you will not go anywhere near him."

"But it might be the only way we'll ever find answers."

"And if he's guilty, it might blow us out of the water. Your promise, Vicki. And no splitting hairs. Absolutely no contact. I don't want the good senator to know you're anywhere around."

"You act as if you don't trust me."

"I trust your integrity, but not necessarily your judgment. I'm waiting for your promise."

"Oh, all right, I promise. But what if we can't find anything? If the senator's the only way?"

"Then I'll be the one to contact him."

"I don't see why," Vicki protested. "He's more likely to confide in me."

Caine sighed. "For the present, the senator's off-limits to both of us, okay? And before I do anything, I promise I'll discuss it with you first. Deal?"

If only Caine wasn't so prejudiced against politicians, Vicki thought. She was sure, well, almost sure, that the senator was not involved, and he was the one man who might be able to give Caine the answers he wanted. But Caine was adamant, and there seemed to be little else she could do but agree.

"All right, it's a deal," she said, albeit reluctantly. "So now what are we going to do?"

"Go into the foundation's offices and take a look around. I'd like to examine the files on the projects where the money was skimmed. I know they've been looked at before, but maybe I'll see something new. Hindsight sometimes helps."

"Good idea," Vicki agreed, "especially if we go in tonight. It's Friday. The office closes at five for the weekend, so no one should be around. If we time—"

She stopped in midsentence. Oh, Lord, how could she have been so dumb! "Caine..."

"What's wrong?"

"Nothing's wrong," she almost shouted, "except for the fact I'm so stupid. The personnel files. Henderson's personnel file—it'll contain his original application. If we want to know who recommended him, all we have to do is look at who he named as references!"

Caine bolted from his seat. "You're not stupid," he said, his voice exuberant. "Not stupid at all. In fact, you're damn near a genius." And before Vicki could react, he leaned down and kissed her solidly on the mouth.

CHAPTER FIFTEEN

HE NEVER SHOULD HAVE kissed her.

There'd been nothing passionate, not even anything particularly sensual, about it. It was a spontaneous gesture of excitement and exuberance, an act of mutual celebration.

But still, he never should have kissed her.

Heaven knew he was having a hard enough time dealing with the here and now. A glance, an accidental touch, and his testosterone shot up to previously unknown levels. The sexual heat between them was enough to blister the paint from a steam boiler. But that kiss... that kiss was something he'd never before experienced, not even remotely. It was frightening in its simplicity and its complexity. It made him think of friendship, companionship, shared futures, all possibilities that could never be.

In the closed confines of the rental car, the delicate aroma of honeysuckle that Caine had come to associate with Vicki was making it even more difficult to concentrate on the business at hand.

He'd wanted to leave her behind on the excursion into the foundation's offices, but in the end had been forced to accept her argument that, alone, he would be guilty of burglary, while she, as an employee, had a right to be there.

All in all, he thought their expedition had gone well. The only person they'd encountered was Fred, the night watchman, who'd seemed both pleased and relieved to see Vicki.

"Been that worried about you, Miss Vicki," the old man had said, "especially what with Mr. Henderson turning up dead."

"I'm fine, Fred," Vicki had assured him, "but I'd rather no one in the office knew I was around. I'm not sure I'm ready to come back yet."

"You take your time, Miss Vicki. I won't be telling nobody around here I've seen you. Don't expect they'd have any reason to be asking me, anyhow."

Not only had Vicki been able to retrieve and copy Henderson's personnel file, they'd also made copies of the project files that had led to her original discovery of embezzlement, hoping that a reexamination would reveal something new.

He knew Vicki was disappointed that Henderson's résumé had contained no personal references, only a listing of previous organizations he'd worked with.

"Interesting to note that he moved on every two or three years," Caine said now. "I wonder if there were any cash shortfalls after he left?"

"But we're no closer to identifying who he was working with," she said, disappointment evident in her voice.

"Not to worry," he told her. "I'll get Charlie to dig out names of corporation officers and boards of directors at the organizations where he was employed. I'll bet we'll find a name that's familiar. I won't be surprised if it shows up several times. I'm beginning to suspect he'd been at this for a while."

Yes, at last they had something to work with, Caine decided.

"Caine," Vicki said suddenly in a voice he'd learned to identify as trouble, "before we go back to the van, could we go by my apartment?"

It was the last question he'd expected her to ask. For a moment he was speechless. Didn't she realize how vulnerable she was? At least she'd asked, he tried to reassure himself. She hadn't simply decided to go off on her own. Not that there was any guarantee she wouldn't if he said no. He could almost feel his hair turning gray.

"Just for a few minutes," she pleaded. "I can't believe they'd have anyone watching, not after all this time, and especially after they've already searched the place. Please? I'll be careful, do exactly what you say."

Caine pulled onto a side street and parked. He couldn't deal with Vicki and Friday-night traffic at the same time. He turned in the seat to face her. The dim glow from the streetlights failed to hide the combination of anxiety and entreaty in her expression.

"Exactly what is it you want from the apartment?" he asked, managing to keep his voice calm.

"A few clothes, for one thing. I left for Little Falls with nothing but what I was wearing. I'm tired of borrowed castoffs, and if we're going to be out in public at all, well, red flannel shirts and worn-out jeans are not inconspicuous, not in Washington.''

Personally he liked her in worn-out jeans, the soft denim hugging her curves like a second skin. She didn't need fancy clothes to enhance her beauty.

He studied her for a moment. Tonight she must be wearing her original getaway outfit: gray tailored slacks, silky cream blouse and a blue wool jacket that for some reason made her eyes look even greener. Except for a few rebellious tendrils that curled around her face, her wild hair was confined in a sophisticated arrangement low on the back of her neck.

He had to admit she was gorgeous in her understated elegance, very much the professional cosmopolitan. But he suspected he'd always remember her as he first saw her at the cabin—her long legs clad in faded denim, the collar of her flannel shirt open to expose the pulse beat in her throat, her hair loose and tousled around her shoulders and her eyes bright with anger and anxiety. Or as she'd appeared in the cave—in jeans again and wearing his oversize shirt, the wild tangle of curls around her face, the bemused expression on her face when he—

''I'd also like to get my computer,'' she added while he was still trying to catalog the images of her that were already indelibly printed on his mind.

''William said it appeared to be undamaged. When I discovered the theft, I didn't dare keep the information at work, so I set up a couple of hidden files at home. If whoever broke in didn't find them and erase them, I thought it might be worthwhile to go through them again. There might be something I've forgotten. Or maybe missed the significance of at the time.''

''You haven't mentioned computer files before.''

''They're mostly just notes to myself. I didn't remember them until you and Harve started talking about what I might know that I didn't realize.''

Caine thought for a moment. He suspected the two men who'd showed up in Little Falls were Vicki's burglars, and it was unlikely that those thug-for-hire types would be able to turn on a computer, much less access hidden files. Her idea to retrieve the computer had merit. He could even sympathize with her desire for her personal belongings. But it wasn't going to be as easy as simply stopping by for a few minutes.

''Caine?''

''I'll admit it's not a bad idea,'' he said thoughtfully, ''but we can't go in tonight. Even if we were able to get into the building without being seen, the lights would tip off anyone watching that someone was there. But let me think.''

There was an possible alternative, he realized. They could use the apartment he'd rented next door and wait until daylight to enter hers. The more he considered it, the more he felt the idea had merit. Although he suspected his house and office might be under watch, he doubted that anyone would know about the second apartment. He could also risk using the phone to get hold of Charlie and have him start running checks on Henderson's past associates.

No, not a bad idea at all, he decided, but first he would have to explain to Vicki about renting the apartment next to hers. He imagined she had no idea he was watching her before he chased her to Little Falls.

He took a deep breath. "Do you remember when your apartment was broken into and you asked if it was Henderson?"

Vicki nodded. "You said it wasn't."

"Did you ever wonder how I knew?"

"I... No, I don't guess I did." The look she gave him was puzzled. "How *did* you know it wasn't him?"

"Because I had you under surveillance before you split for Little Falls. I'd installed security cameras in the hallway outside your apartment door and on the fire escape. We had videos of the break-in. As a matter of fact, I suspect the burglars were the same two who tangled with Sweetpea's relative, but I can't be sure, because when they broke into your apartment they were wearing ski masks."

He had her attention now.

"Security cameras? At my apartment? But when?"

"Right after the trial. You were still in a safe house." He waited for her reaction and was surprised when she didn't seem angry. Then he realized she'd accepted the need for surveillance the same way she'd come to accept her need for his protection.

"Okay," she said, "but why tell me now?"

"I was simply trying to explain that I was already watching you, or trying to, anyway, before you slipped out of town."

"I still don't understand what this has to do with whether or not we go to my apartment."

"As part of my surveillance, I also rented the apartment next door to you."

The look on her face was almost comical. "The apartment next door? But I never saw you."

"You weren't supposed to. However, if you remember, you only waited a day or two after you came out of protective custody before taking off for Little Falls. Now, I don't want lights showing at your place, but we could stay at the other apartment tonight, then get into yours in the morning—in the daylight."

"Caine Alexander, are you asking me to spend a night with you in your apartment, to actually give up the efficient, compact camper van for a real bed with box springs and mattress and a bathroom with both tub and shower?"

Even in the dim light, Caine could see the sparkle in her eyes.

"Actually," he said, "it's a waterbed."

She gave a dramatic sigh. "That sounds absolutely decadent."

"I was thinking the same thing myself," he said, his voice a low growl. The image of Vicki in the waterbed was playing havoc with his concentration.

A short time later Caine left Vicki waiting in the alley behind her apartment building. He didn't like the idea of leaving her alone, not even for the few minutes necessary for him to park the car, enter the front door, then let her in through the fire exit at the back hallway. But there was no help for it. He didn't want anyone, even the doorman who owed him a few favors, to know she was here.

He checked the alley carefully before letting her out of the car, and in spite of her assurances she would be fine, felt a rush of relief when, minutes later, he opened the fire exit and saw that she was safe.

Carrying the bag of groceries they'd purchased at a small convenience store a few minutes ago, he quietly opened the door into the emergency staircase. "I don't want to use the elevator," he said softly. "We can't take a chance on anyone seeing you."

Vicki nodded and began climbing the stairs.

There were only two apartments to a floor, the entries directly opposite each other. He saw Vicki glance longingly at hers as he shifted the bag of groceries to his hip and unlocked the other door.

"It'll still be there in the morning," he told her.

"I know. It's just... Dammit, Caine. I'm tired of this. I want my life back."

She looked so discouraged it took all his control—and the handicap of a sack of groceries—to keep himself from taking her in his arms. "You were right when you decided to go on the offense," he told her. "We'll find the connection, Vicki, I promise. We've now got several new places to look for leads. It will all be over soon."

Somehow he managed to repress his thoughts about what would happen then. Once they had the answers, once she was safe, she'd be out of his life. It was something he didn't want to contemplate.

VICKI UTTERED a soft oath as she finished scrolling through the notes in her hidden computer files for the second time. She'd hoped to find a clue, something she'd previously missed or forgotten.

But there was nothing here, nothing new or significant, she realized with growing despair. If Caine didn't find something in Henderson's employment records, they'd be back where they started. Exactly nowhere.

With a sound of disgust, she switched off the computer. When she and Caine had entered her apartment early this morning, she'd been relieved to see little damage from the burglary. Her personal papers and business files had been mostly destroyed, but she could find nothing actually missing except a few dishes and several photographs and certificates she'd had hanging on the wall. Reason told her those had probably been smashed during the search.

She'd retrieved several changes of clothes, some toiletries and her computer. Most of her computer files had been wiped clean, but the burglars had been too stupid to destroy the backup diskettes she kept in plain sight on top of her desk. They'd also been too inept to realize there were a couple of hidden files on the hard disk.

Not that it made much difference, she thought, as she wandered into the kitchen to pour herself a cup of coffee. There was nothing new in them, at least nothing she could find. Another dead end, unless Caine could spot something she'd missed.

Caine had left this morning as soon as they'd retrieved her possessions and moved them across the hall, but only after extracting her promise not to leave the safety of his apartment.

"Don't stick your head outside the door until I get back," he'd ordered. "Don't even open the drapes. I want your word."

She'd promised, even if it did seem unlikely anyone would be peeking in windows on the fifth floor. But she'd learned one thing in the past few weeks. It was almost impossible to deny Caine when he was in his protective mode.

Besides, if she hadn't agreed, he probably would have refused to leave her alone at all, and she knew he was anxious to get started on tracking down information on Henderson's former employers.

He'd called his friend Charlie first thing this morning and put him to work gathering preliminary information, but personally she had more faith in Caine than in his friend. If there was a connection, Caine would find it.

It was surprising, she realized, how much she'd come to trust him, to trust his judgment in the short while she'd known him. Of course, she'd managed to fall in love in the same amount of time.

She'd been living with that knowledge for more than a day now—since she'd seduced him, in fact. Even thinking about her siren act was enough to make her blush. She tried to convince herself that she never would have succeeded if Caine didn't care something for her.

He'd made love to her again last night, and it had been ... wonderful. Never had she felt so cherished, so sheltered, so complete. She loved the strength of his body, the weight of him on her, the security of being in his arms. She loved the way the look in his eyes softened with tenderness. She loved the way he caressed her, his callused hands moving over her skin.

Could he have made love to her with such intensity if he didn't care? At least a little?

Vicki carried her coffee back into the living room and sat down in front of the computer again. Both Harve and Caine insisted that whoever was threatening her believed she knew something that could connect him to Henderson. She'd have to go through the files one more time.

Vicki was engrossed in rereading the files when there was a sudden pounding at the door. Her heart slammed against her ribs.

Caine?

No, not Caine. He'd have used his key.

No one else knew she was here!

But someone was definitely pounding on the door.

It was a mistake, she tried to reassure herself. No one could possibly know she was here. If she stayed quiet, whoever it was would give up and go away.

Suddenly she realized that the pounding wasn't on this door, but on the door across the hall—the door to her own apartment.

But why would someone be doing that? She'd hadn't stayed here in more than a month. She wasn't supposed to be here now. As far as the doorman knew, she wasn't here now. And he wouldn't have let any door-to-door salesmen into the building.

Maybe it was a mistake. Someone who'd gotten off the elevator on the wrong floor?

Or could something have happened to Caine? Could he have sent someone with a message and forgotten to tell them she was in his apartment, not hers?

Fear clutched at her, not fear for herself this time, but fear for Caine. She had to know who was at her door.

She looked at the blank screens of the two monitors sitting on the other side of the room. Caine had explained they were part of the video setup he'd installed to guard her doors, but he hadn't shown her how to work them. The equipment positively bristled with dials—there was no way she could figure it out herself. Wait! There was a much simpler way.

Thankful that the carpeting muffled the sound of her footsteps, Vicki moved cautiously toward the door. All the apartments in the building had peepholes. If she was careful she should be able to see who was in the hall without being seen.

Holding her breath and praying the cover over the peephole wouldn't squeak, she opened the shutter and put her eye to the lens.

Damn! All she could see was his back.

Whoever he was, he was wearing an expensive-looking business suit, and his sandy-colored hair was conservatively trimmed above the collar. She couldn't help thinking he looked familiar.

Even as she told herself to have patience, that he would turn in a minute so she could see his face, the man raised his hand to knock again. "Vicki," she heard him say, "Vicki, let me in. I need to talk to you."

It was then he turned slightly, and she saw his face.

She gave a muffled gasp.

What was Ben Sinclair doing here? Foundation business? But his legal work for the foundation was pro bono and usually at the request of the board. He was rarely around the staff. Why would he be looking for her?

He turned, his eyes scanning the hallway. Vicki froze. Did he sense someone watching him? She held her breath, afraid to move, afraid to blink. After a moment, he returned his attention back to her apartment.

"Come on, Vicki," he pleaded. "I know you're in there. It's me. Ben Sinclair. I need to talk to you. It's important."

Knees trembling, Vicki softly closed the shutter and leaned weakly against the door. How did he know she was here? she asked herself again. What did he want to talk about? And most importantly, what was she going to do about it?

CHAPTER SIXTEEN

CAINE PUSHED the pile of papers across Charlie's desk. "That's it then. Two familiar names, both appearing once and both years ago."

"That's all we've got so far," Charlie confirmed, "but you can't expect miracles. Hell, Caine, what's wrong with you? You know there are no shortcuts in this business. If you try to cut corners, you're likely to miss the very bit of information you need. You peel off a layer at a time. And it *takes* time." He glanced at his watch. "We've only had three hours on this. We'll find more when we dig deeper."

Caine knew Charlie was right. As a private investigator, Charles Abbott was one of the best. He'd done an incredible job gathering so much so soon. That pile of papers contained the names of the senior staff and board of directors for every company and organization Henderson had worked for in the past fifteen years—current officers, as well as the personnel at the time Henderson was employed. It was a phenomenal effort.

"I'm sorry, Charlie. I shouldn't be taking my frustration out on you. You've done a great job. It's incredible you were able to get together so much so quickly."

Charlie leaned forward. "It's the age we live in—computers and the information highway. In my dad's day, it would have taken weeks and an inch of shoe leather to collect this. Today, a few key strokes and bingo. Nice in my line of business, but you know, in some ways it's a little scary. One thing for sure, once the man on the street realizes how much of his life is an open book, it's going to make for a lot of smarter criminals or a lot more honest men."

"You're too young to be turning philosophical on me, Charlie."

"Ha. I'm six months older than you, boyo, and don't you forget it."

"Yeah? Well, right now, I'm aging a lot faster than you. I've got a bad feeling about this and I'm in a hurry."

"Okay. I'm with you. Already got a man on the senator—I'll put one on our second possibility, too. We ought to have a better picture in a few hours."

"I've suspected the senator all along," Caine said, "but I'll admit, I also expected more of a visible connection than this. The only time we have them linked is twelve years ago. According to what you dug up, Van Brock resigned his seat on that bank's board of directors and put his stock into a holding company to run for congress only six months after Henderson signed on as an assistant to the bank president. We can't even be sure they knew each other. Van Brock wasn't working in the bank, and Henderson was just a lackey. It's unlikely he ever attended the board-of-directors' meetings."

"Right now I have to agree the senator is more likely," Charlie said. "Our second guy's connection with Henderson is even more nebulous—and he's a preacher, to boot. You know that shelter down on skid row? He runs the place. I doubt if we'll find any evidence of hidden assets there."

"Unless he's siphoning off funds for his charity work."

"Be kinda like robbing Peter to pay Paul, wouldn't you say? The foundation's in the same business."

"You're probably right," Caine acknowledged, "but dig, anyway. The way my luck's running, a missed paper clip will be the key to the vault."

"Already working on it. What are you going to do now?"

"I think I'll go talk to the senator. Maybe he'll make a mistake." Caine lifted himself from the chair and stepped toward the door. "Thanks for everything, Charlie," he said over his shoulder. "I'll be in touch."

"Have you got the lady stashed somewhere safe? If you need any help at covering, I can loan you a good man."

Caine froze. "What makes you think there's a lady involved in this?"

"Come on, buddy. It wasn't hard to figure out when you put me on to digging around in Henderson's records. She was front-page news during the trial, and your brother-in-law was very visible. I figured you took over after the marshal's office was closed out. How'd he con you into it, anyway? I know you don't do bodyguard jobs."

Caine sighed. Charlie knew him too well. "Danny was concerned she wasn't safe. When Danny's bothered about something, Maggie's bothered, too. She's due to deliver any day now and I didn't want her worried. So I volunteered."

"Little Maggie's going to be a mother? Last time I saw her she was still in braces and pigtails."

"Well, she isn't so little now. Looks like she's carrying around a basketball team—front and center."

Charlie laughed. "Imagine that, Maggie a mother. Hey, that's going to make you an uncle."

"Yeah, imagine that." Caine grinned.

"I wasn't baiting you when I offered you some help," Charlie said in a more serious tone. "I admire the lady. It took guts to do what she did. Besides, you know I've always had a weakness for redheads."

"And just how the hell do you know so much about her?" Caine asked, his voice gone grim.

"Easy, Caine. I did a little snooping when this thing first broke. The foundation's right at the top of my mom's charity list. Hell, it's high on mine, too. I don't like being taken for a sucker."

Caine felt himself relax. That sounded like something Charlie would do. He'd want to know if the whistle blower was legit or had a personal agenda, and he'd have been too impatient to wait for the results of the trial.

"So you checked her out?"

"Yep. Victoria Winslow is solid gold, a real classy lady. I've got the file around here somewhere if you want to look."

For a moment Caine was tempted. "No," he said. "No thanks. I know all I need to know. Besides, my job's keeping her safe."

"Have you been with her since the trial?"

"Most of the time. I was on the scene when she came out of the safe house, but she slipped away. Took me a few days to catch up with her again."

"Slipped away? From you?" Charlie laughed. "Resourceful, isn't she? Has Caine Alexander at last met his match?"

"I'm supposed to keep her safe, that's all," Caine said quickly. Maybe too quickly, he thought, when Charlie gave him a penetrating look.

"Well, call me if you need me," Charlie said. "Go on now. Get out of here. We've both got work to do."

He was going to take Charlie up on his offer of a man, Caine thought as he headed back to the apartment. He didn't like leaving Vicki alone. He'd done it this morning, but he hadn't been happy about it. No one should have tumbled to their presence in town, at least not yet. But the word would be out soon, and the longer they were here the greater the chance of discovery became.

Feeling increasingly anxious, Caine zipped through an intersection on a yellow. He'd left Vicki alone longer than intended, and even though logic told him she was perfectly safe, he was still uneasy.

She wasn't going to like being back under guard, but he was definitely calling in Charlie's man. She'd have to accept it, just as she'd have to accept that he was going to talk to the senator.

Dammit, she'd better agree because he had a gut feeling they were running out of options and time.

VICKI DEBATED what to do. She'd promised Caine she wouldn't leave his apartment. On the other hand, neither of them had anticipated anyone coming to look for her—at least not openly. The doorman had to admit anyone without a pass key, but only after permission from a resident. How had Ben gained entry?

Regardless of the reason, the doorman had let him in and would be able to identify him, Vicki reasoned.

Whatever Ben wanted to talk about, it must concern the foundation. Had he discovered something new about the embezzlement?

Ben, like the senator, had been somewhat disbelieving when she'd first approached him with her suspicions. But once she'd found Henderson's dummy accounts, she'd received his full support. He'd even helped her search the books to verify the source of the funds in the secret account.

He had to know she was in hiding, even if it wasn't official knowledge, she thought. So if he'd come looking for her today, it must be important. She'd have to talk with him.

Decision made, Vicki retrieved her apartment key from her purse. Talking with Ben was one thing, but she was going to be careful about what she told him. And she wouldn't reveal that she wasn't actually staying in her own apartment.

When she opened the door, Ben was halfway down the short hallway, heading toward the elevator. "Ben," she called. "I thought I heard someone out here. Were you looking for me?"

Ben turned at the sound of her voice, surprise clearly evident on his face. "Vicki! There you are. I thought... Did I get the wrong apartment?"

"This one's mine," she told him, digging into her pocket for her key. "I was visiting a neighbor when I heard someone knocking." She opened her door, glad of the excuse to look away. She'd never been a very good liar. "Come on in."

"I thought the other apartment was vacant," he said, following her inside.

Vicki punched in the override code for the front door on the security panel, leaving the rest of the system in place. A sense of uneasiness was making her cautious. "Why did you think that?"

"Several weeks ago I asked the doorman if I could speak with your neighbor to see if you had left an address. He said there was no one there."

"You must have misunderstood," Vicki told him, trying to invent a logical story. "The doorman probably meant she wasn't at home. My neighbor is an elderly woman. She spends the winter months with her son in Florida. She only returned a few days ago."

"Oh. Well, I guess that explains it." He glanced around the room. "How are you, Vicki? And where have you been? I've been worried." He took her hand.

"I'm fine. Really. After the trial I needed to get away for a while. So I've been traveling, visiting relatives. That sort of thing."

She pulled her hand away, then gestured toward the couch. "Go on and have a seat. I'll make us some coffee. If I have any, that is. I only got home last night. Haven't had time to shop yet."

Instead of sitting down, Ben followed her into the kitchen.

"I can't imagine how you knew I was here," she added, hoping he would volunteer an explanation.

"I worked late last night, and when I bumped into Fred, I asked him if anyone had heard from you or knew when you were coming back. I probably shouldn't tell you this because you'll be upset with him, but Fred told me you had stopped by the office earlier in the evening. He said you'd asked him not to say anything at the foundation about seeing you."

He paused for a moment. "He really didn't mean to break a confidence, Vicki. He doesn't consider me a part of the foundation staff. Besides, he knows how concerned I've been. We've discussed the situation several times. What's going on, anyway? Don't you plan to go back to the foundation?"

"I haven't decided yet, which is why I asked Fred not to broadcast my return," Vicki said. "But I'm glad you explained. I couldn't help wondering."

"I hope you aren't mad at him. He's been worried about you. All of us have."

"No, it's all right. He meant well." Actually, she thought, it was a relief to know there was such a simple explanation for Ben's showing up on her doorstep. Still, she'd continue to be careful what she told him.

Vicki offered up a silent thank-you when she saw the coffeepot in its usual place. Now if she could only find the coffee. Checking such mundane things hadn't been high on her list of priorities this morning. Ah. There it was—the bright red canister in the cabinet.

"Well, I'm glad you're back safe and sound," Ben told her. "I've been checking every few days, hoping you'd show up." He leaned against the kitchen counter.

"Every few days?" Didn't the doorman tell you I wasn't here?"

"And announce to the world that your apartment was empty? That would have set you up for burglary. I'm sure management rules prohibit that."

Management rules also prohibited anyone being allowed into the building without occupant approval, Vicki thought, a sudden chill running down her spine. Fred might have told Ben she was back, but how had he gotten into the apartment house? Something was wrong.

"There," she said, turning on the coffeemaker. "Let's go to the living room where we can sit down. It'll be a few minutes before the coffee's ready."

She brushed past him, acting on an impulse that demanded more space between them. Her sense that something wasn't right was growing stronger.

When he sat on the couch, she took a seat in the armchair facing him and willed herself to remain calm. "Why have you been looking for me, Ben? Is something wrong at the foundation?"

"I told you, I was worried, especially after Roy was found dead. You heard about that, didn't you?"

Stay calm. Stay calm. The command sang in her head like a mantra.

"Yes, I knew he was dead."

"And you weren't concerned? The police think his murder is somehow connected with the embezzlement. I was afraid you were in danger, too."

Uneasy at the turn of the conversation, Vicki swallowed against the tightness in her throat. "I don't understand what you mean," she said, hoping her voice didn't betray her. "I'm sorry he was killed, but I don't see how his death could concern me. Quite frankly, Ben, after the last six months, I'd be happy if I never had to hear or think about Roy Henderson again."

There, she thought, that ought to be a strong enough hint for Ben to change the subject.

"The police must think you're in danger," he persisted. "They sure are keeping you under wraps."

Was he being deliberately dense? The thought made her go cold.

"That was before the trial and because they said Roy had threatened me. If I was ever in any danger, it was over after my testimony."

"You're sure? That's a relief. I assumed you were still being threatened, or they wouldn't have assigned you a bodyguard after the trial. And when Fred said Mr. Alexander was with you last night, well, I needed to see for myself that you were all right."

Vicki managed a smile as her previous uneasiness exploded into full-blown panic. "As you can see, I'm fine."

She hadn't told Fred that Caine was a guard, hadn't introduced him at all. So how did Ben know his name? Dear God, it was Ben! It had been Ben all along!

"I don't know where Fred got the idea Caine was my bodyguard," she heard herself saying. "He's just a friend."

Careful, Vicki, she warned herself. *Don't let him see you know.*

"The coffee should be ready," she said, pushing herself out of the chair, praying her knees would hold her. "Stay where you are, Ben, and I'll get it. You take it black, don't you?"

Ben stood, too. "Sorry, Vicki," he told her, slipping his hand from his pocket.

Vicki gasped at the sight of the dull black pistol.

"Now you know why I'm not a trial lawyer. I always give too much away. I think you should sit back down. You look a little shaky. When is Alexander due back?"

Bluff. She had to bluff. "What on earth are you talking about? Caine's a friend, not a guard," Vicki improvised. "We have a date for dinner tomorrow night. I don't expect to see him until then. You can put the gun away, Ben. I told you, I'm not in any danger."

Ben shook his head. "Nice try, but it won't work." He sighed. "I'd hoped to persuade you to leave with me, but now I think we had better wait for Mr. Alexander. Sit down, Vicki." His voice had sharpened.

She shook her head, trying to ignore the gun pointed directly at her heart. "Ben, why? You'll never get away with this." She took a step backward. He wouldn't shoot her here, she told herself. He wouldn't dare.

"I'll do what I have to do. Now sit down!"

Oh, Lord, she should have listened to Caine. He was going to kill her when he found out what she'd done. If Ben didn't kill her first. She had to get away. Mentally she calculated the steps to the door.

"Last warning, Vicki. Sit down. Or else . . ."

Vicki lunged for the door, her heartbeat thundering in her ears. She couldn't let Caine walk into a trap. She had to get away.

She felt the cold metal of the doorknob in her hand. She was almost—

Ben lunged into her from behind, slamming her body against the door.

A blinding pain exploded in the back of her head. A gray mist swirled before her eyes. She was falling. She felt her knees hit the floor and reached out to catch herself, then everything went black.

CAINE PARKED the car on the street in front of Vicki's building, then, impatient as he was to see her, forced himself to stop by the doorman's desk.

"Afternoon, Jackson," he said as he picked up the visitor's sign-in book. "How's it going?"

"Good afternoon, Mr. Alexander," the doorman answered. "Things are pretty quiet."

Caine laid book aside. "Looks that way. Not a single visitor all day."

"Most of the tenants are gone for the weekend," Jackson explained. "Haven't seen a soul except for Mr. Sinclair. He stops by every couple of days to take care of the fish tank up in 6-A. Colonel Bolton's a new tenant. Rented the place about six weeks ago, then took off to spend the rest of the winter in the Bahamas."

Good. No strange visitors. Caine allowed himself to relax. "Well, you take care, Jackson."

"I'll do that, Mr. Alexander. It's nice to see you back."

"It's nice to be back," Caine answered over his shoulder as he walked toward the elevator.

His good mood dissolved as soon as he stepped into the apartment. Vicki wasn't there. He could feel her absence even before he looked.

Dammit, he'd told her to stay put. Anger overrode his usual caution as he hurriedly checked out each room. She'd promised. Where was she?

She'd promised, he reminded himself, and she always kept her promises. Slowly his anger receded. Had she ducked into her apartment to pick up something she'd forgotten this morning? It made sense. Knowing Vicki, she'd consider a quick trip across the hall in keeping with the spirit of their agreement.

That was it, he reasoned. She wouldn't have gone anywhere else. She'd even left her purse in plain sight on the couch. She'd be back any moment, and if she wasn't, he'd simply go get her.

Almost automatically Caine punched the rewind button on the security camera video, rolling it back to the time he'd left this morning, then began running the film at fast forward. When a flickering movement on the lower monitor, the one that covered the hallway, caught his eye, he punched the freeze button, then played the film at regular speed.

His gut twisted as he watched the silent drama unfold—Vicki coming out of his apartment, calling down the hall, then unlocking the door to her apartment and inviting a strange man inside.

He rewound the film, noting the time line at the bottom of the image and checked his watch. Forty-five minutes ago. He replayed the film, his face growing grim as he again watched Vicki and the man enter her apartment. Then he hit fast forward to the end. Whoever the man was, Vicki apparently knew him, was comfortable with him. It didn't make him feel a damn bit better. He'd been convinced for a long time that Vicki's enemy was someone she knew.

According to Jackson, no one but the fish tender had entered the building today, at least not legitimately. What was his name? Sinclair?

Sinclair! Caine's blood ran cold. What was the name of that attorney Vicki had mentioned—the one who did occasional work for the foundation? Sinclair. That was it. Ben Sinclair!

Sinclair was a common name, he tried to tell himself as he dialed the doorman's desk, but Caine didn't believe in coincidence.

"Jackson," he said, as soon as the doorman answered, "who did you say was taking care of the colonel's fish? Sinclair? What's his first name?"

"Anything wrong, Mr. Alexander?" Jackson asked.

Caine forced himself to sound calm. "No, nothing's wrong, but when you said Sinclair, I thought it sounded familiar. I know a Sinclair. Haven't seen him in a while. Thought it might be the same guy. My friend's an attorney. First name's John. He's into fish, too."

As he talked, Caine scanned the video from the fire-escape camera. Nothing there. Vicki and the man must still be inside.

"...not your friend, Mr. Alexander," he heard Jackson say, "although he is a lawyer. His first name's Ben. Kind of a coincidence, isn't it, them both being lawyers and all. He knows Miss Winslow, your neighbor from across the hall, too. They work in the same building. Fact is, I've seen Mr. Sinclair bring her home a few times when the weather's been bad."

"Thanks, Jackson," Caine said, his knuckles white as he hung up the phone. His string of curses did nothing to relieve his anxiety or his guilt. He'd goofed,

goofed big time, and he was painfully aware it could cost Vicki her life.

Why hadn't he picked up on Sinclair? Vicki had mentioned the fellow, but so casually he hadn't given the man a thought. He'd been so stupid, so focused on the board, on Senator Van Brock in particular, he'd completely dismissed the volunteer lawyer.

The perfection of the setup alone should have tipped Caine off. The man was connected with the foundation, but so remotely he'd never fall under suspicion. But Vicki knew both Sinclair and Henderson well. Chances were a remembered remark, an idle observation of the two men together, had been enough to make Sinclair fear her adding two and two together.

There was no question in Caine's mind that Sinclair was his man. He didn't need proof. The sharp knot of fear in his belly was enough. If Sinclair had hurt her, he'd kill the man with his own hands and the devil take the consequences.

Focus. He had to focus, to get himself back under control. He had to think of a way to get Vicki out of there.

Caine looked at his watch. She'd been in there with him almost an hour. On the tape Vicki had greeted Sinclair as a friend. It was obvious she hadn't suspected him. Not then. But Caine reasoned that Ben's sudden appearance was an attempt to find out what she knew.

He couldn't worry about how Ben had known she was here. Not now. He could do a postmortem later. He had to worry about the present.

An hour was too long. Sinclair would have tipped his hand by this stage and Vicki would have caught it. She was smart and perceptive.

Did Sinclair know about him? Of course he did. He'd even known about Sweetpea. So that was his game. Sinclair was waiting for him. A trap. What did he plan to do? Kill them both, then make it to look like a murder-suicide?

It was the only option Sinclair had if he meant to get away. He'd already killed once. Even if it hadn't been his hand on the gun, Caine was sure Sinclair was behind Henderson's death.

Okay, so Sinclair was setting a trap. Now all Caine had to do was avoid walking into it. Somehow he had to bypass Sinclair, get into the apartment and rescue Vicki.

He looked around his apartment. It was a simple reverse of Vicki's—living room, kitchen-and-dining L, one bedroom and bath. There were only two ways in, through the front door or the fire escape. He'd feel better if he knew where Sinclair had Vicki. Probably under restraint in the bedroom. And Sinclair would be guarding the front door.

If Caine had been sure of that, he'd have chosen to go in through the fire escape. But that entry would set off the security alarm, and if she was in the living room with Sinclair, she'd be too far away for him to rescue when the alarm sounded. No, he'd have to go in through the front door. Take out Sinclair and then get to Vicki. It was his only chance.

Caine punched in the number to Charlie's office to fill him in. "Call the cavalry for me, Charlie," he said. "If I speak to them, they'll tell me to wait, and I can't take that chance. I'm going in."

He pulled his pistol from his shoulder holster and released the safety, then eased open the door, stepped across the hall and flattened himself against the wall.

Caine listened intently for a moment, but could hear no sound from inside Vicki's apartment. Careful to keep himself out of range of the peephole, he slowly leaned down to look at the lock.

The gods were smiling! The key slot was horizontal. The door was unlocked.

And why wouldn't it be? Caine asked himself. The man had baited his trap with Vicki. Sinclair wanted Caine inside. He'd issued an open invitation.

He'd also made a mistake. The unlocked door cut valuable seconds from Caine's entry time. There was a bitter smile on Caine's face as his fingers closed around the knob and slowly, very slowly, began to twist. Sinclair's invitation was one he couldn't refuse.

CHAPTER SEVENTEEN

VICKI'S HEAD ACHED, a pain so intense it made her senses swim. She could feel her pulse beating against her temple, each throb a new wave of agony.

Eyes closed, she tried to think past the pain and nausea swelling with each breath.

Where was she?

What had happened?

Why did her head hurt so?

Open your eyes, Vicki, she told herself. *Open your eyes and at least you'll know where you are.*

Her efforts to think increased the pain. She wanted to call out, but her lips wouldn't move.

Panic produced the incentive that reason had failed to provide. Her eyes flew open and for a moment new waves of pain nearly defeated her.

Her first rational thought was that she was in her apartment lying on her bed. Then came the knowledge that she couldn't move her arms and that something was tied across her mouth.

No, not tied. Taped. There was tape across her mouth, and her arms were tied behind her back. She was bound and gagged and lying on her own bed in her own apartment.

en!

Vicki moaned, her returning memory so frightening, so shattering, it overrode the pain in her head.

Ben Sinclair is the enemy. He killed Henderson. He hit me on the head. Now he's waiting for Caine. He'll kill us both.

Fighting back tears, Vicki pulled against the restraints on her wrists. Her shoulders ached. Her head pounded.

She had to do something. She couldn't simply lie here, waiting for Caine to walk into Ben's trap.

A new pain stabbed between her shoulder blades, and she shifted instinctively, then realized what she'd done. He hadn't bound her legs! He'd tied her arms behind her back and taped her mouth, but he hadn't bound her legs—a small enough boon, but under the circumstances, a boon nonetheless. She wasn't completely helpless.

It wouldn't be easy, she realized, but theoretically she should be able to move. Ben Sinclair had made a mistake. He'd left her a small degree of mobility. Somehow she'd find a way to use it to her advantage.

Vicki slumped back against the pillow, her head spinning. She'd have to act quickly. Caine would return soon, and when he discovered she was gone, he'd know something was wrong. He'd figure out where she was, that she was in trouble and come charging to the rescue.

And Ben will kill him!

She couldn't let that happen.

Willing herself to ignore the pain in her head, she looked around the room. Her gaze settled on the window. The fire escape? No. With her arms tied behind her, she would be awkward, clumsy. The steps were steep. She wouldn't be able to hold on to the banister. She wouldn't even be able to call for help. Besides, she'd never manage the window.

The window! How could she have forgotten? All her windows were wired to the security system. One solid bump against any glass pane and the apartment alarm would start screaming like a banshee. She should know. She'd accidentally activated it once.

She remembered leaving the security system on when she turned off the door alarm. Would Ben realize it was still active? Would he try to turn it off? Or dismantle it?

No, she decided after a moment. If he realized she'd left the alarm on, he'd be afraid to tamper with it, afraid he'd set it off.

Vicki lay still for a moment, gathering her strength and listening for any sound from the front room. Ben had closed the bedroom door, but she was still going to have to be careful. Any sound would bring him running.

Slowly, awkwardly, using her shoulders and hips, she got herself closer to the side of the bed.

Dear God, her head ached.

She rested for a second, waiting for her dizziness to subside, then slowly, carefully, swung her legs over the edge of the mattress. At last she managed to push herself into a sitting position.

Her head swam. Black spots danced in front of her eyes. Her stomach rolled.

Please, God, she prayed. *Don't let me throw up.* With her mouth taped she'd choke.

The black spots faded to a gray mist, then cleared completely. Her stomach steadied to a more controllable simmer. Her head still throbbed.

Vicki took several deep breaths through her nose, then shifted her weight to stand. She swayed on her feet. *Don't fall, don't fall,* she chanted mentally. Ben would hear the thump and come to investigate. Only her determination kept her upright until the world stopped spinning.

There were only four or five steps to the windows, she told herself. One foot in front of the other. Once, twice, third time's a charm. She could do this. She had to do this.

In front of the windows she stopped, eyes searching for the opening in the draperies. She'd have to touch glass to make this work. There it was. One step sideways.

Carefully balanced she turned around, positioning her back to the windows. She'd need her hands to pull open the draperies.

Her efforts sent fresh waves of agony through her skull. Again the gray mist threatened her vision. She swayed, then caught herself and waited for her tilting world to stabilize.

Her shoulders ached. Her arms tingled. Her hands were all but numb. She tried to flex her fingers, wasn't sure she could feel them move. But they were there, she told herself, and they would do what she commanded.

Hurry, she urged herself, her eyes focused on the door across the room.

Stepping backward until she could feel the draperies brushing against her arms, she groped blindly to separate the overlap.

Then she saw the doorknob on the other side of the room slowly turn.

He was coming! She was out of time.

Where was the damned opening? As the gray mist pressed closer, she felt the material part beneath her hands. She threw herself backward, touched smooth cool glass.

"Ooouh-eee, ooouh-eee, ooouh-eee." The pulsating shriek of the alarm, decibels louder than hearing comfort, swelled to overwhelm other senses.

Vicki fought the gray mist. Some part of her brain recognized the movement on the other side of the room as a door swinging open. Then she felt her knees wobble and the world went black again.

THE UNEXPECTED SOUND of the alarm galvanized Caine into action. Bending low, he crashed thorough the door. As he dived for the floor his mind registered the image of Sinclair standing in the open doorway of the bedroom, registered the image of the gun in his hand as, in what seemed like slow motion, the man turned toward him. Without thought, without hesitation, Caine fired.

The bullet caught Sinclair high in the shoulder, the impact jerking his gun arm upward, spinning him around. He slumped to the floor. A second explosion sounded as Sinclair's shot slammed into the ceiling.

Caine sprang to his feet and in three strides stood over the fallen man. A kick sent Sinclair's gun spinning across the carpet. Without waiting to see the extent of the man's injuries, Caine burst into the bedroom.

In a single glance, his eyes absorbed the scene—the rumpled bed cover, the draperies hanging askew at the window, Vicki's still form on the floor. With a muttered curse, he was beside her in seconds, his curses increasing in vitriol and volume when he saw her bound wrists and the gag across her mouth.

He felt for a pulse in her neck, and relief flowed through him. He shoved his gun into its holster. Carefully he lifted Vicki and laid her on the bed. Using his pocket knife, he slashed the cords binding her wrists, then wincing in sympathy, peeled the tape from her mouth with trembling hands.

She was so pale, the slight rise and fall of her chest the only signs of life.

Please, God, he prayed, *let her be all right.* He ran his hands down her arms and legs, checking for hidden injuries. So far, so good. Then he gently cradled her head, discovered the sticky patch of hair and a lump the size of a golf ball.

Rage coursed through him. Never before had he felt such an intense desire to kill. He could feel his fingers wrapped around Sinclair's throat, feel them squeezing, slowly, deliberately, choking the life out of him. Only Vicki's presence and his inability to leave her side prevented his fantasy from becoming reality.

How had she done it? Arms tied behind her, gagged, a huge lump on the back of her head, and still she'd managed to get off the bed and sound the alarm!

Out of the corner of his eye he caught a movement on the floor in the doorway. His right hand slid the gun from his holster in the same instant his gaze locked on the man trying to roll to his side. "Move another half an inch, you bastard," he growled at Sinclair. "Half an inch. That's all the excuse I need."

Sinclair lay still.

The alarm continued to scream. *Hurry, Charlie,* Caine silently pleaded, straining to hear the sound of approaching sirens over the din.

He heard noise from the front room, then the sound of the doorman's voice. "What's going on here? Mr. Sinclair? What— You're bleeding!"

"Jackson," Caine bellowed, "in here. Leave that bastard where he is."

"Mr. Alexander, but what— That's Miss Winslow!"

"Call an ambulance. Turn off the alarm. Then get back downstairs. The police are already on their way. They'll need directions to the right apartment." His orders left no room for misinterpretation.

Jackson's face blanched. "Yes, sir. I'm going, Mr. Alexander." He backed away from the door, carefully avoiding the fallen Sinclair.

At last the alarm stopped. Now Caine could hear the sound of sirens getting closer.

He looked down into Vicki's pale face, wanting to gather her in his arms, but afraid to move her.

"Hang on, Vicki," he implored. "Please hang on. Help's on the way."

REALITY RETURNED to Vicki in slow increments. Enveloped by a shadowy mist that seemed to stretch forever, she had no sense of time or place, only a perception of being. She heard a moan and around her the shadows shifted and changed.

Another moan, and this time she knew it was hers. The mist receded, dissolving into a dull incessant ache that seemed to have no beginning and no end. She longed to retreat back into the shadows, but there was no return. Caught like a piece of flotsam, she rode the currents of pain and sound toward awareness.

She could hear a strange whooshing, whirling noise interrupted by an intermittent clicking from somewhere close beside her and an even stranger bleep-bleep noise, like the sound of a computer cursor gone wild, from somewhere above.

Where was she? There was something she had to do, something she had to remember— "Caine!" Her scream came out only as a soft whisper.

"I'm here, Vicki. I'm right here. Open your eyes."

It was his voice, that low growl that always sent shivers down her spine. She felt the warmth of flesh against flesh as someone gently squeezed her hand, and she dared to believe. "Caine," she said again, and opened her eyes.

Her world spun before finally slowing, and his face swam into focus. "Caine," she said a third time, the sound of his name reinforcing her belief that he was here. "What—" Her tongue stuck to the roof of her mouth. She tried to swallow.

"Shh. Don't try to talk." He punched a red button on some kind small control panel, then slipped his arm beneath her shoulders to raise her head.

"I know your mouth's dry," he said, "but you can't have water yet. It might make you sick. The nurse said I could give you an ice chip when you woke up." He slipped a plastic spoon between her lips.

The ice was cold and wet—ambrosia as it melted in her mouth and the moisture slipped down her dry throat. He lowered her back onto the bed and again took her hand in his. She felt his fingers slide between hers, felt his thumb tracing circles against the inside of her wrist.

"Are . . . are you all right?" she murmured.

He made a harsh sound in his throat and shook his head. "That's a question I should be asking you. My God, Vicki . . ." There was a peculiar look in his eyes. "I'm fine."

Her gaze rested on him. His was a face of bold features, a face that reflected strength and purpose and character, a face she would never tire of seeing.

She became aware of other things now, the IV pole beside her bed and, on the wall beyond, a monitor with an ever-changing series of jagged lines bleeping their way off the display.

"I'm in a hospital, aren't I?"

"Yes. You hurt your head, but you're going to be fine now. The nurse'll be here in a minute."

"Ben?"

Caine's expression settled into hard planes and angles. "He'll live."

"What happened?"

"It's over, Vicki. You're safe, and Ben is being taken care of. Don't worry about anything now. You'll hear the details later."

Her gaze caught his—warm melting chocolate, no shadows, no secrets. She let out a breath she hadn't realized she was holding. It was finally over.

"So we're awake, are we?" The owner of the unfamiliar voice moved into her line of vision, a short, stout woman dressed in white. "You can wait outside for a few minutes, Mr. Alexander."

"I'll wait over in the corner, out of the way," Caine said.

"You'll wait in the hall, or I'll have you escorted off the floor. You're not even supposed to be here. Don't push your luck." Then, in a softer voice. "Outside, Mr. Alexander. You can come back in a few minutes. I promise. Let me do my job."

Vicki almost smiled when she saw Caine's fierce frown. Then with obvious reluctance he stepped into the hallway.

"Stubborn, isn't he?"

"Very," Vicki agreed, her lips twitching.

"Well, if you can remember that, I suspect you're going to be fine."

Vicki endured the next few minutes with a stoic resolve to get it over and done with. She gave the nurse her name and birthday. She was poked and probed, then finally allowed another ice chip.

"You're doing fine," the nurse assured her. "Had us worried there for a while, but your tests show no internal injury. Just a good-size lump on your head. I'm going to let Mr. Alexander back in now, but don't talk too long. You need rest."

CAINE CAME quietly back into the room. She looked so vulnerable against the white sheets. Dear God, he could live another hundred years and never be as terrified as he'd been the moment he'd felt that lump on her head.

He returned the chair to the side of the bed and sat down, taking her hand in his, reassured by the simple contact.

"You really know how to scare a fellow," he said lightly, the words slipping out without thought.

"Oh, Caine, I'm so sorry. I nearly got us—"

"Hush. Damn me for a fool. I need lessons on bedside conversation. Don't think about anything right now but getting well. You've got that little machine bleeping and blipping all over the place. If you're not careful, we'll have the battle-ax back in here to throw me out again."

Thank you, God, he offered silently when Vicki gave him a weak smile. "She's not a battle-ax. She's nice."

"I know. She simply doesn't appreciate my congenial personality."

Her smile grew broader, and for the first time Caine could see a sparkle in her eyes. Now he could believe she really was going to be all right. His heart turned over.

"You don't have a congenial personality," she teased.

"I know that, too. You shouldn't be talking so much. The nurse said you needed rest."

"Will you stay with me until I go to sleep?"

He squeezed her hand. "Of course."

"You promise?"

"I promise, Vicki. I'll wait right here until you go to sleep."

It was what she needed to hear. "Thank you, Caine," she whispered, and closed her eyes.

He continued to hold her hand until her breathing became deep and regular. Still he sat, too tired to think about anything except the fact that Vicki was going to be all right. For now, it was enough.

Finally, as the first hint of morning showed behind the window curtains, he roused himself enough to slip her hand from his. Standing, he leaned over, his lips touching her brow. "Goodbye, Vicki," he murmured, then without looking back, walked out of the room.

CHAPTER EIGHTEEN

SPRING HAD ARRIVED in Little Falls. Vicki could see Aunt Abby's garden from the window of her upstairs bedroom. Purple flags of bearded iris nodded in beds bordering the long driveway leading to the house. Apple and pear trees were in full bloom, and only the forsythia bushes growing in deep shade retained any hint of yellow. The spherical buds in the peony beds swelled larger each day.

Vicki watched as the various plants in Aunt Abby's garden matured from bud to bloom, but she saw none of the beauty, only the marking of time.

She'd been in Little Falls four weeks now, been out of the hospital nearly five. She'd mentally crossed the passing days off the calendar and told herself Caine would come tomorrow. But finally she was forced to accept the truth.

Caine Alexander wasn't coming. Not tomorrow, not the next day, not ever.

Vicki wandered aimlessly downstairs, remembering the last time she saw him. He'd sat by her bedside holding her hand until she'd fallen asleep, had stayed by her, according to the hospital staff, even longer, all through the dark lonely hours of the night. At dawn he'd walked out of her hospital room and out of her life. When next she'd awakened, Harve was sitting by her bedside.

Vicki accepted Caine's absence for the first few days easily enough. He was busy. He was spending hours with police.

The newspaper headlines told the continuing story: Attorney Held for Attempted Murder; D.A. Drops Shooting Charges Against P.I.; Sinclair Charged In Henderson Death; Attorney Linked To Stolen Funds; Foundation Funds Found In Secret Account.

Neither Colonel Bolton nor his fish tank had ever existed. Sinclair had, according to police, rented the apartment through the building's management company to give him easy access to Vicki. Harve speculated that Sinclair was afraid Henderson had mentioned they'd worked together before he'd taken over the foundation directorship.

Days passed and Caine continued to stay away. Vicki began to worry. "Inge said, 'Worry is interest paid on trouble before it comes due,'" Harve told her, and whisked her back to Little Falls.

As the investigation continued, Caine's suspicion that Henderson might have worked his embezzlement scam before proved correct. Identifying Sinclair as Henderson's partner provided the key to unraveling the complicated web of fund transfers and secret accounts.

"You can take credit for unmasking the villain," Harve told her.

"Credit for stupidity?" Vicki protested. "It was sheer luck I didn't get both Caine and myself killed."

"We Tremaynes have always been lucky," Harve said. "There's an old Arabian proverb—pitch a lucky man into the Nile and he will come up with a fish in his mouth. I'd say Sinclair was one big fish."

Vicki gritted her teeth. Sometimes she suspected Harve trotted out his encyclopedic knowledge of quotations simply to provoke. But he was right on one count, she acknowledged. Sinclair—she could no longer bring herself to think of him as Ben—was indeed a big fish, or at least a fat one. Auditors were busy verifying transfer of funds from the foundation to Henderson to Sinclair. It appeared the foundation would be able to reclaim most of its pilfered money.

They might never know why Sinclair had killed Henderson—a falling-out among thieves, or perhaps Henderson had threatened to bring Sinclair down with him. It no longer mattered. Henderson was dead and Sinclair was in jail for what looked to be a long, long time.

It was over.

Vicki had believed she would be happy when she was finally safe, when she was once again in charge of her own life. Now she knew it would take more than that.

Damn Caine, anyway, she thought. He could at least have said goodbye. He owed her that much.

"At last," Aunt Abby said when she saw Vicki at the foot of the stairs. "I was afraid you were going into a decline and would waste away like some Victorian heroine. Silly creatures."

"I'm out of my blue funk," Vicki said. "Now I'm plain old-fashioned mad."

"What are you going to do?"

"I'm going back to Washington. I'm going to make Caine Alexander tell me face-to-face that he doesn't love me."

"Balderdash! The man's tush over toenails in love with you."

"Tush?" Vicki laughed.

"I thought it quite appropriate, given the man's assets," Aunt Abby said, in her best grande-dame manner. "It's good to hear you laughing again, child."

"I've been feeling sorry for myself, Aunt Abby," Vicki said. "I'll get over it."

"He's been calling, you know."

"Caine called?"

Aunt Abby nodded. "Every day for the first two weeks. I believe he's limiting himself to every other day now."

"But . . . but why didn't someone tell me?"

"Because that fool grandson of mine promised he wouldn't. I, however, am under no such constraint."

Vicki threw her arms around the old woman. "Oh, Aunt Abby. I love you."

"Wait a minute. Where are you going now?" Aunt Abby called as Vicki ran up the stairs two at a time.

"To pack. Will you phone Harve and ask him to give me a ride to the airport?"

"Well, it's about time," her great-aunt said.

IT HAD TAKEN Vicki forty-eight hours to make arrangements and flight connections from Little Falls to D.C., and in her impatience, each hour seemed twice as long. Now that she'd finally arrived, she still had to locate Caine. She couldn't find a listing in the telephone book, and the address for Alexander Security Consultants was a post-office box.

Vicki had briefly debated calling for an appointment, then decided that when she confronted Caine, she didn't want a business setting. She'd find a way to beard him in his den.

A short time later she was standing in front of Danny Carelli's small but neat bungalow in one of Washington's suburbs, gathering her courage to knock on the door. Most likely the marshal would be at work, but Caine's sister should be home. The question was, would Maggie Carelli help her?

She recognized the small, dark-haired woman who opened the door, although Maggie Carelli was noticeably thinner now than she'd been in Caine's photograph. But even if Vicki had never seen that picture, she would have known this was Caine's sister. They shared the same chocolate brown eyes.

"You're Vicki Winslow," the woman said as soon as she opened the door. Then she smiled, and Vicki knew she'd found a friend.

"Do you love my brother?" Maggie asked as soon as she'd seated Vicki and handed her a cup of coffee.

Vicki saw no need to deny the truth. "Yes, I do."

"Thank the good Lord," Maggie said fervently. "He loves you, too, you know, but you're going to have trouble making him admit it."

"He's going to have to tell me straight out that he doesn't," Vicki told her, "and then he's going have to convince me."

"I'm betting on you, Vicki Winslow." Maggie grinned. "I've been waiting for a long time for my brother to fall."

The sound of a baby crying in another room temporarily interrupted their conversation. Maggie returned minutes later carrying a small blanket-wrapped bundle. "Meet Daniel Alexander Carelli. We call him Alex."

Vicki held out her arms. "He's beautiful," she said as young Alex clenched her finger with his tiny hand. "I have this little fellow to thank for meeting Caine, you know. Your brother told me that he didn't want the marshal leaving you to come looking for me."

"Imagine that." Maggie laughed. "A matchmaker before he was even born. And you might as well start calling my husband Danny. We're going to be family, after all."

"I wish I was as sure as you." Vicki sighed. "I know I talk a good game, but deep down, I'm scared. I can't understand why he simply disappeared like he did."

"He feels guilty," Maggie said softly. "He says he almost got you killed."

"But...but that's ridiculous!" Vicki protested. "If anything, it was the other way around. I was the one stupid enough to let Sinclair into my apartment. I'm the one who nearly got us both killed.''

This time it was Maggie who sighed. ''My big brother always feels guilty. He blamed himself when our father deserted our mother. He was only five then. Later he blamed himself every time mother got sick and lost another job. When he was in the service, he blamed himself whenever any of his buddies was injured or killed. He even blamed himself when I fell off my bike and broke my arm. He wasn't even there, but he said it was his responsibility because he hadn't taught me to ride well enough.''

Vicki shook her head. ''He's not responsible for everything that goes wrong in the world.''

''Well, I hope you can convince him of that. I've never been able to. He's a stubborn, obstinate, pigheaded fool. Are you sure you want him?''

''Oh, yes, I'm sure,'' Vicki said. ''Can you tell me where I can find him?''

''I can do better than that. Hold on to Junior for me. I'll be right back.''

Maggie returned with a key and a piece of paper on which she'd written Caine's address and the code to the house security system. Of course, Vicki thought as she glanced at the paper. She should have suspected he'd have a security system.

''Surprise him,'' Maggie told her. ''You know, I think he half expects you to come looking for him. He made Danny promise he wouldn't tell you where to find him.''

"He did?"

"He did," Maggie said. "I, however, made no such promise."

Vicki laughed out loud. "Oh, Maggie, my great-aunt Abby is going to love you."

ONE MORE MILE, Caine told himself, only one more mile. He was determined to jog himself into exhaustion. Then maybe he'd be able to stop thinking.

It had been five weeks since he'd walked out of Vicki's hospital room, and every day had seemed like a lifetime. He'd known when he said goodbye he would never forget her, but he'd believed he'd be able to put her into one of those locked corners of his mind as he had so many other memories.

It hadn't worked.

Neither had handball, weight lifting, rowing, jogging or cold showers. His weight was down. His muscle-to-fat ratio was up. He'd set a new personal bench-press record, then promptly broken it. He'd also shot four consecutive 380s on the firing range. He was in better shape than he'd been in years.

He was miserable.

Vicki Winslow wouldn't get out of his head.

He'd expected her to be fully recovered by now, busy, happy to have her life back. But Harve had reported that while physically she was well, completely recovered from the knock on her head, she was nevertheless quiet and depressed. Harve's voice had held an accusing note.

It was his fault, Caine realized. He'd handled it all wrong. He should never have simply walked away, leaving the situation between them unfinished.

But he'd been afraid.

He was still afraid, afraid if he confronted her he wouldn't find the strength to deny her. Or himself.

He wished she'd get mad. He could handle mad. She was magnificent mad, her green eyes flashing, her fiery hair almost sparking with anger when she tossed her head.

Another half mile. Caine adjusted his running speed to a cool-down pace.

He could feel the heat of the concrete through the soles of his running shoes and remembered the comfort of running on the dirt trails around the cabin. He passed a spindly-looking tree growing in a concrete box between the sidewalk and the street and longed for the untamed woods around Little Falls. He drew a deep breath and nearly choked on the exhaust fumes. Oh, Lord, he was in trouble.

He entered his house through the mudroom in the back, cursing when he realized he'd forgotten to set the security system. He was losing his mind. Even seven hundred miles away, she was driving him crazy. This had to stop.

He peeled out of his damp shirt and jogging shorts, throwing them in the direction of the washing machine, and stepped under the shower next to the laundry room.

The hot spray beat down on him until his muscles felt like jelly, then he turned on the cold water, wondering why he continued to punish his body this way. It wasn't doing a damned bit of good.

He wrapped a towel around his waist, stepped into the hallway—and froze. He blinked once, twice, not sure he was actually seeing what he thought he was seeing. He swallowed, his eyes locked on the furry black-and-white animal confronting him. He took a step backward. The skunk took a step forward.

Caine stopped, his breath coming into short gasps. Disbelief. Fear. Wonder. Hope. "Sweetpea?" he said, finally managing to find his voice. The animal chittered in answer and wound herself around his ankles.

"Vicki!" he yelled.

"I'm right here, Caine." Like a fantasy, she walked down the hall, stopping right in front of him.

She was real! All he had to do was reach out and touch her. The thought made him dizzy. "But how... why... what are you doing here?"

"You seemed disinclined to come and see me. So I decided to come and see you."

She was even more stunning than he remembered. Her eyes were flashing green flame. "You're mad."

"You're damn right I'm mad."

"And I thought I could I could handle mad." Holding on to his towel with one hand, he bent down to pick up Sweetpea. It was the only thing he could think to do to prevent himself from dragging Vicki into his arms.

"What did you say?"

Caine sighed. "Never mind. Let me get some clothes on. We need to talk."

"You could've fooled me."

Never had he felt so close to complete defeat as he did at this moment, standing in front of her practically nude. "Yeah. Well, I think I fooled myself, too." He'd been right to be afraid of confronting her. Subconsciously he must have known he would lose.

"You don't have to get dressed, Caine. Our conversation may not take long. I came here to tell you I love you and to ask you one simple question. Do you love me?"

Oh, God. She wasn't making this easy.

"It isn't a trick question, Caine. All you have to say is yes or no."

"Of course I love you, but—"

"No buts, Caine. Either you do or you don't," she said.

"Dammit, Vicki. I'm no good for you. I nearly got you killed."

"No, I nearly got *you* killed. I'm a big girl, Caine. I can decide for myself who and what's good for me. And I'm still waiting for an answer."

"This is ridiculous. Here." He thrust Sweetpea into her arms. "I'm going to get dressed, then we'll continue this conversation."

"Yes or no?"

"Yes, dammit. Now are you satisfied?"

"Yes," she said, breaking into a grin.

He wanted to pull her into his arms. He wanted to hold her, kiss her, love her, until neither of them could remember the last miserable weeks. "Put down the damn skunk," he growled.

"I've got a better idea," she told him. "Instead of you getting dressed, why don't I . . ."

Sweetpea hid under the bed as they made love with a desperation that needed no words, and then again, with a sweetness and tenderness unlike anything Caine had experienced before.

Whatever resolution he'd made, it didn't matter anymore. He couldn't let her go. Not now. Not ever.

He pulled her close against his side and, raising himself on his arm, took a deep breath for courage. "Vicki, will you marry me?"

Her lips parted in a wide smile. "I thought you'd never ask."

"It's not a trick question," he teased. "All you have to say is yes or no."

"Yes, but—"

"No buts, Vicki. Either you will or you won't."

"I was only trying to tell you I come as a package deal."

His breath caught in his throat. "You mean you— Are you—? Vicki?"

"Are you asking if I'm pregnant?"

"Yes."

"Does it matter?"

Caine shook his head. Although he had doubts about being a good husband, he'd never been apprehensive about fatherhood. A child of his and Vicki's would be doubly loved. "No," he said. "Not a bit. I want it all, a wife, kids, a place in the country, aunts, uncles..."

"Oh, Caine, I love you."

"Does this mean we should start shopping for a cradle?"

Vicki shook her head. "No, I'm not pregnant. At least not yet."

"Then what was all that about a package deal?"

"It's Sweetpea." She grinned. "Harve's giving her to us as a wedding present."

Caine laughed and began revising his list. "A wife, kids, a place in the country, aunts, uncles, cousins, dogs, a skunk, a Jeep station wagon..."

"And his-and-her Harleys," Vicki added as she kissed him.

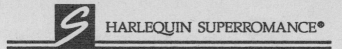

HARLEQUIN SUPERROMANCE®

**Four men of courage
Four special men
Four men who'd risk anything
For the women they love**

Next month, meet the fourth of our Strong Men!

Major Nick Apostalis is used to danger. A member of the
Canadian peacekeeping force, he'd been assigned to some of
the world's most hellish places. But none of his tours of duty
prepared him for the hell he's going through now that Kara
Hartman has disappeared from his life.

Kara knows he'll try to find her but she also knows he won't be
prepared for the secret she's carrying…

**Watch for PEACEKEEPER, Harlequin Superromance
#655 by Marisa Carroll. Available August 1995
wherever Harlequin books are sold.**

4SM-4

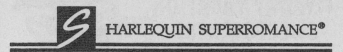

HARLEQUIN SUPERROMANCE®

Join bestselling author
Lynn Erickson
in
Apache Springs!

Gabriela and Brian Zimmerman run the Apache Springs Hotel, relying on the spectacular scenery and local legend to bring in the tourists. Then two of their guests die under very suspicious circumstances, and Deputy U.S. Marshal Jed Mallory comes to town. Gabriela doesn't know which bothers her most, the investigation of the hotel or the man who is conducting it—an old flame she's never quite forgotten....

First love...last love.

Look for *Apache Springs*, Harlequin Superromance #656, this August wherever Harlequin books are sold.

FLYAWAY VACATION SWEEPSTAKES!

This month's destination:

Glamorous LAS VEGAS!

Are you the lucky person who will win a free trip to Las Vegas? Think how much fun it would be to visit world-famous casinos... to see star-studded shows...to enjoy round-the-clock action in the city that never sleeps!

The facing page contains two Official Entry Coupons, as does each of the other books you received this shipment. Complete and return all the entry coupons—**the more times you enter, the better your chances of winning!**

Then keep your fingers crossed, because you'll find out by August 15, 1995 if you're the winner! If you are, here's what you'll get:

- Round-trip airfare for two to exciting Las Vegas!
- 4 days/3 nights at a fabulous first-class hotel!
- $500.00 pocket money for meals and entertainment!

Remember: The more times you enter, the better your chances of winning!*

*NO PURCHASE OR OBLIGATION TO CONTINUE BEING A SUBSCRIBER NECESSARY TO ENTER. SEE REVERSE SIDE OF ANY ENTRY COUPON FOR ALTERNATIVE MEANS OF ENTRY.

VLV KAL